Will   Irma   Taranee   Cornelia   Hay Lin

The Beginning:
The Power of Five
The Disappearance
Finding Meridian

Adapted by ELIZABETH LENHARD

HarperCollins *Children's Books*

Lydia
    well done for getting a brilliant
P5 report. July 2006

    love Mum

Congratulations for a great year of
Hockey + play.
    love Dad

W.i.t.c.h.

Will   Irma   Taranee   Cornelia   Hay Lin

The Power of Five

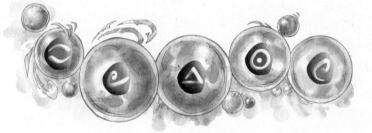

Adapted by **ELIZABETH LENHARD**

HarperCollins *Children's Books*

DISTANT AND DEEP...

THIS IS CANDRACAR...
AN ELSEWHERE WITH
NEITHER TIME NOR SPACE.

A VAST
NOTHINGNESS
IN THE
CENTER
OF WHICH
RISES UP
THE TEMPLE
OF THE
CONGREGATION...

ALLOW ITS
SPLENDOUR TO
DAZZLE YOUR EYES.
COME CLOSER
IF YOU DARE,
BUT DO SO
IN SILENCE....

THE ORACLE IS ABOUT
TO SPEAK....

ONE

Taranee Cook walked into the courtyard of her new school. She cringed as she looked at the sign looming over the entrance – a big, green archway that read SHEFFIELD INSTITUTE.

Institute. Taranee still wasn't used to that word. She remembered when her parents had told her the name of her new school.

Oh, yeah, Taranee thought, rolling her eyes behind her tiny, round specs. That was just before they made me pack up my entire life and move to a new city where the air always smells like salt water and the sidewalks are overflowing with skinny fashion models.

"The Sheffield Institute's one of the best private schools in Heatherfield," her mother had said, nodding briskly.

1

"You're putting me in an institution?" Taranee had wailed back.

Turned out, a lot of schools in Heatherfield were called institutes. It was just one more way this city was totally different from Sesamo, Taranee's *real* hometown.

She shivered as she winded her way towards Sheffield's front door, tiptoeing around the puddles still left over from that thunderstorm the night before. It had been a wicked downpour. Taranee must have spent an hour watching the lightning bolts zapping the ocean just beyond her bedroom window. With every strike, the lightning had seemed to inch a bit closer to her new cliffside house. But for some reason, Taranee had barely flinched.

Scared of fire? she thought. Not even. Scared is knowing that the tofu stir-fry Mum packed for me is going to be reeking by noon. Which means the stylish Sheffieldians will have yet another reason not to sit with me at lunch. The first reason being, of course, that they don't know I'm alive.

Taranee hopped around another puddle. But for all the leftover rainwater this morning, one would never know the storm had happened.

The sun was shining and the sky was so blue it didn't look real. The stream of kids trotting up the school's stone steps all seemed to be wearing the latest fashions.

Just looking at all those strangers laughing and shouting hello to each other as they rushed into the school made Taranee shiver again. It was only her third day of school, and she was already dreading it. She yanked the cuffs of her orange turtleneck over her hands and gazed up at the Euro-style pink stucco building, complete with a mottled green copper roof and a big clock. A big clock that read 8:08. As in, two minutes till she'd be late for history class.

By the time she made it into Sheffield's main hallway, most of the kids had rushed off to class. Taranee caught her breath and made a dash for the big marble staircase. She was just about to launch herself onto the bottom step when she skidded to a confused stop.

"Oh, man . . ." she whispered. "I have no idea where to go!"

After only two days at Sheffield, Taranee realised, as dread swirled in her stomach, that she still hadn't mastered the maze that was her class schedule.

She tore open her cloth book bag and began pawing through it. Tofu in Tupperware. Lip gloss. Eyeglass cleaner. Two shiny, new notebooks. And her schedule? Nowhere to be found.

Just when Taranee was breaking into a cold sweat, she heard the familiar *clomp-squeak-clomp-squeak* of frantically late sneakers behind her. She glanced up to see yet another stranger. But this one was a skinny girl with half a dozen cowlicks in her red hair and a chest that was almost as flat at Taranee's. She looked lost, too. The girl dug her schedule out of her jeans pocket and blinked at it. Then she spun around looking for an arrow, a trap door, a sign from the heavens – anything to save her from the dreaded first day of school. (How did Taranee know this? That had been *her*, forty-eight hours ago. She recognised the signs.)

Finally, the new kid's brown eyes flashed. She threw out her hands and screeched, "So, what does a girl have to do to get to room 304?"

Taranee grinned as the girl stomped her green sneakered foot in frustration.

"How to get to room 304?" she answered. "Hope to get promoted out of room 303, maybe."

The girl's skinny shoulders shot up to her ears as she spun around to stare at Taranee. Taranee tried to act casual. She didn't want the new kid to think she was *too* excited to be making actual human contact or anything.

"Two days ago, I had the same look on my face," Taranee said, tossing the longest of her randomly assorted, beaded braids over her shoulder. "I'm new, too. My name's Taranee."

"Nice to meet you," the girl said quietly. Slowly, her shoulders unclenched themselves. "I'm Will."

Taranee felt herself thrill inside. New-friend moment, she thought. Totally worth being late to class.

"Would you *please* explain what you're still doing out here in the hallway, young ladies?!"

Taranee cringed, and Will's shoulders shot back up to her ears.

"It's the principal," Taranee whispered to the terrified newbie, as the source of that very angry voice bustled toward them. "Mrs. Knickerbocker."

Ugh! Being late to history class, Taranee thought. That's no biggie. But a discipline session with Sheffield's big cheese? Taranee tried to think of things she'd rather do. Drink warm milk? Run a three-minute mile?

Ugh. Taranee shuddered. Okay, even doing time with Mrs. Knickerbocker is better than that, she thought.

Mrs. Knickerbocker stalked around the school with her ample chest thrust out before her and her even more ample backside swishing from side to side with terrifying force. It reminded Taranee of the swirling brushes of a street sweeper, dead set on ridding the hallways of filth (otherwise known as loitering students).

And then there was Mrs. Knickerbocker's hair. It was fascinating – a towering, shellacked pompadour. Snowy white. As translucent as spiderwebs. It was definitely one of the wildest old-people oddities Taranee had ever seen. She couldn't help staring at the stiffly glistening beehive as Mrs. Knickerbocker pointed a plump finger towards the east hallway.

Oh, yeah, Taranee suddenly remembered. *That's* where my history class is. . . .

"Lessons have already begun, Miss Cook," Mrs. Knickerbocker sputtered. "Straight to class."

Taranee was one step ahead of her. She'd already spun around and begun hurrying away.

She glanced over her shoulder as she slunk down the hallway.

Poor newbie, she thought, watching Will grin nervously up at the principal. I wonder what lunch period she has.

"As for you . . ." Mrs. Knickerbocker was saying, leering down at Will.

"M-m-my name is Will Vandom, ma'am," Will said, flashing the woman with the widest, fakest cheesy grin Taranee had ever seen. She liked Will already. "I think I'm a bit lost."

"Miss Vandom," the principal announced. "We're off to a bad start!"

Taranee sighed as she saw Will's chin drop to her chest. She knew *exactly* how the new kid must have felt: gawkily, nauseatingly, please-let-the-floor-open-up-and-swallow-me bad.

Come to think of it, Taranee thought as she finally located her history class and walked inside, that's just about how I feel right about now.

Taranee gave an embarrassed little wave at the twenty-one pairs of eyeballs that were, well, eyeballing her as she stumbled through the door. She looked wildly around the room, searching for an empty desk. Luckily, there was one right behind two girls she already recognised.

She had two other classes with them. They usually sat in the back of the room, the better to keep up their constant, whispered gossip sessions. Taranee was a little suspicious of the sassy early bloomer with the tousled, brown hair and pug nose, but she liked the Asian kid with the kooky clothes. Today – the kid was using a pair of green, bubbly goggles as a headband. The goggles clashed with her fuchsia sweatshirt in the most brazen way. She was beyond cool.

"Better late than never, Miss Cook," Mr. Collins called out from the blackboard. Even from the back of the room, Taranee could see his thick, red mustache twitching with amusement.

"Students are always welcome here," he continued. "Especially on days when there's a pop quiz!"

"A pop quiz?" the early bloomer cried. "Yesterday you said there would be a review!"

"I lied," Mr. Collins said, skulking down the aisle with another mustache-shimmying smile. He leered with vampirelike glee at the girl and said, "You should know by now, Irma, that we history teachers are mean by nature."

The Asian girl giggled and gave the early bloomer – Irma – a wink.

"I thought that was only maths teachers," she piped up cheerfully.

Irma, meanwhile, was pouting big time. She slumped onto her desk and whispered, "This is just plain *cruel*. It's completely different."

Taranee sank into her desk chair and searched for her history book in her book bag. Actually, she felt grateful. In one fell swoop, Irma had shifted all the attention away from Taranee and onto herself.

Perhaps more attention than she'd bargained for.

"Why so upset?" Goggle Girl whispered to Irma. "Doesn't your spell work anymore?"

Taranee blinked. Spell?

Irma blinked, too. Then she glared at her friend.

"What on earth are you talking about?" she muttered, narrowing her blue eyes to malevolent slits.

"Oh, come on," Goggle Girl said, giving Irma's shoulder a playful nudge. "I mean rigging the quizzes."

"Did you say 'rigging the quizzes'?" Taranee whispered over Irma's shoulder. As soon as the question left her mouth, she gritted her teeth.

Way to go, she thought. As if I don't have enough black marks with Knickerbocker today. Now I have to walk into the middle of a cheating scandal.

Of course, Irma's reaction was no surprise. She whirled around and clamped her hand over her friend's grin.

"She didn't say anything," Irma said, somehow managing to glare at Taranee and Goggle Girl in one sweeping motion. "She just likes the sound of her own voice."

"Rmmmph," Goggle Girl gasped, before she squirmed her face out of Irma's palm. A second later, Irma unleashed a piercing yowl. She snatched her hand away from Goggle Girl and started shaking it around. She wiped it on her sweater with exaggerated disgust. Then she waved it high in the air.

"What's going on back there?" Mr. Collins yelled.

"Mr. Collins!" Irma yelled back. "Hay Lin bit me!"

Taranee stifled a snort of laughter while Hay Lin fiddled with one of her long, glossy pigtails and fluttered her eyelashes innocently.

Clearly, Mr. Collins knew how to play dumb, too. Ignoring Irma's bite marks, he simply homed in on her hand.

"That's a raised hand," he said. "Congratulations, Irma. I needed a volunteer, and it looks like I've found one."

"Burn!" Taranee whispered to herself. She'd learned the antique dis from Peter, her surfer-dude brother. And never had it been more appropriate than at this moment.

As Mr. Collins began to ponder his quiz question, Irma's injured hand started trembling. She sank into her chair.

"B-b-but that's not fair," she squeaked.

Hay Lin just giggled again and turned to Taranee.

"Watch and learn," she whispered from behind her hand. She wore a glittery purple ring that sparkled in the fluorescent light. "When Irma's quizzed, first she gets angry. Then she gets desperate. Then she shuts her eyes tight, crosses her fingers . . ."

"Shut up!" Irma snapped.

That would be "angry," Taranee thought.

"I didn't study at all," Irma whined to Hay Lin. "All I know is a little about Charles the Great."

Hel-lo, desperation, Taranee thought. Then Irma did just as Hay Lin had predicted. She laced her fingers together, clenched her eyes shut, and began chanting.

"Ask me about Charles the Great," she breathed in a rush. "Please-oh-please-oh-please-oh . . ."

Hay Lin continued to narrate to Taranee.

"See? And if there's only one single thing she's studied, that's exactly what the teacher is going to ask her about," she said. "I don't know how she does it. All I know for sure is that it works every time."

Taranee was . . . totally confused. So, it wasn't cheating that Hay Lin was talking about. She was saying Irma had . . . what? Some psychic power? A voodoo spell? A chunk of kryptonite hanging from her neck?

All three girls stared hard at Mr. Collins as he scanned his textbook.

"Hmmm," he said.

Charles the Great? Taranee thought.

"Let's see here," Mr. Collins muttered with agonising casualness.

"Charles the Great," Hay Lin whispered impishly.

"Irma Lair . . ." Mr. Collins began.

"Charles the Great," Irma pleaded in a hoarse whisper.

"Why don't you tell us," Mr. Collins demanded finally, "about Charles the Great?"

"Yes!" Hay Lin cried, bursting into loud laughter. It would have been a sure detention-getter if Mr. Collins hadn't been so focused on Irma.

Irma, meanwhile, practically clapped her hands with glee as she launched into a long, show-offy speech about some Holy Roman emperor.

Not that Taranee listened to a word. She was too busy freaking. Maybe she had much more to fear from this curvy in-crowder than school yard snubbing.

Maybe . . . Taranee thought. But before she let the idea form fully in her mind, she shook her head hard enough to make her braids click together.

What was she thinking? That Irma, with her hippie, flower-power jewelry was . . . magical?

"Naw," Taranee muttered, slumping back in her desk chair with yet another shiver. "That's just not possible."

TWO

When Sheffield's final bell rang, Cornelia Hale looked down at her notebook page.

It was blank.

There was a physics test in three days, and Cornelia hadn't taken one note. In fact, she'd heard not one word of Mr. Temple's lecture.

Where have I been for the last fifty minutes? Cornelia wondered, blinking sleepily as she began to put her notebook and pens into her magenta messenger's bag. A long lock of blonde hair fell over her eyes, and she shook it away impatiently.

I wish my hair wasn't so straight, she thought irritably, shoving the lock behind her ear even though she knew it would slither back into her face in about three seconds.

And then Cornelia felt a chill. Because suddenly she realised where the past hour had gone.

She'd been doing it again.

It had begun so gradually, Cornelia couldn't even remember when it had started. In fact, she didn't really know what *it* was. Not exactly. But she remembered the first time she'd been aware of it.

She'd been in English class. Martin Tubbs had been droning on about the symbolism of the night in *Huckleberry Finn*. Cornelia had sighed heavily – leave it to four-eyed Martin to find something obscure, then analyse it to death.

I wish it was night now, Cornelia had thought wearily. Then this whole, lame school thing would just be a distant mem–

Huh?

Just over her head, Cornelia had heard a sputter, then a pop. And then the classroom had gone dark.

Their teacher, Mrs. Nelson, leapt out of her chair.

"There must be a blown fuse," she'd said, going to the classroom door and looking out the window. "Although . . . that's funny. Ours seems to be the only classroom without light. Sit quietly, and I'll go get the janitor."

Of course, the class practically threw a party when Mrs. Nelson left. There was *nothing* like a reprieve in the last ten minutes of an excruciating English lecture. Cornelia had gotten up from her desk with a big grin and done a few stretches. (Being a figure skater, she craved constant motion.) Then she'd loped over to her friend Elyon's desk to show her the new lip gloss she'd bought the day before.

But, behind her happiness, Cornelia had felt a tiny kernel of unease. She'd glanced up at the dark, slightly hissing fluorescent lights. And a tremulous, almost silent voice in the back of her head had whispered, "Did I do that?"

That's when she'd suddenly remembered the broken pencil that had seemed to have sharpened itself, the bell that had rung just a few minutes early, the boy who had smiled at her *just* when she had willed him to.

And just now, during her physics lecture, Cornelia realised with a start, something even stranger had happened. She'd been staring out the window, gazing at the green-red leaves of a maple tree as they fluttered in the breeze. But then the leaves had begun to swirl around and form shapes. First she'd seen a squirrel. Then the face of a cute guy, winking at her. And then her little sister, Lilian, sneering. But when Cornelia had wished to see the cute boy again, there he'd been.

Part of Cornelia knew that, somehow, she was making these things happen. But most of her, the *real* her, the one who got things *done* instead of daydreaming her days away, managed to shake the knowledge from her head every time it wormed its way in.

It's not true, she told herself. Not true, not true, not true – impossible. She'd listened to enough physics lectures to know *that.*

Cornelia knew what would clear these thoughts from her head immediately – people. She headed out of the classroom to join the throng of kids in the hall. Most of them were already slamming their locker doors shut and running, not walking, toward every available exit door.

Cornelia noticed several people – most of them boys – glancing her way as they passed by. She shrugged it off. She knew she was part of

Sheffield's Infielders. As opposed to the Outfielders, as the school's rebels and misfits were known. Or the dreaded snufilupigi – invisible to all.

So, she was popular – big whoop. Cornelia didn't put too much stock in it. She knew who her *real* friends were. Friends like Elyon, whom she'd just spotted down the hall. She was plodding slowly through the crowd, looking even more wistful than usual.

Just as Cornelia started to wave to her, she was swept up into the whirlwind of Hay Lin and Irma.

"Ha!" Hay Lin was saying to Irma as they scurried out of their history class. "I can't believe you did it again!"

"Hey! It's a secret," Irma said, glaring at Hay Lin, whose slouchy jacket was falling off her skinny shoulders as usual. "You can't go around telling the whole school."

Then why are you talking it about it so loudly? Cornelia wondered. Then she pasted on a smile and turned to her buds.

"What can't she tell us?" she asked Hay Lin.

"Cornelia!" Hay Lin squealed. "The remote-control quizzes. She did it again."

Cornelia hid a tiny smile by turning to open her locker.

Remote-control quizzes, she thought with a little laugh. Irma thinks she's a big shot. But she's just a beginner. If she only knew what I can do.

For an instant, her mind flashed upon the cute, brown-eyed boy with the flouncy hair who'd appeared in the swirling leaves outside her classroom window. She felt as if she'd seen him before. Perhaps in a dream . . .

Then Cornelia shook her head sharply.

Impossible, remember? She admonished herself. She scowled into the mirror hanging inside her locker door, narrowing her blue eyes to slits. Then she slammed her locker door shut and spun around in time to see Hay Lin waving at an African American girl in an orange turtleneck and a cockeyed assemblage of beaded braids.

"See you tomorrow," Hay Lin called to the girl.

"Who was that?" Cornelia asked, watching the girl cautiously negotiate the pack of Sheffielders barreling through the door.

"Her name's Taranee. One of the new arrivals," Hay Lin said. "The other one is in class with you and Elyon, right?"

"Yeah," Cornelia said, noticing that Elyon had finally made her way through the throng and reached them. "I think her name's Will. But ask Elyon. She always has all the news."

Not that you could tell this afternoon. Elyon's eyes were downcast and her straw-coloured bangs were even more limp than usual.

"Hi, guys," she practically whimpered. Then she fell into step with them as they all trooped out of school. Irma put a finger beneath Elyon's chin and turned her face toward hers, staring deep into Elyon's pale blue eyes.

"Look at me," Irma said. Then she nodded and glanced at Cornelia and Hay Lin.

"I've already seen this face before," she said.

"Me, too," Cornelia joked. "It was in a doc-umentary about Easter Island." She stuck out her lower lip and glowered.

"Oh, no, Cornelia," Irma said, contradicting her as usual. She ducked behind Elyon and pointed at her wan expression with mock concern. "I recognise a *flunked* look when I see one. And I'd say that what we have here is a big, fat, hairy *F!*"

Elyon yanked herself out of Irma's clutches and glared at her.

"All right, already," she said through gritted teeth. "I got a bad grade in maths. Satisfied?"

"Of course, I am!" Irma said. "Because you know what that means, right?"

Uh-oh, Cornelia thought with a grin. Here it comes.

"*Punishment!*" Irma and Hay Lin screamed. They grabbed Elyon by the elbows and began to drag her through the Sheffield arch. Elyon made the most of her suffering, sighing heavily, rolling her eyes, dragging her feet – the whole bit.

"Come on," she complained. "You could look the other way, just this once."

"The law's the law, Elyon," Cornelia said with a giggle. "You know the rules of the group."

"And for a really terrible grade, we need something really nasty!" Irma said.

Suddenly, Cornelia had a stroke of genius. She gave Elyon a sidelong glance and then put on a puzzled look.

"Hmm, that's strange, though," she said. "I thought Matt-ematics was your favourite subject!"

Elyon stopped in her tracks and gasped.

"Leave Matt out of this," she cried.

"Of course!" Hay Lin said, bouncing tauntingly in front of Elyon. "He'll be your punishment. You'll have to convince the biggest hottie in the school to study with you."

"Begging and pleading," Irma added.

Cornelia covered her mouth to keep from guffawing. After all, she was probably the only one here who knew how big a crush Elyon had on Matt Olsen, who was scruffy and painfully cute, even if he was married to his guitar.

Hay Lin put her fists on her bony hips and swung around to face Irma.

"Let's get this straight, Irma," she said. "Either Elyon begs or she pleads."

"She should beg," Irma decided, nodding forcefully. "I said it first."

"And if we had her beg pleadingly?" Hay Lin proposed.

"That's silly!"

"But it's a compromise!"

Who needs *Mad TV* when you've got these goofy friends, Cornelia thought, letting one chuckle escape her pink-glossed lips before she gave Elyon a wave.

"Good luck," she called as Elyon slumped over in defeat. Then she turned left and followed the Institute's wrought-iron fence down the sidewalk. She'd parked her bike at the rack around the corner.

As she strolled along, feeling the breeze ripple her long lime-green skirt, she gave a little sigh. The change in season always made Cornelia a little sad, especially when summer gave way to fall. Cornelia couldn't help taking it a little personally when the trees lost their leaves. She knew it was silly, but she felt for those trees in the winter, all bare-limbed and damp and chilly. They seemed so . . . vulnerable. Leaves were like insulation, like the cosy, blue turtleneck she'd put on for her bike ride home.

A girl's yell jolted Cornelia out of her daydream.

Okay, time to ditch the vulnerable thoughts, she said to herself. Something's going down by the bike rack.

Another girl's voice, shrill as a bird, joined the first. Cornelia sped up.

What's going *on* over there? she wondered angrily.

As she rounded the corner, she saw one of the girls – hey, it was Taranee, the new kid in the orange sweater. Crouching on the sidewalk next to Taranee was the other new girl – Will. And they were both glaring at . . . ugh, Uriah's gang of thugs. Greasy hair, lots of zits, tattered skate duds, and a collective I.Q. of about 22.

They'd be the terror of Sheffield if they weren't so uncreative, Cornelia thought with a sigh. As it is, they're just a major pain in the neck.

This time, the thugs had tangled a bunch of bikes into an elaborate knot. Cornelia had seen it all before. But she wasn't sure if Taranee could handle it. She'd seemed pretty timid in the hallway.

"Did you guys do this?" Taranee demanded while Will yanked at one of the bikes angrily.

Oh, Cornelia thought, I guess she *can* hold her own.

"Hee-hee!" Kurt squealed. He was the tubby one with scuzzy brown hair. He and Laurent, with his blond buzz cut and barrel chest, were two dumb, giggling peas in a pod.

"Looks like somebody's going to be walking home today!" he teased.

Cornelia couldn't help noticing that Nigel, the only halfway presentable member of Uriah's crew, stood by silently. He issued no taunts, no name-calling. In fact, he looked a bit bewildered.

Kurt, on the other hand, was laughing so hard he was snorting like a pig. His fuzzy brown eyebrows waggled tauntingly at the new girls.

"So, you think that's funny, do you?" Will growled.

"Could be," Kurt bellowed. Then his eyebrows started wiggling . . . in a different way. He leered at Will.

"You're new here, aren't you?" Uriah said. "You're cute!"

"And you're the same old lamebrain, Uriah!" Cornelia burst out as she stepped over to the gang and tapped their leader on his bony shoulder. He spun around and stared at her, giving her way too close a view of his oily chin, his overgelled red spikes, and his pimply nose. Cornelia threw her shoulders back and returned his stare. She pointed at Uriah and then pointed at her blue bike, which was twisted around Will's red one.

"Is that my bike in the middle of that mess, too, Champ?" she asked him threateningly.

He scrunched his face into a snarl and blurted, "So deal with it! Let's move, guys."

Cowards, Cornelia thought, as the gang scurried after Uriah, guffawing and elbowing one another in the ribs before they disappeared around the corner.

"You've just met Uriah and his pals," Cornelia said to Will and Taranee. Ruefully, she blew a strand of hair out of her face.

"I sure could have done without it," Will said, biting her lip as she finally freed her bike tyre from Taranee's handlebars.

"Don't worry," Cornelia replied breezily, pulling her own bike out of the mess. "Not everyone around here is like that. You'll see, at tonight's party."

Just saying that was enough to make Cornelia forget about all the creepiness and aggravation of the last hour. The Halloween dance. It was going to be sweet! She couldn't wait.

The new girls clearly did not agree.

"Oh, no! The party," Taranee cried.

"I forgot all about it," Will said. Then she turned and began working furiously on reattaching her bike seat to her bike, as if she'd like to *re*-forget all about it. Cornelia gazed at Will curiously. She had no idea what it was like to be the new kid in school. After all, she'd lived in Heatherfield all her life.

It must be awful, it occurred to her, not knowing anybody, not knowing how to get to places.

But Cornelia also thought it might be kind of awful to say something like that out loud. So, instead, she put on a cheerful smile and turned to the other new kid.

"Taranee, right?" she said, extending her hand. "I'm Cornelia."

"Nice to meet you," Taranee said with a shy smile.

"We're all meeting at the gym at eight o'clock," Cornelia told her. When she saw Taranee's smile begin to fade away, Cornelia squeezed her hand reassuringly.

"You'll see," she said. "It'll be a party you won't forget!"

"As far as I'm concerned," Will muttered behind Cornelia, "I just want to forget about today as soon as possible."

Cornelia decided to ignore the crack.

"And don't forget to wear a dress," she added. "Scary or wonderful or whatever. Just make sure it's special."

"I'll see what I can do," Taranee said drily, looking down at her slouchy jeans and baggy turtleneck.

Cornelia hopped onto her bike. Okay, so the new girls were a little frumpy. But that didn't matter – Cornelia had a hunch that underneath their new-kid crabbiness, they might be kind of cool.

She felt her usual "in control" mood returning as she propped a purple sneaker on her pedal.

"See you later, then," she said.

"I don't know, Cornelia," Will blurted suddenly, leaping to her feet with a panicked look in her huge, brown eyes. "I haven't been to a party in ages."

"Then this will be your chance to get back into the habit," Cornelia called over her shoulder as she began to ride away. Soon, she was halfway down the street, leaving behind the physics fiasco, Uriah, and all the other bummers of the school day. And suddenly, all she could feel was joy. She was surrounded by beautiful weather, her bike was picking up speed, and she had the coolest dress to wear to the dance tonight.

And, she realised, she might have two new friends on her hands. Turning around, she shot the girls a final grin and waved.

"Bye!" she called. And then she raced toward home.

THREE

Uriah stomped around the corner, pretending not to care if the guys were behind him or not. Besides, he knew they were. They always trailed him like loyal dogs. And besides – he could hear Kurt's fat feet clomping on the cement and Nigel's sneakers shuffling along timidly.

Nigel. What's *up* with that dude? Uriah thought, curling his thin upper lip. Nigel's been such a loser lately. Never wants to have any fun.

Thinking about losers, of course, sent Uriah straight back to his standoff with Cornelia Hale. He, uh, hadn't exactly won that battle.

But wait'll she sees what I've got in store for her, Uriah thought. And all the other Infielders who think they're better than me.

Uriah didn't know much, but he

knew there was one great equalizer in the world.

Fireworks.

And he had some.

Uriah snickered as his gang slumped into their usual after-school terrorising positions on the front steps. Then they dug the day's junk-food supply out of their backpacks and commenced with some full-on slouching.

"Aaaaaarrrgggh," Laurent yawned loudly, five minutes later.

"Grrrgle," Kurt grunted through a mouthful of corn chips. "The show is over."

"Guys," Uriah cackled, jumping to his feet. "The show hasn't even started. Come with me."

As the last students trickled out of Sheffield, Uriah and his boys slithered back in. They sneaked – well, as much as one can sneak when the gang is made up of huge, sloppy lunks – into the west hallway and crept up to Uriah's locker.

Uriah nodded at his boys, and they each stationed themselves at a corner of the hallway. Uriah felt a surge of energy – he had power over these guys. Even if they were a bunch of duds, that meant something.

"The coast is clear, Uriah," Nigel said, looking over his shoulder.

"Keep on the lookout," Uriah snapped. Kurt glared down the hallway as Uriah quickly twirled through the combination on his locker. Then he reached in and paused. All three guys turned their attention to him.

"What is it?" Laurent whispered. At the moment of prime dramatic impact, Uriah pulled out three small rockets. He thrust them towards the boys and laughed maniacally.

"Whaddya say to these?" he said. "I took 'em, and a whole lot more, from my old man's boat."

"They're Bengal lights," Laurent said dully. "Flare rockets. Whaddya wanna do with them?"

Uriah sighed. He was working with amateurs here.

"At tonight's party," he explained slowly, "the school's taking care of the music and the eats."

"Yeah," Kurt said, totally bewildered.

"Yeah?" Nigel said edgily.

Uriah cackled again. Then he flashed his boys a triumphant grin.

"But," he announced, "I'll take care of the fireworks myself!"

FOUR

Irma sighed happily. She was in her favourite place in the whole world – the bathtub.

Well, actually her *favourite*, favourite place was the ocean. She grabbed every opportunity to hit Heatherfield Beach and soak up the salt water. She'd bodysurf for an hour or just float effortlessly on her back, feeling her hair fan out into the water, giggling when a fish skimmed by her toes.

So, let's call this her favourite place in her *house*, which, let's face it, was a pretty average, saltbox type of place. Certainly nothing like Cornelia's fancy high-rise apartment or Hay Lin's funky flat above her parents' Chinese restaurant.

Still, Irma's bathtub was glam.

She'd stacked every available surface with beautiful bottles of bubble bath and flowery salts and shells she'd collected from the beach. Sometimes she even propped her pet turtle, Leafy, on the tub's rim. He would dunk his claws into the hot bathwater and scowl at her over his little horny nose.

The two-hour soak was a key part of her getting-ready-for-a-big-night ritual. Sometimes, Irma wished it were the *only* part.

It wasn't that she was nervous about the party. That part would be a blast.

No, Irma told herself. It's the agonizing half-hour pawing through my closet that I'm dreading.

Irma dunked her head beneath the bathwater and blew a dramatic stream of bubbles. When she popped up, she swaddled her head in a pink towel and reached for the cordless.

"Hi!" Hay Lin's voice chirped through the phone.

"How'd you know it was me?" Irma asked.

"Didn't," Hay Lin said with a giggle. "I just wanted to psych out whoever it was. Whatsup?"

"I still don't know what to wear tonight," Irma wailed. "What about you?"

"No, I haven't decided yet what I'm going to wear," Hay Lin said. "But it's certainly going to be something spectacular."

Irma could just picture Hay Lin in her bedroom. She'd be perched in her favourite spot – the window seat – gazing out at the rain, totally oblivious to the chaos around her. And that chaos most likely consisted of, say, one Rollerblade and about a dozen comic books scattered on the floor, crusty paintbrushes drying next to her easel, and action figures hanging all over the computer terminal like little monkeys.

"All I can tell you," Hay Lin continued, "is that it's a new outfit and when I pass by, everyone's head will turn."

"Wow," Irma said, trailing her finger glumly through the bathwater. "Another creation by Grandma, huh? Is it gonna be ready on time?"

"Of course, it'll be ready by eight," Hay Lin said with a nervous laugh. "You'll see. It'll be something unique! Something extraordinary! Something . . . something *bewitching*. And with a couple of stitches, it'll be ready in ten minutes."

Then Irma heard a rustling and some quick, peppy footsteps.

"Right, Grandma?" she heard Hay Lin say.

"Ten minutes, as always."

That was Hay Lin's grandmother's voice – high-pitched, reedy, and thickly accented. The older woman both fascinated and frightened Irma. She was the tiniest grown-up Irma had ever seen, with the *biggest* ears she'd ever seen. They jutted out from her long, wispy white hair like a mother lion's – always cocked and listening.

Hay Lin was back to Irma.

"Well, I better hop in the bath myself," she said. "Just wait'll you see my dress!"

Click.

Irma tossed her cordless onto the fuzzy toilet seat and pulled her knees up beneath her chin. She turned on the hot-water tap to warm up the water a bit. Then she breathed deeply as steam swirled around her head. She let one hand drape across her knee, the fingertips just touching the water. As usual – lately – the connection sent a warm jolt flowing up her arm. It was almost like electricity. Not a shock, really. More like a pleasant power surge.

I'm really curious about her dress, Irma thought, as she wiggled her fingers lightly. Hay Lin is always full of ideas. As for me, as always,

I don't know what to wear! It should be something dark that fits the occasion. Something that matches my mood!

Irma stretched out her arm and dipped a single finger into the water. She twirled it around lightly.

I always get nervous when something that I don't understand happens, Irma thought unhappily.

Then, hesitantly, she raised her finger out of the water.

Yup – there it was. The water was rising out of the tub, like a cobra hypnotised by a snake charmer's music. Steadily, a thin stream of water bobbled through the air – coiling and flipping over itself. It was as if Irma were a conductor and her finger a baton.

Something really *incomprehensible* is going on here, she thought as the rocking rivulet danced past her eyes. She had more control over the water than she'd had at first. The day she'd discovered the water following her command – about two months earlier – Irma had, of course, lost her head. It was so exciting! Before she knew it, she'd created a small tidal wave, leaving the tub empty of everything but her shivering self and the bathwater sloshing all over the floor.

Since then, every bath had been a chance to experiment with this wild water dance. She'd gotten better and better. Now she could make fountains, whirlpools, and bubbles frolic obediently around her.

Should I talk to the others about this? Irma wondered as she flicked an overenthusiastic arc of water away from her hair.

"Maybe not," she muttered to herself. "After all, playing with water is so nice. It's so. . . so . . ."

Magical, she thought. Because she couldn't even bring herself to say the word out loud. It was too crazy. Of course, making six streams of water do the cancan out of the tub was just a little crazier than calling it magic, wasn't it?

Irma was just giggling to herself when a buzz kill barreled through the door in the form of her father's voice.

"IRMA!"

Splooosh! Splish! Splash!

Irma winced as her lovely cancan dancers collapsed into a big puddle on the floor. Her arching fountain missed its target and landed over by the sink. Her magical water was now just . . . wetness. All over the floor.

"Are you done?" her dad bellowed through the door from the hallway. "You've been in there for more than an hour!"

Irma sighed. I *had* to get a police sergeant for a dad, she thought. I couldn't have gotten, oh, a club DJ or a nice, laid-back hippie?

"Just a sec!" she called out. She jumped out of the tub and grabbed her fluffy pink towel, wrapping it around herself. Then she gaped at the monstrous puddles all over the floor.

"Come on," she whispered to the water. "Evaporate. You wouldn't want Dad to see this mess."

"Irma! I'm warning you! I'm losing my patience."

"H-here I am," Irma called back as sweetly as possible while she whipped the towel turban off her hair and began flapping it through the air, trying to clear the steam.

"IRMA!"

"I'm coming!"

She wrapped the towel back around her head, put on her best pout and indignantly slid open the bathroom door. Then she slipped her feet into her (okay, slightly damp) pink slippers and minced past her dad into the hallway.

"The next time, I'm going to break down the door," her father said to her back. But she didn't have to see his face to know he was teasing her. "You know I can do it!"

"Oh, yeah," Irma tossed over her shoulder. "And by what law, if you please? It's not a crime to take a two-hour bath."

Her dad grimaced and rolled his eyes. Then he squinted at her smooth hands. His bushy, steel-grey eyebrows got all smushy with confusion.

"If only you got pruny fingers like everyone else," he said, "you wouldn't act like this. But nooooo!"

Irma had to giggle. Her dad liked to growl a lot, but she knew he was just a big teddy bear. Annoying? Often. But Irma still had a soft spot for him. Sometimes, on their long walks down to the beach, she would even hold his hand. That is, if she was *sure* that no Infielders were lurking about to see.

"The little lady can stay in there soaking all afternoon like it was nothing," her dad went on. "Good grief."

"I know my rights, Inspector," Irma teased.

Then she saw her dad's eyes shift to the left – towards the bathroom!

Danger, she thought. Eye contact has been made. Proceed to bedroom – immediately!

"Irma . . ." her dad was growling as he poked his head into the bathroom for closer inspection. "There's a *lake* in here!"

"I'll only speak in the presence of my lawyer," Irma squeaked as she trotted down the hall. She slipped inside her bedroom door before her dad could get himself into lecture mode. Slamming the door behind her, she leaned against it and sighed.

"Whew," she muttered. "It's tough being a teenager."

Kicking her slippers off, Irma slouched over to her desk and sank into her chair. She rested her head on her forearms and gazed into the black, reptilian – yet somehow inviting – eyes of her pet turtle.

"I envy you, Leafy," she sighed. "I'd like to have a nice shell, just like yours. The same out-fit, every day, for your entire life. But me? I have to choose!"

Leafy looked less than moved. He turned his back to her and swam over to a piece of lettuce he must have overlooked earlier.

Rolling her eyes, Irma flounced out of her chair and opened her wardrobe doors. Her favourite dress – the one with the ruffly collar, sheer flowy sleeves, and swirly skirt – suddenly looked just awful. It was yellow. Yellow! What *had* she been thinking?

"Why can't I ever find what I want," she complained, flopping backwards to sprawl on her pink, smooshy comforter.

"A nice, dark blue dress!" she said. "Now, is that asking for too much? That's all I could wish for."

And then . . . something happened.

Irma felt a familiar thrum. Her fingertips and toes tingled, and she felt a little spark at the back of her neck. It was exactly the feeling that coursed through her when she was conducting her little water ballets. The strange thing was – there wasn't a speck of water in the room. Not unless you counted the murky puddle in the bottom of Leafy's bowl.

But suddenly, there was *something* in Irma's room. It looked like a firefly, and it was hovering right in front of her nose! Irma gasped and stared at it. Where had it come from?

As the little spark of light shimmered and danced before her bulging eyes, Irma realised it was decidedly blue.

Irma blinked and groped for an explanation. Was she seeing spots from gazing up at the lightbulb? Or maybe she was having a weird reaction to her lavender bubble bath.

Before Irma could come up with more theories, the sparkly, floaty thing flew away. It made a shimmering arc across the room, then swirled into the wardrobe.

And that's when her yellow dress, along with all the other clothes in her wardrobe – turned blue.

Navy blue. Just what Irma had asked for.

Stifling a scream, she leaped off the bed and slammed her wardrobe doors shut. She could feel her heart pounding through her fuzzy towel.

She had no idea what to make of this! She shook her head and tried to catch her breath, racking her brain for some logical explanation. But her mind remained stubbornly blank, except for one phrase, that irritating thing her mother always said to her when she was pouting: "Careful what you wish for!"

FIVE

Will watched Cornelia's long blonde hair trail behind her as she rode off down the sunny street. She heaved a big sigh and then returned her attention to her bike seat.

Thwip.

Finally, it snapped into place.

Well, Will thought, I think that was the first thing to go right today. Of course, I never would have had to play bike surgeon in the first place if Uriah hadn't shown up. Jeez, I had to have a run-in with the school bully – *and* the principal – on my first day!

Will felt her shoulders sag wearily as she and Taranee walked their bikes around the corner. As they passed Sheffield's big courtyard, Will's eyes drifted over to the gym – a boxy, modern building next door to the school. The decorating committee was scurrying around like, well, kids on Halloween. One girl was trying to cram an enormous bunch of balloons through the double doors. A jock was teetering on the top of a ladder as he glued ominous black bats to the gym wall. And a whole throng of Sheffielders were slapping papier-mâché onto a giant jack-o'-lantern. Its jagged grin made Will shiver.

"I don't know if I feel like going to the party," Will said quietly as she straddled her bike. "I'm tired. And I might have to help my mum connect to the Internet."

The minute the words left her mouth, she cringed. Lame, lame, lame.

"Well," Taranee said, turning to eye Will, "if you're not going, I'm not going, either!"

Slowly, Will began pedaling down the sidewalk. Taranee rode along next to her.

Will knew she should fight to fit in at Heatherfield, the same way she fought to beat the clock at swimming practise or fought to get along with her mum, even when her mum was driving her crazy.

But the thing was, back in Fadden Hills,

where Will and her mum had lived until just yesterday, Will had gotten accustomed to *not* fighting. In fact, she'd sort of gone into hiding. Will and her mother both had.

The issue? Dad.

Dad refused to let go after the divorce. He called and called and called. He never gave Will's mum a moment's peace.

Finally, her mum had moved them to Heatherfield, where they had an unlisted phone number. And it had worked. There'd been no phone calls since they'd arrived. Not a one from Dad *or* Will's "friends" in Fadden Hills.

Will sighed a shuddery sigh. She couldn't even really accuse her friends of dissing her. After all, she'd been the first one to pull away. During her parents' messy divorce, Will had gotten more quiet, more timid. She definitely was not much fun to be around. She knew that was why her friends had stopped including her in their after-school burger runs and Friday night basketball games. And that was why not one of them had called to check in since she'd moved.

Will's mum said the silence was a relief. But when Will thought of all the quiet in their new apartment – a place right in the city that her mum had chosen for the twenty-four-hour security guard at the gate – she imagined being wrapped in a big down comforter. It was protecting her from the world, but at the same time, it was muffling her, too.

A Halloween party, Will thought. Well, that would be a way to come out from under the covers in full force, wouldn't it?

Before she could change her mind, she whipped her cell phone out of her sweatshirt pocket. Expertly, she dialed with one hand while she steered her bike with the other.

"Let's hear what the boss has to say," she said to Taranee as she mashed the SEND button with her thumb.

"Wow," Taranee said, her eyes widening behind her glasses. "You've got your own cell phone?"

"Yeah," Will said. "My mum works for Simultech. She's never at her desk. So . . . the cell phone is like my second mother."

Will glanced at the sky as the phone rang.

That's funny, she thought. Look at all those black clouds rolling in. Just a minute ago, the sun was blinding.

"Susan Vandom," her mother said, picking up after the third ring.

"Hi, it's m—"

"Will!" Her voice shifted from clipped and professional to warm and gooey in a millisecond. "How was the first day?!"

"Listen," Will said, wanting to avoid the whole first-day rehash for as long as possible. "There's going to be a party at school tonight, and–"

"Fabulous!" Her mother gushed. "That's a great place to make new friends, Will! What luck!"

"Wait," Will said, panic suddenly rising in her throat. She realised that she'd called her mum hoping to get some negative vibes. It would have been a perfect excuse to scrap the whole party plan.

But Will had forgotten how irritatingly cool her mother could be sometimes.

"I'll drive you!" she said.

"Would you let me–" Will stammered.

"You should wear that black halter dress."

"It's just that–"

"What?" Her mother interrupted again. "I assume it's a Halloween party? So the black will be perfect. Plus, Halloween is only your favourite holiday. Well, back when you were trick-or-treating it was, anyway."

"But–"

"I *knew* Heatherfield would be a great place for you," her mother said cheerfully. And suddenly Will knew – there was no getting out of this party. Not unless she wanted to totally worry her mum.

"Okay," Will said, feeling weary once again. "Talk to you later."

Will gave her cell phone a withering glare and pushed END. Then she stashed it back in her pocket and struggled to look at Taranee.

"Did she say no?" Taranee asked. Will could see a familiar seesaw between hope and fear in Taranee's eyes.

"She said yes," Will replied flatly.

"So . . . aren't you happy?"

Will cringed and shot Taranee a wobbly, totally fake grin.

"Can't you tell?" she said and crossed her eyes.

Taranee laughed out loud. And Will found herself smiling for real. For the first time, it occurred to her – maybe she wasn't totally alone in Heatherfield, after all. Maybe she and this fellow newbie could become fast friends.

Will grinned at her new bud. And Taranee responded with a squeal.

"Aaaigh," she cried, looking skyward. "It's raining!"

"Day complete," Will muttered as a fat raindrop hit her on the nose. Her one happy moment was being washed away by a sudden shower.

"I live on the next block," Taranee called as the rain quickly morphed from drizzle to downpour. "Want to come take shelter?"

"Sounds great to me!" Will said. She pedaled after Taranee. A minute later, they pulled up to Taranee's house, which was shiny, white, and ultramodern. It was all about crazy angles and glass bricks. The girls ran inside.

"Tea," Taranee declared, trotting to the kitchen and kicking her wet sneakers under the kidney-shaped, white island. "My parents are still at work, and my brother's probably at the beach. He's completely addicted to surfing. So, we've got the house to ourselves."

She filled a kettle with water and broke out a

couple of mugs and a can of instant chai tea. Then she flounced onto a tall stool and smiled at Will.

Will smiled back. And suddenly, they were deep into chat. They talked about Sesamo, where Taranee was from, and about Fadden Hills. They giggled as they recalled the bizarre bod of Mrs. Knickerbocker. And before Will knew it, an hour had gone by and the sun had reemerged.

"It's stopped raining!" Will said, peering through the kitchen's sliding glass doors in surprise. "I'd better be going. But thanks for having me over, Taranee."

Taranee slumped a little, gazing into the dregs of her chai.

"How are you going to look tonight?" she asked. "Scary or elegant?"

"I always look scary," Will said, pulling on her navy sweatshirt and swiping at her rain-damp red hair. "I've decided to try something new."

Taranee laughed as they headed outside. Will grabbed her bike off the front porch and bounced it down the steps.

"So," Will said, shrugging at Taranee, "I'll pick you up at seven-thirty, then."

Taranee shrugged back with a smile and

said, "On your bike?"

"By car. My mum will take us," Will said, knowing her mum would be psyched to meet her new bud.

"Great," Taranee said. "See you later, Will."

Will grinned and waved as she set off down the street. For a moment, she felt light as air, loving the sizzling sound her tyres made as they skimmed over the wet sidewalk. But the minute Taranee faded from the little rearview mirror on her handlebars, Will felt her grin collapse. She frowned as wet leaves and twigs whipped around her pedaling feet. A mist still hung in the air, making her messy, chin-length locks even more lank than usual.

Maybe I spoke too soon, she wondered as she turned off Taranee's tree-lined street onto one of Heatherfield's main streets. I don't think an elegant dress was such a bright idea. I'd feel a lot better wearing a sweat suit.

She smiled wryly as she rode past a stretch of boutiques, the kind that sold exactly the sort of little, strapless nothings that Will could *not* picture herself wearing.

"I should ask around," she muttered. "Who knows if they sell evening sweats somewhere. If they exist, I bet they're sequined."

Just to make sure there *wasn't* such a thing as sparkled sweats, Will peered into the next window she passed. But she couldn't make out what was inside. All she saw was a reflection of her own whizzing bike wheels and–

"Huh?!" Will gasped. She grabbed her brakes and skidded to a halt. And then, she gaped into the window.

She blinked a few times.

Then she stared some more.

The reflection blinked and stared back at her. But that reflection wasn't her! Or was it?

The girl looking back at her was more like . . . a woman. Her hair was Will's same red mop, but it was straighter, chunkier, cooler. It seemed to flutter perfectly in a breeze that wasn't there. And the face – that was Will's, too, if you added cheekbones and plumped up the lips and put a cool knowingness in her eyes.

And then, there was that body. Her figure was definitely, um, *enhanced*. This fantasy Will was taller than the real Will and had curves at every spot where Will had angles and flat planes. Will's too long, baggy Adidas pants and red T-shirt had been replaced by a tight, belly-button-baring purple top with bell-shaped sleeves. And her long, muscular legs were wrapped in blue-and-turquoise-striped tights and amazingly rad, knee-high boots.

Her backpack, though she could still feel the straps looped around her shoulders, had disappeared from her reflection. And in its place were . . .

Wings.

They looked more flowery than feathery – thin, dark stalks dotted with delicate, translucent petals. As Will stared, the wings undulated lightly, swayed by the same invisible breeze as fantasy Will's mod hairdo.

Will's eyes traveled up and down, and up and down this bizarre reflection until she realised that she'd stopped breathing. She gasped, sucking in a gulp of air. Then, finally, she tore her eyes away from the window. She glanced around quickly to see if anyone else could see what she did, but luckily, this stretch of sidewalk was empty after the rain. She looked up at the sign above the window. No, it wasn't some freak show or occult shop. Just a shabby-looking place called Ye Olde Bookshop.

Almost against her will, Will's sneaker – or was it her purple leather boot? – found her bike pedal. She stood on the pedal so fast that the bike gave a little hop as it began speeding down the sidewalk.

Will pedaled as hard as she could. Her breath came in ragged gasps. She kept her eyes on the cement in front of her, not daring to even glance into any other window she passed. Already, her altered image was beginning to waver in her mind. Perhaps the day's stresses had warped her vision. Maybe fantasy Will hadn't been there at all!

The problem was, Will didn't feel as if she were hallucinating. Or even crazy. Slightly neurotic, yes. But unhinged? No.

Which meant that this figure, this alternate Will, had somehow been . . . real?

Will's mind was racing as fast as her bike. She shook her head, blinking her tousled hair out of her eyes. Through rattling teeth, she muttered, "Th-that can't be!"

SIX

Cornelia couldn't believe this was her life. She was standing in the upstairs hall of her apartment, actually wearing her dress for the party, and her mother was telling her she couldn't go out.

"Forget it, young lady," she was saying, glaring down at Cornelia through her oversized glasses. "Tonight, you're not going anywhere. At least, not until you've cleaned your room!"

The two of them glared through Cornelia's bedroom doorway. Okay, Cornelia had to admit it to herself, the room was a total sty. There were sweaters strewn on the floor and dangling off the dresser after that morning's what-should-I-wear-fest. Research for a biology report was scattered around her desk. Stuffed animals were crashed out at the foot of her unmade bed. Even her ice skates were tossed under the windowsill, and some of her old skating trophies were overturned.

Well, Cornelia thought, I like it that way. So sue me for being a free spirit.

Not that *that* approach would work with her rigid mother. Instead, Cornelia would opt for bargaining.

"Come on, Ma!" she yelled. "I'll do it tomorrow!"

"What's keeping you from doing it now?" her mother said, pursing her lips and crossing her arms. Through a haze of rage, Cornelia was dimly aware of how alike they must look. Both had heart-shaped faces with pointy chins thrust out in identical, angry pouts. Both had long, skinny arms crossed stubbornly over their chests.

This knowledge only made Cornelia angrier. "My genetic coding," she growled, "doesn't let me give in to blackmail!"

"As you like, Cornelia," her mother replied coolly. She turned her back on her daughter and began to head down the stairs to the open, high-ceilinged living room. "If this is a challenge, you're the one who's got everything to lose."

There's only one thing that could make this moment more completely annoying, Cornelia thought.

"Neat!" piped up a squeaky voice behind her.

And *that* would be her, she thought. She turned to glare at her sister, Lilian – six years old and irritating enough to be twins.

"Looks like tonight, we'll all be at home together, huh, big sister?" Lilian said. She sneered slyly up at Cornelia.

"Shut up, you little toad!" Cornelia yelled. Then she began to stomp toward her bedroom. Even stomping made her mad, because stomping on the Oriental rug made no noise whatsoever.

"Why can't rooms just clean themselves?" she groaned.

Slam!

Cornelia reared back in shock. Her bedroom door had just slammed in her face! She whipped around to see Lilian hopping down the stairs, making little toadlike noises.

"Ribbit. Ribbit. Ribbit," Lilian said with each little hop.

Cornelia scowled. Lilian was just trying to get to her. And actually, it had worked. Because if Lilian was out here, that meant she hadn't slipped into Cornelia's room and locked her out. So, who had?

Cornelia frowned and reached for the brass doorknob. She rattled it back and forth, but the door wasn't budging.

Swiiiish, swooosh, swiiish.

Cornelia pressed her ear to her bedroom door. Something was definitely going on in there. It sounded like a wind flapping through crispy autumn leaves.

Feeling the first tremors of panic, Cornelia rattled the knob some more and banged the door with her shoulder.

"Urrrgh," she grunted. "Stupid door. I wonder why it won't . . . aaagh!"

Abruptly, the door opened and Cornelia almost fell inside her room.

Her . . . spotless room.

Cornelia clutched the doorknob weakly and gazed around. Her sweaters were folded on the foot of the bed, which was neatly made. The stuffed animals were smiling sweetly from her pillow. Her books were arranged in precise stacks on the desk. Her trophies had been polished and evenly spaced on the shelves. Her shoes were lined up like soldiers on the rug. Even the rug's fringes were neatly combed!

"Wow," Cornelia whispered. Whispering was all she could manage, considering that she was practically hyperventilating. She took baby steps into her gleaming room.

And that's when she felt a grin slowly work its way across her face.

I can't believe it, she thought, skimming a palm over her dust-free desk. All it took was the thought to make it happen! What Irma can do in class is nothing compared to what I've been able to do lately. In class, I control everything just by wanting it.

She walked, as if in a trance, to her newly organised vanity. Absently, she picked up her lip gloss and plopped a dab of it on her lower lip.

And now this, she thought, pursing her lips together contemplatively. Suddenly, she slumped onto the bed, creasing the perfect quilt.

What's happening to me? she wondered. What does this mean?

She glanced up and caught sight of herself in her vanity mirror. Her cheeks were as pink as her floaty dress, and her eyes were sparkling. The sight of her dress made Cornelia remember what had started this whole mysterious room-cleaning. Her mother. Her *smug* mother, who thought Cornelia would be spending the night sulkily scrubbing her room.

Ha! Cornelia thought, bouncing off the bed. I know exactly what this means. It means I'm going to the Halloween party!

She went to the closet for her hot-pink shawl, which was – naturally – dangling from a hanger. She swept the shawl triumphantly around her shoulders and bounded out of her room. Then she hurried down to the living room and made a beeline for the front door.

"Cornelia!" her mother said.

Oops. Cornelia hadn't seen her mum lounging on the couch on the other side of their cavernous living room. Mum was reading a magazine, and Lilian was camped out next to her. "Where do you think you're going?"

"To the party," Cornelia called out breezily. "My room's clean."

As Cornelia bolted for the door, she saw her mother leap off the couch.

"Cornelia?" she called threateningly. "For your own sake, that had better be true. Cornelia!"

But Cornelia didn't stop. Why should she? It *was* true. Her room was clean.

Flying out the door, she practically crashed into her dad, who was just arriving home from work. He looked a little tired, but cheerful, in his damp raincoat and windswept brown hair.

"Hi, Pop!" Cornelia called, waving goodbye to him as she ran to catch the elevator.

"Hey," her father said jovially. "Did I miss something?"

There was no time to answer before the elevator doors closed, with Cornelia safely inside. She hit the lobby button and heaved a big sigh, leaning against the mirrored wall.

"Oh, boy, Pop," she muttered, shaking her head in disbelief. "Did you ever!"

SEVEN

After she'd arrived home from the most bizarre bike ride of her life, Will had gone to her room and collapsed onto her bed, banging into a half-unpacked box as she did. She kicked the box onto the floor and then looked around, gazing at this strange new room of hers. All she saw was chaos – rain-damp boxes, her frog collection scattered across her furniture, clothes tossed around the room.

The pile of clothes reminded her of what Cornelia had said before she rode away. "Don't forget to wear a dress.... Just make sure it's special."

A miniskirt, purple boots, and a pair of wings, Will thought. Well, *that's* pretty special.

Then Will shook her head. She just couldn't

forget the image she'd seen reflected in the bookshop window.

But she also couldn't *stand* to think about it. It was too much to handle today! Will flopped onto her stomach and stared at the phone on her nightstand. She loved her old-fashioned white phone – it was called the Princess style – and she loved her creaky, old, wooden nightstand. If she squinted at them hard, she could tune out everything else in this room. She could pretend that she was back home in Fadden Hills. And her phone was just about to ring. There'd be a bunch of friends giggling on the other end, inviting her out for a movie.

Ring, she willed the phone. Ring . . . ring . . .

Will awoke with a start and blinked blearily. The first thing she saw was her telephone – her utterly silent telephone.

It's *so* silent, Will thought, rolling over to the edge of the bed, that I must have dozed off for a minute. Rubbing one eye, she looked around for her frog with the clock in its belly. It was gone, just like the rest of her stuff – lost in the mess somewhere.

Yawning loudly, Will heaved herself off the

bed and stumbled to the window. Then she woke up completely.

It was pitch-black out! What *time* was it?!

She rushed into the hallway and glanced at the wall clock: 10:04! She'd fallen asleep for hours! With a yelp, Will ran into the bathroom, discarding clothes as she went. Then she jumped into the shower.

Five minutes later, she was rushing around her room in her underwear, her hair dripping into her eyes, looking desperately for something to wear.

After throwing the contents of about six boxes onto the floor, she unearthed a dress – a short, red velvet shift with wide shoulder straps. She pulled it over her head and spun in front of her full-length mirror.

Okay, this is not good, Will thought. She skimmed her hands over the dress, flattening it against her hips. She caught a hint of curve, but as soon as she let go, the dress hung away from her body again, as lifeless as ever.

She turned sideways. Okay, *that* was even more depressing. She was a two-by-four in red.

"Will!"

Her mum's voice startled her out of her

gloom. Will turned and glared at the door. She could just picture her mum leaning against it, rolling her big brown eyes and gazing down her long, Roman nose at her watch.

"It's super-late," her mum said through the door.

"Who cares about the party?" Will yelled, whipping the red dress off and clenching it in her fist. "I didn't want to go, anyway. You're the one who insisted."

She held the straps up to her shoulders, dangling the dress over her body. She glared down at the lifeless fabric.

"On top of that," she ranted, "I have *nothing* to wear. Everything makes me look like a surfboard and . . . and . . ."

Will's voice trailed off to a bewildered squeak as she caught a glimpse of her reflection in the mirror.

The face in the mirror wore Will's surprised expression. The hand clutched the withered, red velvet dress. But the body . . . once again, it was utterly foreign – tall and shapely, with a waist that nipped in and hips that flared out. Will's eyes traveled to her reflection's chest and blushed. This *had* to be a figment of her imagination.

"That's . . . that's not me," Will whispered, reaching out towards the mirror. The reflection's hand touched her own with strange, manicured fingers. Will stared at this . . . this ghost and was powerless to do anything but tremble.

"Will?"

In the top corner of the mirror, Will spotted her mother's face, peeking around her open door and gazing at her questioningly.

What will she think? Will thought in a nervous panic. Her daughter has suddenly been replaced by a stranger!

"Aaaaagh!" Will screamed, covering her face with the dress. "Don't come in! Don't come in!"

"What?!"

Will peeked out from behind her dress to see her mother, fully inside her room now. She was looking at Will in irritation. Will searched her mum's face for shock and horror, as well. But there was none.

Will bit her lower lip and glanced back at the mirror. She was back – the real Will, flat chest, knobby knees, and all. She looked disheveled, scared, and just a little bit nuts.

"Why aren't you dressed yet?" her mum

asked, glancing at her watch. She pointed at a filmy, black dress crumpled in the bottom of a box – Will's halter dress with the little rose at the neck. "Aren't you going to put that black one on? It used to be your favourite."

"The only thing in black that would look good on me is a garbage bag," Will said, feeling the sting of tears springing to her eyes.

"What are you talking about?" her mum said, gently laying a hand on Will's shoulder. "What's wrong?"

"I look like, no, I *am* a broomstick," Will said through a choked sob. She batted the red velvet dress angrily against her skinny leg.

But she had to admit, she felt a tiny bit better when her mother gave her shoulders a little squeeze.

"You are a special girl who will meet new special friends at the party, just as you are." Then she grabbed Will by the shoulders and turned her towards the mirror. Will looked at her mother. She saw a pretty woman with long, wavy black hair and big hoop earrings. And next to her, she saw a girl. A skinny girl with a scruffy head of hair and wan, red-rimmed eyes.

"Look at yourself, Will," her mother said. "You have to love yourself, because only in this way will you allow other people to appreciate your qualities."

Will squinted at her reflection. Was it *possible* to love herself in this state? She decided to give a small smile a try. She lifted a corner of her mouth.

Not bad.

She raised the other corner.

Will didn't want to admit it, but it *did* help.

She grabbed the black dress out of the box and held it up against her body. Not bad, again. *Definitely* better than that old red dress.

"Now, let's get going," her mum said. "The party won't last forever."

"And we have to pick up Taranee," Will added. Thankfully, Taranee was not mad about the late ride. She was happy that Will still wanted to go.

Twenty minutes later, Mrs. Vandom and the two girls pulled up at Sheffield. Will and Taranee hopped out of the car and waved good-bye to Will's mum, who hung her head out of the window and grinned.

"Have a great time," she called. "Hey,

Taranee, take good care of Will for me. She's a shy girl. Put a little fire into her!"

"See you later, Mum," Will said, feeling her cheeks go hot. She felt a surge of gratitude for Taranee's sweet smile. It would have been so easy to snort with laughter, point at Will and shriek, "Mama's girl!"

Instead, Taranee just waved at Mrs. Vandom and said, "Maybe I'm not the right person for the job, but I'll try!"

The girls followed the orange-and-black signs taped to fence posts, pillars, and any other available surface. They all pointed to the party. With each step closer to the pounding music and shrill chatter of the dance, Will's mouth got drier.

"We're still in time, Taranee," she hissed into her friend's ear. Or what would have been her ear if Taranee hadn't dressed as a sort of neopunk Amelia Earhart. She was wearing a leather aviator's cap, complete with goggles and earflaps, and a zebra-striped coat over her simple pink dress. "Let's turn around and get out of here."

"Looks like it's too late," Taranee said, sounding just as tremulous as Will did.

"Cornelia!"

Will gasped and peeked over Taranee's shoulder. Yup – there was the blonde goddess herself, looking as gorgeous as ever in a tiny purple camisole and voluminous pink skirt. She looked every bit the popular girl. But Cornelia's smile was as warm and welcoming as it had been that afternoon.

"Hours late," Cornelia said with a grin. "Fashionably late, you might say. That's okay. The party's just hitting its peak."

EIGHT

Irma looked down at the filmy, indigo skirt of her once-yellow dress and willed it to shimmy back and forth, or spin around or . . . *something*.

You're at a party, she told herself irritably. She glanced at the costumed kids milling around the gym in hockey masks and devil's horns and dramatic, flowing dresses. Cobalt Blue was on the stage, slamming out an Alicia Keys cover. The overhead lights had been covered with gold cellophane and candles burned in the rafters, giving the entire room a hazy yellow glow.

A party, Irma reminded herself again. As in *fun*? As in dancing and flirting with boys and raiding the cupcake platter?

But it's hard to dance when you're seething. Which is exactly what Irma had been doing ever since she made the mistake of confiding in her friends about her wardrobe's magical transformation. Hay Lin and Elyon had laughed so hard, they'd almost collapsed on the floor.

"Your dress turned from yellow to blue," Hay Lin snorted. She looked down at her own silky kimono, which was just as gorgeous as she'd promised. "And I'm actually a Japanese geisha."

"Next thing you know, she'll come to school as a blonde and tell us, 'I didn't dye it. It was *magic,*'" Elyon squealed.

Elyon's just picking on me to distract us from her punishment, Irma had thought angrily. She gave the band's lead singer, Matt Olsen – otherwise known as Elyon's big crush – an angry glare.

And now, to top it all off, Irma's friends weren't paying *any* attention to her. They'd all traipsed to the gym door to greet the new girls, Will and Taranee. Cornelia was planting a pointy black witch's hat onto Will's sheepish head.

"It's my fault we're late," Will said. "I lost track of time, and. . . ."

"Hear that, Irma?" Elyon said, turning to grin at her. She was dressed as an elf, or imp, or fairy – something mischievous, anyway. She wore a feathery green tunic and a crown of leaves. "This is what I call an original excuse!"

Hay Lin glanced at Irma and giggled.

"She got here late, too," she told Will and Taranee. "And do you want to know what excuse she made up?"

"There's nothing to laugh about," Irma retorted with a scowl. "All of the clothes in my wardrobe *did* change colour."

Hay Lin and Elyon burst into another round of hysterical giggles. Irma squirmed some more. She knew if it had been anyone else telling such a crazy story, she'd be the one laughing loudest. But, well, the shoe was on the other foot now. And boy, did their laughing make Irma mad.

"It's the truth!" she yelled at Hay Lin and Elyon. "And if you don't want to believe it, that's your problem."

Will stepped in from the doorway and met Irma's eyes.

"I believe it," she said quietly.

Before Irma could flash her a grateful smile, Martin Tubbs appeared.

Martin! Any time Irma least wanted to see him, which was, well, pretty much always, there he was. And each time he was goofier than the last. Tonight he was wrapped in about a hundred yards of tattered bandages. Behind his Coke-bottle glasses, he blinked dreamily at Irma.

"Hi, Irma," he whispered. When she glared at him with what she hoped were icy eyes, he leaped back and whipped out a Polaroid camera. At least Martin *sometimes* knew how to read Irma's "get lost" signals.

"How about a picture, gals?" he called.

"Yeah!" Hay Lin cried. She slung her arms over Will's and Taranee's shoulders, and Elyon and Cornelia squeezed in. Then Hay Lin grabbed Irma and yanked her into the shot.

"I'll never tell you any secrets again," Irma hissed to Hay Lin. "So there!"

"Smile, ladies!" Hay Lin called, grinning into Martin's camera and pointedly ignoring Irma.

As soon as Martin's flashbulb popped, Cornelia and Taranee drifted off toward the refreshments, leaving Irma, Hay Lin, Will, and Elyon to groove to Cobalt Blue's throbbing music. The last note of Matt's song seemed to echo through the gym, causing Elyon to go all pale and trembly. Irma rolled her eyes and glanced at Will.

What's this? she thought. Looks like Will's getting a little misty-eyed, too!

Will gazed at Matt as he heaved his guitar out of the way and grabbed the microphone.

"Thirty minutes till midnight, my friends," he yelled into the mike. "Halloween is here! A big hello to the great pumpkin, yeah!"

"Oh . . ." Will said quietly.

Uh-oh, Irma thought. I smell a new crush!

"Cute, huh?" Hay Lin said to Will. "His name's Matt. He's the one that Elyon likes. He's a little older than us."

"I thought the older guys were all like Uriah," Will said breathily.

"Speaking of," Irma broke in, "hope you're not too hungry, Will. Uriah and his drones practically cleaned out the sandwich buffet earlier. Totally on Knickerbocker's radar, too. I heard her talking to them." Then Irma added in her best Mrs. Knickerbocker impersonation,

"'*Bon appétit*, boys. From the looks of your booty, I'd say you all like the buffet.' And then Uriah was all, 'It's not how it looks, Principal. We're only stocking up on our winter supplies.'"

"Ugh," Will said.

"That's what Knickerbocker thought," Irma continued happily. She *loved* when she had good gossip to dispense. "So she was all, 'I guess that means you're ready to spend another school year in hibernation? Excellent!'"

"Go, Knickerbocker," Hay Lin squealed with a laugh.

"Yeah, Uriah was really bugged," Irma giggled. "Haven't seen him since."

"But I *do* see someone new," Elyon interrupted. By now, their group had migrated further into the party. They were hanging in a cluster, halfway between the dance floor and the gym door. And walking through that door was a guy who looked so cool it was hard to believe he was in high school. He totally wasn't Irma's type, but even she couldn't help staring at him. He was so *dramatic*, with straight, silky brown hair that hung from a blue stocking cap all the way to his waist. He wore a long, deep purple coat and an angular turtleneck straight out of *Star Wars*. A bright pink mask hid his eyes, but Irma could still tell he was a hottie, with a chiseled chin; fine, small nose; and skin that was pale and perfect.

"So what do you think of that guy who just came in?" Elyon said. Irma could practically see Matt being erased from her mental crush book, to be quickly replaced by this mystery man.

"Never seen him before!" Hay Lin gasped. "He looks out of this world!"

"But he's wearing a mask," Cornelia said. She'd just returned from the snack table, empty-handed.

"He still looks out of this world," Hay Lin gushed.

"They all seem out of this world to you, Hay Lin," Irma said, giving her friend a sidelong glance.

"That's not true," Hay Lin retorted. "For example, the one who's walking up to you now is *uuuugly*."

"How about another picture, sweet thing," said an all-too-familiar male voice behind Irma. "Just you and me?"

"Martin!" Irma said, spinning around to

glare at the oh-so-geeky pest. "Disappear!"

Irma immediately turned back to her friends. Taranee had just rejoined them, carrying two cups of lurid pink punch. She handed one to Will.

"You know something, girls," Cornelia was saying. "I'd say that guy over there is cute enough for Elyon's punishment."

Elyon looked not at all unhappy at the prospect. In fact, she had that heavy-lidded, flushed-cheek look that screamed "boy crazy."

"I'm sure he gives great maths lessons," Elyon cooed. She gave her friends a little goodbye wave and began making her way through the crowded gym to talk to the stranger.

"You go, girl," Irma cried with a laugh.

"Okay," Cornelia said, rubbing her fingertips together and turning to the group. "We're accepting bets on Elyon, ladies. I say she won't do it."

"Well, she did look pretty determined," Taranee said, taking a shy slurp of her punch. "What do you think, Will?"

"I . . . I . . ." Irma watched in alarm as Will's eyes went blank. She suddenly seemed overwhelmed by the crush of people around her.

Irma couldn't blame her. Some seventh-graders had started slam dancing nearby. A wacky kid in a Donald Duck costume was jostling Will as he pushed by with a platter of sandwiches on his head. And an enormous, surly-looking guy – must have been a football player – was looming over her in an ugly, blue, monster mask.

But then, Donald Duck slammed into the blue guy and knocked him back into the crowd, giving Will some space to breathe. It must have helped, because her eyelids fluttered and she seemed to shake the fog out of her head. Then she slowly grinned at her friends.

"I say Elyon can do it," she said. Irma felt a stab of affection for the scruffy new girl. First, she'd been the only one in the group who'd believed Irma's story. Now she was struggling to be cool, even though she was clearly freaked by the wildness of the party.

Cornelia must have sensed this, too, Irma grudgingly admitted to herself. Because she shot Will a look of concern.

"Everything okay?" she asked.

"I guess so," Will said, pressing a palm to one ear. "But don't you guys hear a strange humming noise, too?"

"The music is too loud," Taranee shouted. "Let's get away from here."

As the girls edged towards the door, Irma glanced over her shoulder, then blinked in surprise. Elyon – shy, sweet, awkward Elyon – was showing all the signs of expert flirtation. (And Irma certainly knew how to recognise them.) She was waggling her fingers at the new hottie and shooting him a lopsided grin. Irma even thought she saw Elyon wink.

But before Irma could get closer to spy on Elyon's close encounter of the cute kind, she heard a plopping noise. She spun around just in time to see Will lurch. She looked like she was about to faint!

"Uuuhhh," Will groaned. She'd dropped her cup of punch on the floor, and Taranee was grabbing her arm.

"Will," she exclaimed. "Do you feel okay?"

Will shook her head blearily. Over her head, Irma noticed that blue guy again. He was coming straight toward them.

Ewww! Irma thought. What a creep! Why doesn't he get lost? Then she returned her attention to Will, who looked a bit better.

"Just a short dizzy spell," Will was saying.

"Maybe a breath of fresh air would do me some good."

"We'll go with you," Cornelia said as Irma nodded.

Anything to get away from this scene and that pushy blue dude, she thought.

She was also still feeling a little cranky after the whole blue dress humiliation, not to mention two annoying buttinskies by the wretched Martin.

At least *he* seems to have evaporated, Irma thought. As she followed her friends out of the gym, she scanned the room. She didn't see a trace of the nerd-turned-mummy.

Well, Irma thought with a sigh, I guess this time, getting my wish was a good thing!

NINE

The Oracle was floating, suspended in a place both ethereal and solid – a platform that hovered in the very center of the Temple of Candracar. This was the Oracle's place of respite, where artwork created by a thousand otherworldly craftsmen decorated every inch of the walls; where the air was so thin and clean, it almost sparkled; where the Oracle's powers to see all, and know all, were at their most crystalline.

He knelt on the tiny platform, peace suffusing his face as he closed his eyes and focused his energy. His adviser, Tibor, stood sentinel behind him as always. Tibor's spine was ramrod straight and his eyes alert. His white beard and mustache were so long they nearly brushed against the Oracle's back. But the Oracle knew that age was irrelevant to Tibor's strength. The man was powerful. He was the brawn that allowed the Oracle to concentrate all his mental powers on the new Guardians, the young girls whom he had anointed to protect the Veil. Only this quickly thinning Veil separated evil – which had been exiled to the world of Metamoor – from good, which existed on earth.

If the girls failed at their mission, life as all knew it would be destroyed. The balance was growing more tenuous by the day – the Oracle could sense it. And the disruptive storms showering Heatherfield served as concrete warnings.

But the Oracle was not afraid.

For their salvation had begun.

In his unlined, outstretched hand, a small square suddenly appeared. It was a photograph of six girls. One wore an indigo dress, another, a flowing kimono. There was the mysterious one in an impish green costume. And then, of course, the one, the heart, she with the hair like flames and the sad, brown eyes.

"The new Guardians, Tibor," the Oracle

said. His voice sounded more like a dozen voices, all singing in harmony.

"Look at them!" the Oracle continued, gazing at the picture. "They are close."

"But not yet united," Tibor noted in his rumbly growl. The two gazed into the picture and saw the evil that lurked beyond its frame.

They saw Lord Cedric disguised in a stocking cap and a long cloak, which were both blue, the colour of royalty. With him was the hulking monster Vathek. His skin was bright blue, his skull a lumpish monstrosity with beady, deep-set eyes. He loomed over the partygoers.

And then he spoke to his master. The Oracle could hear Vathek's words, though they were issued in the most guttural whisper.

"She's coming towards us, sir," Vathek said. He motioned with his scaly, blue chin towards the girl in green, the one called Elyon. The Oracle gazed at Elyon's shy smile. He read her thoughts: "He's so cute. He couldn't possibly be interested in someone as minor as me. But what do I have to lose?"

The Oracle almost chuckled at all that Elyon – and her friends – did not know.

"I'll take care of her, Vathek," Cedric whispered to his thug. His voice was as silky as a snake's hiss. "You think about the redhead. You know what to do."

"You can count on me, sir," Vathek said, baring his razorlike teeth in a grim smile. "In all this confusion, no one will notice me."

The music surged louder. The dancers grew more frenetic. The Oracle felt a stab of negative energy. At that moment, Lord Cedric and Elyon – the dark and the light – made their first contact.

"Umm, hi!" Elyon squeaked, waggling her fingers at the dark lord.

"Hello, Elyon," he replied. In the dim light, Elyon couldn't see the death in Cedric's icy blue eyes or the tightness of his smile. She did go wide-eyed, however, at the mention of her own name.

"You know my name?" Elyon said softly. "Who are you?"

"My name's Cedric," the evil lord replied.

Meanwhile, across the room, the outspoken one in the blue dress – Irma – was wielding power she didn't even know she had.

"Martin," she said to a hapless admirer behind her. "Disappear!"

And he did – literally going invisible in the blink of an eye. The Oracle could sense the boy's aura, continuing to move through the party, oblivious to his magical state of nothingness. There was no need to worry, the Oracle knew. This invisibility was only temporary.

Also oblivious was the heart, Will, who was swayed, but not conquered by the lurking presence of Vathek. He had come at her through the crowd, hurling toxic psychic waves in her direction.

The first time he'd lunged at her, he was intercepted by a boy with the head of a duck and a plate of food.

I almost had her! the Oracle heard Vathek think.

A few minutes later, Vathek made another pass, this time causing Will to drop her drink and waver, almost fainting. Her dizziness caused the Oracle to close his eyes and gird himself against a wave of pain.

As Will's friends whisked her out of the gym for fresh air, Vathek stormed after them in a rage. He pushed past a child who grinned at him and said, "Hey, cool costume, Bud!"

Humans! Vathek thought, his disdain searing the Oracle's mind. Maybe they wouldn't be so friendly if they knew that this is what I *really* look like.

Then something – or rather, *nothing* – stopped the blue brute in his tracks.

"Ouch!" cried a disembodied voice. Only the Oracle could see the spirit of the boy, the one wrapped in rags called Martin.

"Why don't you look where you're going, you big ox!" Martin yelled.

"Who . . . who said that?" Vathek growled, spinning around in confusion.

"I did!" Martin said. Suddenly, he shimmered into view, just as the Oracle had known he would.

"By the moons of Gaahn," Vathek said, invoking one of Metamoor's evil gods. "An invisible being!"

"Okay, so I'm not very popular here at school," Martin complained, glaring up at Vathek, "but you don't have to rub my nose in it."

Vathek gaped at Martin, who shrugged the disrespect away. He was used to it, the Oracle knew.

"In any case, great mask," Martin said, lifting his camera to his eyes. "You deserve a photo!"

His camera's flash exploded, bathing Vathek in a blast of light.

"Aaaaagh," the thug cried, clutching his enormous head. "My eyes! AAAARRRGGH! I can't stand light."

Vathek staggered heavily backward, crashing into a table of refreshments and sending drinks and bowls of potato chips flying. While nearby children screeched and leaped out of the way, Martin merely peered at his Polaroid as it developed in his hand.

"It came out a bit blurry, I'd say," Martin said.

Vathek growled. Smoke puffed out of his nostrils as he lunged for the skinny boy.

"You'll pay for this, microbe!" he growled. But, then, an echoing, amplified voice startled him out of his attack. It was the boy on the stage, the one Will had been gazing at admiringly.

"Your attention for a moment, guys," he yelled into his microphone. "Only three minutes left till midnight!"

An elderly woman in a voluminous robe and a large bubble of white hair took the microphone from the boy.

"And now it's time to burn the giant jack-o'-lantern in front of the school," the woman, the leader of these children, said. "But first, we'll award the prize for the best costume of the evening. And by unanimous vote, ladies and gentlemen, the winner is . . . that very large blue boy over there."

That would be the very large, blue Vathek, who was in the middle of contemplating his revenge against Martin.

"Let's see," Vathek was muttering. "I could turn you into a wart, but I'm not so sure that anyone would notice the difference – huh?"

With a start, Vathek noticed all eyes turning to him. And slowly, he comprehended the ridiculous fact that *he* had just won a Halloween costume contest. A crowd of chattering children grabbed the blue beast away from Martin and began shoving him through the gym door towards the giant pumpkin that rested on the front lawn.

"And there, on the grass," the Oracle said to Tibor, "the Guardians are waiting. The secret will soon be revealed, and the five will be together at last."

"Five?" Tibor said, peering over his master's

shoulder at the photograph in his hand. "I see six, sir."

"One of them will betray the others, my friend," the Oracle said quietly. "The moment they unite will also be the moment of betrayal."

TEN

Taranee gazed worriedly at Will, who was still a little shaky after her dizzy spell in the party. They were standing with Cornelia, Hay Lin, and Irma on the lawn just outside the gym door. And secretly, Taranee was relieved. The throbbing noise of the party and all those carefree, dancing people – they'd made her feel so out of place. The fact that most of these strangers wore costumes that blew away Taranee's simple, short-sleeved pink frock – *that* Taranee could handle. But dancing and totally letting go of all cares? Taranee had just never seen the point. She'd always been more comfortable being on the outside, peeking in. That was probably why she was happiest behind a camera, capturing the actions and images of other people.

Speaking of images, there was one out here that was totally creeping Taranee out – that giant papier-mâché jack-o'-lantern with its slit eyes and jagged grin. It was nothing but a big, fake pumpkin, but it made her shiver. Why did it seem so . . . sinister to her?

Taranee's brooding was interrupted by a chorus of whoops and yowls coming from inside the gym.

"And now what's going on?" she asked, watching anxiously as a crowd of people came tumbling out onto the lawn.

"It's the grand finale," Hay Lin explained. "The person with the best costume gets the honour of setting fire to the jack-o'-lantern."

Taranee watched as Mrs. Knickerbocker marched over to the jack-o'-lantern. She looked just like a circus tent in her billowing witch's robe and pointy black hat. High over her head she held an old-fashioned torch. Taranee was mesmerized by the violent, barely contained flame at the end of the torch. It looked so strong, almost as if it wanted to leap out of Mrs. Knickerbocker's grip. A plume of angry smoke billowed off the flame, clouding up the clear night air.

Close behind the principal, a bunch of kids were laughing and shoving that giant guy in the blue mask out of the gym.

Wow, that *is* some costume, Taranee thought. Those lumps all over his big, blue head are really disgusting. And he even got himself some big, blue hands with long, cracked claws. *Ewww.* They must be latex, but they sure look real.

For some reason, however, this kid wanted none of his "best costume" glory.

"Let me go!" he shouted, struggling to squirm away from the grip of half a dozen giggling kids. "Put me down. You're making a big mistake. You'll be sorry for this!"

"Halloween! Halloween!" the crowd was chanting. They formed a circle around the jack-o'-lantern, sweeping Taranee and her friends into their midst. The boy in blue staggered a bit. He gaped at the crowd as if he were an alien from outer space, encountering modern teen life for the first time.

What's up with this guy? Taranee wondered. She looked at her new friends. Hay Lin and Irma were jumping up and down and chanting along with the crowd: "Halloween! Halloween!"

Cornelia was smiling serenely, clapping in time to the chant. And Will was looking at the spectacle in a daze. Her shiny brown eyes reflected the red, dancing flames of Mrs. Knickerbocker's torch.

The principal turned to the reluctant honouree.

"Come on, be a sport," she said, reaching up and grabbing the guy's lumpy blue mask by one of its pointy ears. "Before we find out who's behind this great mask, how about getting our bonfire going?"

She held the torch out to the hulking, blue dude. But he only growled angrily in return.

"Oh, wow!" Taranee gasped. "He's giving the principal major lip! I wonder how much detention he's going to ge – *aaaaagh!*"

Taranee let out a little squeal as the blue boy did something even more shocking than talking back. He swatted the torch right out of Mrs. Knickerbocker's hand, sending it flying over his shoulder onto the papier-mâché pumpkin. Immediately, the jack-o'-lantern ignited.

"No one treats Vathek in this manner," he roared. "You have gone too far, you repulsive mass of cells."

Taranee sucked in her breath as Mrs. Knickerbocker stared at the hulking guy. She could see the principal's face move quickly from shock to cool dismissal.

"You're Samson, from homeroom 410, aren't you?" she said threateningly. "I recognise you, and I don't find you the least bit amusing."

Another big, thuggish boy stumbled out of a nearby cluster of partygoers. He was Frankenstein to a T–right down to the fake stitches in his forehead and the bolts poking out of his neck.

"Um, *I'm* Samson, ma'am," he said to Mrs. Knickerbocker.

"Huh?" the principal said in surprise. She turned slowly to the blue guy. And this time, Taranee thought she saw a flicker of fear in the old lady's eyes.

"So, who are you?" she demanded of the stranger.

Fwoooooom!

Before he could answer, a whoosh of hot air rushed out of the jack-o'-lantern. The small fire had really caught now. The flames began to crackle and leap several feet into the air.

But something was wrong.

This doesn't feel like some beachside bonfire, Taranee thought. She felt the hairs on the back of her neck stand up. She turned to her friends, wanting to describe the apprehension she felt. But she was speechless. She felt as if she were slogging through water, suppressed by slow motion. She could only stare at Will, her mouth open, her voice choked, her eyes wide with fear.

And she didn't have to wait long for that vague fear to be realised.

Ka-POW!

The scary-looking jack-o'-lantern exploded, sending rockets whistling into the black sky and shooting plumes of fire out towards the stunned crowd of kids.

The chaos was immediate.

"Aaaaaiggh!"

"Look out!"

"Everything's on fire!"

Like a panicked school of fish, the revelers began to fan out, getting as far away from the pumpkin as possible. Some ran back into the gym while others tore screaming into the street.

SSSsssss-FWOOOM!

The pumpkin unleashed another ominous set of explosions. Another firecracker zipped wildly through the air, trailing sparks. And the flames that engulfed the pumpkin grew hotter, higher, brighter.

But through the fire, Taranee could still see the outline of the jack-o'-lantern, and even its scary smile. Instinctively, she knew this was not the end. She began to think of the great pumpkin as a live being, an enemy, gearing up for a big finale.

Out of her peripheral vision, she saw Irma run and cower against the gym's outside wall. Cornelia gathered her billowing pink skirt around her and grabbed Hay Lin. The two scurried away from the pumpkin, stopping further out on the green lawn to turn and gape at the fiery spectacle.

Meanwhile, Will was staring at Taranee in horror.

"Let's get out of here, quick!" Will cried, starting to run after Cornelia and Hay Lin. That's when Taranee noticed the big blue thug.

He was right behind Will, running at top speed. But he didn't look as if he was fleeing like the rest of the kids. In fact, he was bearing down on Will. His eyes were squinty and malevolent.

"The girl!" Taranee heard him grunt. ". . . My chance!"

What's going on? a voice inside Taranee screamed. What does he want with Will? Why is this happening?

FWOOOOM-pop-pop-pop-pop!

With another tremendous roar, the jack-o'-lantern sent forth yet another flurry of rockets. Before Taranee could even react, one of them hit Will's attacker – right in his big blue butt!

"Yeow!" the guy screeched, his eyes going wild with pain. He reared back as Will ducked from beneath his grabbing hands. She had no idea that she'd even been in danger!

"Eeeeeek!"

Taranee spun around at the sound of the terrified shriek behind her.

Irma was clutching at the gym wall, screaming in terror as a rocket headed straight for her.

"Look out, Irma!" Taranee cried.

Once again, Taranee felt as if time had slowed down. She was aware of her hands flying into the air, reaching out for Irma. She could feel her eyes bulging in fear.

But this time, she wasn't speechless.

"STOP!" she cried.

Fzzzkzzzz.

Taranee gasped as the rocket – stopped! It hovered in midair, literally inches from Irma's nose. Irma stared, then squeezed her eyes shut and hunched her shoulders, preparing for the worst.

But Taranee wasn't going to let the worst happen. She felt something, like a band of energy, connect her with that sizzling rocket. She squinted at it. Every ounce of her being spoke silently to it.

And, somehow, for some reason, it obeyed her silent command. Taranee waved her arms upwards. The firework followed the direction of her wave as if she were a puppeteer, and the rocket a marionette. It veered straight up, skimming past Irma and hurtling into the night sky.

Taranee gazed at the rocket, feeling a mixture of disbelief and incredible power. She had no idea what was happening inside of her. It was as if the front of her mind had checked out. She was all senses and intuition. And those were what had told her to speak to the rocket, to direct the fire.

But even thinking those things somehow caused the bond between Taranee and the rocket to break. She shook her head, as if coming out of a fog, and gazed at the rocket as it whirled and whistled through the sky. Taranee was dimly aware of Will standing a few feet away, bathed in the orange glow of the fiery pumpkin. She was just as transfixed by the soaring rocket.

And Will continued to stand there, paralysed, as the rocket began to shoot back to earth. In fact, it was hurtling right back into the jack-o'-lantern from which it had first sprung.

BWWOOOOOMMM!

As the rocket made impact, the pumpkin's scary smile finally disappeared. In fact, the entire thing exploded in a huge, billowing burst of fire.

A rush of searing air accompanied the explosion. Taranee watched Will's face contort in horror as the heat knocked her peaked witch's hat from her head.

"Will!" Taranee screamed. Bursts of fire, resembling angry, orange claws, leaped out of the jack-o'-lantern. In another instant, those claws were going to engulf Taranee's friend. They were going to kill her!

Taranee threw her hands out in front of her, pushing against the angry heat with all her psychic might. She could hear her voice ring out. She was screaming. She was issuing an order.

"BACK!" Taranee cried.

And – the fire retreated.

Will collapsed onto the grass, her body bathed in the glow of flames that were perilously close, but no longer near enough to harm her. Gasping and sputtering, she crawled away from the fire just as Taranee's history teacher, Mr. Collins, dashed in and began to fight off the flames with a fire extinguisher.

Will gazed up at Taranee in shock. Hay Lin, Irma, and Cornelia stumbled over and stared at her, too.

"I think you owe us some kind of explanation, Taranee," Will said in a haggard whisper. "How . . . how did you do that?"

Taranee was staring at her hands. They had redirected a rocket. They had literally fought fire. But now they were only trembling.

"I don't know, Will," she squeaked. "I really don't know."

Will stumbled to her feet and threw her arms around Taranee. Her body shook with grateful sobs.

"You saved her life," Cornelia said, resting a gentle hand on Taranee's shoulder. Irma and Hay Lin also patted her comfortingly.

But Taranee merely stared over Will's shoulder at the dying flames of the jack-o'-lantern. What did I do? she thought, over and over.

And beneath that incessant question was another of even greater importance.

Who am I?

ELEVEN

Elyon leaned back against a tree in front of the school and sniffed the air. A full school day had gone by since the Halloween fire, but she could still smell acrid smoke in the air.

Even though she'd been inside the gym, flirting with Cedric when the fire had happened, she felt haunted by it. She could have died! Or the school where she'd been a student ever since kindergarten might have burned to the ground.

Most people would cheer at the idea. And sure, Elyon had made plenty of jokes with her friends about being cooped up in the Sheffield *Institution*.

But, she thought, fiddling idly with the tail of one of her straw-coloured braids, I guess that fire made me realise something. Sheffield's sort of a second home to me.

She supposed if she felt a *little* closer to her parents, she wouldn't cling to her school so much. At least, that's what the Institute's counselor had told her once, during one of Sheffield's mandatory "check-ins."

Elyon rolled her pale blue eyes. Best not to go there. After all, there were so many more pleasant things to think about. Like Uriah and his gang stuck in detention for two weeks after it had been revealed that they'd planted fireworks in the jack-o'-lantern.

Elyon spotted the boys reporting to Mrs. Knickerbocker on the main lawn. They each held a huge garbage bag in which they'd collected singed leaves, papers, paper plates and cups, and whatever other gross garbage was left over from the Halloween party.

Ha, Elyon thought. Serves 'em right.

Her gaze lifted from the icky Uriah to the sky, which was clear, blue, and gorgeous.

Just like Cedric's eyes, Elyon thought with a sigh. She still couldn't believe that boy – an older boy with a beautiful face and long silky hair – had singled her out from all the girls at the party. He'd even asked around about her. He must have, or he wouldn't have known her name. And then he'd asked her that magic question. She still couldn't believe it. It was incre–

"Incredible!"

Huh? Elyon blinked in surprise as Irma uttered the very word that had just popped into her own head. She blinked a few more times and came back to earth, or rather, to this post-school gathering of girlfriends under Sheffield's biggest shade tree. Irma, Will, Hay Lin, and Taranee were lounging in a circle on the grass, while Cornelia was leaning against the tree with Elyon.

"It was all so real!" Irma was saying. "I don't know how to explain it. That place, those creatures, the sounds, the noises, even the smells. It was just like being there!"

"What's Irma talking about?" Elyon whispered to Cornelia. "I zoned."

"A dream she had last night," Cornelia whispered back. She had a slightly freaked look on her confused face – something between annoyed and bewildered. "She and Hay Lin were in some bizarre place – a sort of limbo between the Halloween party and the heavens. There was smoke everywhere. Plus a whole horde of demons who looked just like that creepy blue guy who started the fire."

"Hay Lin and I were just hanging on to each other," Irma was saying. "And then, suddenly, all these geometric shapes appeared in a mist over our heads. They were like enormous hieroglyphics. And in the middle was this sort of charm – a glass ball inside this curly bit of metal. And for some reason, that made me feel better. It was terrifying until that medallion charm-thing appeared."

Will leaned forward, her eyes wide.

"And then what happened?" she breathed.

"The alarm went off," Irma said, shrugging.

Elyon glanced at Hay Lin. She didn't seem to be paying any attention. In fact, she was doodling something on her palm with a Magic Marker. Elyon was surprised. Usually Hay Lin was, like, Ms. Supportive.

Finishing her sketch-on-skin with a flourish, Hay Lin thrust her hand beneath Irma's nose.

"Was the medallion anything like this?" she asked urgently.

Oh, Elyon thought. She peered over Irma's

shoulder to check out Hay Lin's inky palm. She'd drawn a pendant. Just as Irma had said, it had a clear orb in the center. Surrounding it was an incomplete circle. The top of it, around ten o'clock, swooped off into a little twirl. And at the bottom, another little loop hung like a pendulum. At twelve o'clock, there was a ring – perfect for a chain.

Irma grabbed Hay Lin's hand and gasped.

"Gosh, yeah!" she said.

"Hang on a second," Will said, looking at Hay Lin's palm as well. "This is the same thing I dreamed about."

"You, too?" Irma breathed. She stared at Will, who nervously pushed a shock of red hair out of her eyes and blinked hard. Then she turned to Hay Lin, who was capping her marker and slipping it back into the pocket of her sweater.

"Neither Irma nor I have *ever* described it in such detail!" she said. "How did you know?"

"Simple," Hay Lin said with a smile. "I saw it in my dreams, too."

"Stop it! Just stop it!"

Elyon gasped and turned to look at Taranee. She'd been sitting by silently as Will, Irma, and

Hay Lin talked about the weird coincidence. But now, she was exploding.

"This . . . this is scaring me!" Taranee whimpered. "What's going on?"

That's when Cornelia sighed huffily and pushed herself away from the tree trunk. She planted her fists on her hips and scowled. Elyon clasped her hands and tuned in, feeling just a little grateful. All this talk was freaking *her* out, too. But finally, here was something familiar – Cornelia, taking charge.

"Let's reason here," Cornelia said. "Strange things have happened to just about all of us. Little things. Unexplainable ones that certainly aren't just our imagination!"

"And so, Sherlock?" Irma said impatiently.

"So, nothing!" Cornelia announced. She glanced around the Sheffield grounds. Besides Uriah and his detention crew, the grass was crawling with kids doing homework on laptops, Hacky Sacking – the usual after-school activities.

"Maybe we all need to talk it over calmly," she continued in a low voice. "But not here and not now!"

"Cornelia's right," Hay Lin said. She still had a little smile on her face.

Leave it to Hay Lin, who's still more interested in comic books than boys, Elyon thought, to be psyched about supernatural phenomenon. To her, it's just a game.

"How about meeting at my house this afternoon?" Hay Lin continued.

That made Elyon catch her breath.

"I don't know if I'll be there," she admitted. Her voice trembled just a bit as she looked at her friends' quizzical faces.

"Have you got something better to do, Ellie?" Irma asked.

"Well . . ." Elyon said, feeling a smile spread across her face. "I've got a date with Cedric! That guy from last night, remember?"

"You don't say!" Cornelia said. Her scowl had disappeared, and her blue eyes were sparkling. "You convinced him to study with you?!"

"He's so fascinating," Elyon said with a giggle. She knew she was blushing, but she didn't care. "He invited me to his bookshop. He says he has to talk to me!"

"A friendly little chat in a bookshop," Irma said with a sneer. "Just thinking about it makes me yawn."

"You're just jealous!" Elyon said, feeling cold resentment worm its way into her gut. Irma always had to be the center of attention!

"Is it that obvious?" Irma said with a mischievous smile.

"Oh . . ." Elyon said, feeling relief wash over her as quickly as her anger had. Irma had just been teasing.

"Ha!" Cornelia guffawed. "Don't worry about her, Elyon. We'd be the last ones to try to stop you!"

Elyon giggled and then, with exaggerated care, pulled up her sleeve to look at her watch. It was 3:45! She had to boogie.

Flashing her friends with a tremulous grin and a little wave, she trotted off the Sheffield grounds. She would have started skipping if she had been, like, eleven. But no, she was a teenager now, and she was on her way to a date.

Elyon rushed down Sixth Street towards Cedric's shop. She smoothed down her favourite green skirt and rustled her shaggy bangs just right. Then, she promptly tripped on a crack on the sidewalk.

"Oooh!" she grunted, catching herself with her hands before she took a major spill.

Oh, man, she thought as she scrambled to her feet. She carefully checked her bare knees. Scuffs – minimal, thank goodness. There was no way she could have shown up for the date with skinned knees. Cedric would think she was a total dweeb!

Elyon took a deep breath and approached the address Cedric had given her. She glanced up at the green sign hanging over the sidewalk – YE OLDE BOOKSHOP. This was it. Elyon checked her watch again.

"Four o' clock, sharp," she thought, taking quick shallow breaths. "I can do it! Take a deep breath and . . ."

Elyon reached for the big, brass doorknob and twisted it. The door opened with a creak. She poked her head into the store. Funny, how she'd never noticed this place before. It was amazing. The room was dark and shadowy and lined with flowery, Victorian wallpaper. There were Asian sculptures here and there, and, of course, tons of books, all of them ancient looking, bound in cracked leather, filling the air with that musty, dusty old book smell. Along the far wall was an amazing, round stained-glass window depicting a golden peacock.

"Umm, hello?" Elyon called squeakily. "Anybody here?"

"I'm right here, Elyon," a voice called from the back of the room. As Elyon crept into the store, letting the door fall shut behind her, Cedric stepped out of the shadows to stand in front of the glowing peacock window. He was holding an open book, looking quite the studious one.

Cedric had lost the stocking cap and the bad-boy mask. Now, his hair was pulled back into a low, loose ponytail, and his eyes were covered with hip, rectangular spectacles. He stood with perfect, even imperious, posture as he gazed over his book at Elyon.

Elyon felt her stomach lurch. If possible, Cedric looked even cuter than he had the night before. But she also noticed something else. His good looks had a glinty edge. His skin looked like fine porcelain, his eyes like cut sapphires.

He's too beautiful for me, Elyon thought.

Elyon shook her head quickly. Where had that come from? So what if Cedric was highly polished, making her feel all the scruffier? It also made her feel all the more flattered.

After all, out of all the girls at Sheffield – from elegant Cornelia to flirty, curvy Irma – Cedric had only asked *her* to the bookshop. He had singled out Elyon.

Only Elyon.

TWELVE

Hay Lin dropped a handful of green tea leaves into her mother's favourite red teapot, the one with the tiny partridge perched on the lid. Then she carefully poured boiling water from the kettle into the pot and watched the tea leaves billow and swirl in the stream. Beneath her kitchen's floorboards, she could hear the faint din of her parents' restaurant – the click of chopsticks on china, the sizzle of crisped rice hitting hot soup, the laughter of customers cracking open fortune cookies. It was a sound she'd grown up with, and it was as comforting to Hay Lin as chocolate milk or the perfect stuffed animal.

But this was no time to get nostalgic. Hay Lin needed to focus on the weird, magical dream that she and her friends had all had. Just the thought of the mysterious medallion made Hay Lin smile. Which was more than she could say for her pals. Cornelia, Irma, Taranee, and Will were all sitting around the big pine table in the cramped family kitchen, nibbling on her dad's crunchy almond cookies and looking seriously nervous.

It made sense that Hay Lin would be the cheerful one in the room. After all, she was the group's comic relief – she knew that. She was always ready with a big grin, a joke, an all-inclusive hug. It was easy for her. To Hay Lin every day was a little adventure, beginning with a fun foray into her closet. She'd find a bungee cord hanging from the doorknob and wrap it around her waist in a cool, crisscrossy pattern. She'd toss her long, blue-black hair under a pair of pink Elvis sunglasses, bunch some retro leg warmers around her ankles, and practically skip out the door.

When she was home, she had anchors all around her – her drawing pencils and paints, her comic books, the whispered conversations she had with her grandmother about, oh, everything. Grandma liked to fill Hay Lin's head with all sorts of stories. She told her that every flower was a vessel for a human soul; that crickets meant the best of luck; that a messy room indicated a creative mind; that magic lurked around the edges of everyday life.

Hay Lin didn't actually believe that. Grandma's magic was like a Buddhist Santa Claus – something fun for Hay Lin to dream about, even cling to, on the rare occasions when she felt adrift.

And Hay Lin did have to admit, she'd been feeling just a *little* floaty lately. After all, she was the only one of her friends who'd never had a crush. She thought talking about boys was fun and all, but it didn't make her get all gushy and moist-eyed and faraway. She would look around her classes at Sheffield and stare at this boy or that. All she saw were their knobby knees and sunken chests and chewed-on fingernails; the way they spewed Fritos in the lunchroom and laughed like donkeys. She found boys totally resistible.

They were also a source of the tiniest gap between Hay Lin and her buds.

Not that it was a biggie. Hay Lin knew her hormones were gearing up. And to tell the truth, she could stand the wait. In her book, things were pretty much fine as they were.

Especially now, when Cornelia, Irma, and the new girls were all glancing at one another anxiously and whispering about unexplainable things.

Welcome to my world, girls, Hay Lin thought as she filled five red cups with steaming, fragrant tea.

"So, what do you think the explanation is?" Taranee was saying.

Hay Lin shrugged and looked at her friends' bewildered faces.

"Well, it's not like there has to be an explanation," she said lightly.

"No!" Cornelia said, anxiously turning a cookie around and around in her long, slender fingers. "There's a reason behind everything, and I want to know what's going on! And by the way, I want you all to know that I don't believe in magic or paranormal phenomena."

Hay Lin turned to put the teapot on the counter and rolled her eyes. That's Cornelia, she thought. Always in control. Well, until now, maybe.

"Mysterious dreams, clothes that change

colour, flying objects, premonitions," Taranee listed, her voice getting quieter with each item. "What do you call these?"

"Growing pains?" Irma interjected, grinning through a mouthful of cookie.

"Maybe that medallion is the answer we're looking for," Will said with a shrug.

Hay Lin glanced at the smudgy drawing on her palm and remembered something. She grabbed her book bag from the corner where she'd tossed it and pulled a sheet of paper out of it. Then she hurried back to the table to show it to Will and Irma.

"Look, I've sketched a better copy of the medallion," she said. "I hope I didn't forget anything."

Hay Lin felt a little thrum of pride as Will raised her eyebrows at her drawing. She knew she was a good artist – always had been. The charm's silvery setting, its craggy glass orb – they looked positively 3-D.

"I'd say it's all there," Irma said, nodding as she grabbed another cookie.

"Hmmm," Will said. "Yep, that looks a lot like it."

Suddenly, Hay Lin heard a faint swishing

at the doorway. It was the trademark rustle of the traditional Chinese robe her grandmother always wore. And when Hay Lin looked up, of course, there her grandmother was. Her copious wrinkles were scrunched into a sly smile.

Hay Lin's own welcoming smile faded a bit as she saw her grandmother pull something out of her pocket. It was a necklace. With a charm. A charm that looked shockingly familiar.

"Grandma!" she cried.

"That's it!" Will said. "The medallion from our dreams. Where did you get it?"

"What matters," Hay Lin's grandmother said to Will in her scratchy, high-pitched voice, "is that you will be keeping it now. This is the Heart of Candracar."

Grandma's sharp, heavily wrinkled eyes swept over the five girls.

"And you are the new Guardians," she announced, gripping the medallion's chain tightly. Hay Lin felt her skin prickle. She'd never seen this side of her grandmother. She'd always been powerful, but quiet, acting from the sidelines. Now, she stood over their group with palpable power, like a queen.

For the first time since all this magic had begun, Hay Lin felt fear.

"Wh-what are you talking about?" she quavered.

Grandma smiled at her reassuringly and motioned for Hay Lin to sit down with the others. Then she stood at the head of the table and began to speak.

"Let me tell you a story, girls," she said. "A story as old as time – a distant time when everything was young, and spirits and creatures lived under the same sky."

Hay Lin felt the familiar tug of comfort that her grandmother's tall tales always gave her. But fighting that contentment was the creeping knowledge that this time, the story might be . . . real?

"The universe was a single, immense kingdom ruled by nature," Grandma continued. "A kingdom that lasted eons. Until . . ."

Grandma paused dramatically before she said, "Spirits and creatures learned evil, and this one world was divided into those who wanted peace and those who lived on others' pain. To separate the two halves, the Veil was created. Evil and injustice were banished to the dark side of Metamoor, which had once been one of the universe's most beautiful worlds."

Hay Lin knew her mouth was hanging open and her hands were trembling. But she didn't care. She could only try to wrap her brain around this incredible news that her grandmother was delivering.

"Before separating for eternity," Grandma explained, "the universe gave life to the Temple of Candracar, in the very heart of infinity. There, the mightiest spirits and creatures are on guard. There, the protectors of the Veil reside and there, if you wish, you also may journey."

Hay Lin gasped and shook her head. Her grandma hadn't just said that they could take a field trip to the heart of infinity – had she? And what *was* the "heart of infinity"?

"It is not by mere chance that you are here," Grandma intoned, pausing to look each girl in the eye, one by one. "You are the new Guardians of the Veil. The most important warriors in a battle that began thousands of years ago."

"The Veil?" Irma piped up.

"The world is made of many different worlds, and the Veil is what divides them," Grandma explained. She held the medallion – the Heart of Something-a-car, Hay Lin told herself – and gave it a reverent look. Then she turned back to the girls, her eyes suddenly flashing darkly.

"It is a barrier that has become dangerously fragile," she said hoarsely. "There are portals between the world of evil and the world that is ours. And those portals are being breached."

Hay Lin saw Will's lip tremble as she spoke up.

"I–I'm afraid I don't understand," she said.

Grandma nodded kindly.

"To understand," she said, "listen to your two hearts. One beats within you, and the other is the Heart of Candracar."

As Grandma spoke, the medallion that she held above her head began to shimmer. Then it trembled. And suddenly, it let loose a burst of light that quickly settled into a warm, pulsating glow. Grandma stepped over to Irma, who gasped as she fixed her eyes on the glowing medallion.

"The forces of nature lie within, and from now and forever, they will be with you," Grandma said to the group. Then she looked down at Irma, smiling kindly.

"You, Irma," she said, "will have power over water – broken and uncontainable."

Hay Lin saw Irma's eyes light up – or maybe that was just the reflection of the glowing, glass orb. In any case, her expression quickly went dark again as Hay Lin's grandmother stepped over to Cornelia, who looked as if she were fighting the urge to leap up from the table and run far, far away.

"To you, firm Cornelia, the power of earth," Grandma pronounced, before turning to Taranee. "And to you, generous Taranee – the difficult gift of fire."

Finally, Grandma stepped over to Hay Lin and placed her dry, warm hand on top of her head. Hay Lin felt herself relax and smile at her grandma's touch. Even in this, the most confusing moment ever, Grandma was a steadying presence.

"And you, my little Hay Lin," Grandma crooned softly. "You will be free and light as air."

Hay Lin's eyes flapped open. She was sure she'd felt a cool breeze skim over her face the minute the word "air" had left Grandma's mouth. She blinked in amazement, before her attention shifted to Will.

"And me?" Will said tremulously, gazing up at Grandma.

"Give me your hand, Will," Hay Lin's grandmother said. Obediently, Will held out her palm. As Grandma slowly lowered the Heart of Candracar into it, she said, "You will find out soon enough."

The medallion came to a rest on Will's palm. Then its warm, pulsing glow began to grow. It became more and more intense until the orb was shooting beams of sparkling, silver light all over the kitchen. Hay Lin held her breath and tried not to scream.

But Will didn't seem scared at all. In fact, she seemed transformed. She still looked the same, skinny Will, swimming in a pair of blue corduroy overalls, but her face was rapturous. Her hair was floating around her head in a luminous halo. And her hand, clasping the magical Heart of Candracar, seemed to float upwards.

"Aaagh!" Will cried, throwing her head back. Hay Lin didn't know *what* was surging through her new friend. Pleasure? Power? Knowledge? Or . . .

"This, this is magic!" Irma breathed.

Hay Lin glanced at Irma and nodded. That's exactly what it was.

And it was also, suddenly, over. Hay Lin's broken gaze, or Irma's voice, or *something* seemed to have broken the spell. The Heart of Candracar became, once again, an inert charm. And Will had returned to being ordinary Will, albeit a very shaken up one.

She turned to gaze at Hay Lin's grandmother, but Grandma was already halfway out the door. Hay Lin bit her lip. She knew this routine. When Grandma was done talking, she was *done talking*. There was no cajoling her to stick around.

So she knew it was a lost cause when Will called to her grandmother's retreating mane of silver hair, "Just a moment. Wait! Don't go away!"

But Grandma had already slipped into the hallway, which was the central artery of Hay Lin's apartment. From that hallway, everything led – bedrooms and bathrooms, her parents' business office and the stairs down to the restaurant. Each door was shut, and Grandma was nowhere to be seen. She'd as good as disappeared.

Hay Lin gently put an arm around Will's shoulders and led her towards the stairs. The rest of the girls followed in silence. No one said a word until they'd formed a small, tight circle on the sidewalk outside the restaurant's big round front window.

"I don't completely understand what just happened," Taranee said wanly.

"Nothing happened!" Cornelia retorted as she arranged her hot-pink shrug around her shoulders. Then she glared at Hay Lin.

"With all due respect, Hay Lin, I think your grandma has a few screws loose," she said. "She told us that ridiculous story, hoping that she'd amaze us using that trick with the shining medallion."

"You're *afraid*, Cornelia, aren't you?" Irma said, giving her a smirk.

Cornelia rolled her eyes and spun on her heel, walking toward the corner. She tossed some parting words over her shoulder, not to mention a glare reserved just for Irma. Irma always got under Cornelia's skin. They were so different! Like fire and ice.

Make that earth and water, Hay Lin thought with a gulp.

Cornelia turned. "I don't believe in fairy tales, Irma," Cornelia called. "This is different. And now, I'm going home."

Taranee glanced at Hay Lin in alarm. Hay Lin, too, felt worried for an instant. Then she shook it off. This was Cornelia. She was just mad that she hadn't figured this all out herself. But she was never one to abandon her friends.

"I know her," Hay Lin said to the remaining girls. "She'll change her mind."

After Cornelia had rounded the corner, Irma turned back to the group, looking a little stunned. But quickly, her trademark grin returned.

"Hey, if we're some kind of supergroup, we should have costumes, don't you think?" she said. Then she giggled and balled up her fists to make her biceps bulge. Not that they bulged that much.

Hay Lin laughed and did a little karate chop in Irma's direction. Then she looked around their little group and gasped. She'd just realised something.

She pulled her felt-tip pen out of her cardigan pocket and began writing on her palm. Then she gazed at the word she'd written there, amazed at how everything seemed to be falling into place.

"We need a name, too," Hay Lin said. "And check this out – what do you think about W.i.t.c.h.? It's our initials put together? Will, Irma, Taranee, Cornelia, Hay Lin! Isn't that cute?"

Taranee gazed at her and clasped her hands behind her back.

"All that ink is going to end up poisoning you, Hay Lin," she said drily.

"It's already poisoned her," Irma cried, grabbing Hay Lin's hand and looking scornfully at the smudgy acronym. "W.i.t.c.h.! I've never heard of anything so dumb. I don't feel like a witch."

Irma turned to Will. They all looked at Will.

"I–I don't know. I'm still a bit confused," Will managed to say, shakily. Hay Lin saw what could only be described as awe in her big, brown eyes.

And that's when Hay Lin remembered exactly what her grandmother had said. They were all Guardians, all elements – earth, air, water, fire. Except Will. She was special. She was the keeper of the Heart of Candracar. Hay

Lin didn't know what that meant, but she suspected it made Will their leader, in some way.

What sort of battle Will would lead them in, though, Hay Lin couldn't begin to imagine.

THIRTEEN

Hours had gone by since the events of the Halloween party, but still the Oracle sat. He was cross-legged and contemplative in the Temple's most sacred space, the mile-high shaft that formed the core of the Temple of Candracar.

Standing behind him – as always – was Tibor. But, for the first time in perhaps a century and a half, the old man's white beard was parted by a smile. He was gleeful.

"Oracle," he exclaimed, "now they are together."

And indeed they were. The Oracle had transposed his vision of the five newly anointed Guardians into the air before them. The girls' awestruck faces floated within a halo of green flame. It was there that Tibor could watch the visions that the Oracle saw in his mind.

"And so, our waiting is over," the Oracle said, nodding peacefully.

Without using his hands or Tibor's help, the Oracle rose gracefully to his feet. The Guardians' image evaporated into a wisp of vapour that unleashed a flurry of scents – ocean water, a floral breeze, a hint of smoke, rain-damp earth.

Then, the Oracle turned to greet his guest – a tiny woman in flowing Chinese robes standing at the sanctuary's door. Her hair was long and white; her ears, large and ever vigilant; her face, at rest in a contented, creased smile.

"The congregation is grateful to you, Honorable Yan Lin," the Oracle said to the air Guardian's grandmother. The old woman smiled wider and bowed her head to her lord.

"Your task is complete," the Oracle continued. He glanced back at Tibor. His ancient adviser fairly glowed with hope. "The waiting is over. We can begin."

FOURTEEN

Will gazed at the questioning eyes of Irma, Hay Lin, and Taranee. She glanced to her right and saw her reflection in the round window of the Silver Dragon – she looked pale and trembly and a bit small, which was exactly how she felt. At least, she wasn't seeing that alternate self, the one with the long legs and the knowing eyes and the wings. *That* would have been way more than Will could handle right now.

In fact, she couldn't even handle Irma's simple question: how did she feel about giving their group the name W.i.t.c.h.?

She looked at her new friends and suddenly felt as if they were very far away. She could barely comprehend all the things Hay

Lin's grandmother had just unloaded on them. But one thing was clear. They were all – what was it called? Guardians. But while four of them had these superpowers of air, water, fire, and earth, Will had absorbed the Heart of Candracar. What kind of power did she have now? She didn't know what the pendant meant. All she knew was it made her different from the other girls.

She was alone.

As usual.

"Guys!"

Will's brooding was interrupted by an elated voice. The girls all turned to see Elyon bounding down the sidewalk across the street.

"Look who's here," Taranee said.

"Elyon!" Irma called as their giddy bud dashed across the crosswalk and hopped over to them. "Is your date already over?"

"Only round one," Elyon said, breathing hard and grinning. "Cedric wants to see me tonight in the school gym."

"I can think of more romantic places," Hay Lin said, rolling her eyes at Irma.

"He said it was just the right place to tell me

a special secret," Elyon gushed, her cheeks flushing.

"Oh, if that's the case," Irma said, winking back at Hay Lin, "there are less ridiculous excuses."

Suddenly, Elyon went pale, and her blue eyes clouded over a bit. Will bet she knew exactly what she was feeling. The initial elation of her triumph had worn off, and now Elyon was good and scared. Will had *so* been there before.

"Why don't you go with me?" Elyon suddenly said. "With you guys there, I'd feel more comfortable."

When you're right, you're right, Will thought, smiling to herself.

Irma nodded enthusiastically.

"Never deny a friend a favour," she announced, "especially if she lets you stick your nose in her business!"

"Same goes for me," Hay Lin said.

"I'll be there, too, Elyon," Will said to her own surprise. Then she shrugged.

Why not? she thought. It's better than sitting home, brooding about suddenly being a magical freak!

"And you, Taranee?" Elyon asked, turning to smile at the last member of the group. "You'll come, too, won't you?"

"I don't think so," Taranee said wistfully. "My folks will never let me go out tonight. I just went out last night!"

Irma slung one arm around Will's shoulders and the other around Hay Lin's. Giving them each a squeeze, she announced to Elyon, "That makes three of us. Do you think that'll do?"

"Yeah, I think that'll do," Elyon said with an emphatic nod. "That'll do just fine."

Will sighed and looked at her new friends, giggling, teasing one another, bonding in a big way. And she realised – she was a part of it! They weren't excluding her just because she was the keeper of the Heart of Candracar.

Whatever scary stuff comes our way now, we'll help one another through it, Will thought. We're *all* Guardians. And maybe I'm not as alone as I thought.

It's a good thing I'm not alone, Will was thinking a few hours later. This is creepy!

She, Irma, and Hay Lin had just arrived at Sheffield's front gate. It was gently swinging back and forth on its hinges, making a faint, eerie, squeaking noise. The whole school was dark. Only a bright, full moon provided a hazy, blue glow on the grounds.

"The gate is open," Hay Lin pointed out. She snuggled deeper into her puffy, blue down coat. It had gotten chilly tonight.

"Elyon must already be here," Will said. "Let's go in, too."

The three girls scurried down the walkway to the gym doors. Will pushed them open and took a few, faltering steps into the gym. Not one light was on. Hay Lin and Irma hovered inside the doorway.

"Elyon?" Will called. Her voice sounded faint as it echoed through the big, and seemingly empty, space. "Are you here?"

"Elyon is at home, sleeping," Irma said, shivering. "Trust me. It's pitch-dark in here. Let's go!"

"Irma is right," Hay Lin whispered. "M-m-maybe it's all a big joke."

Will turned around and stumbled to the wall next to the door. She felt around, looking for a switch plate or fuse box. But nothing beneath her fingertips felt familiar, except that cold, clammy feeling of painted cinder block.

"If only I could manage to turn the lights on," she muttered.

"Aaaaiiigh!"

Will gasped as she heard her friends scream in terror. She spun around just in time to see the gym doors slam shut. Even the faint glow from the moon disappeared, and, for a horrible instant, Will felt as if she were floating in space. She had no sight, no senses, nothing to anchor her.

But quickly, almost . . . magically, Will's eyes adjusted to the light. She almost wished they hadn't, because, through the hazy gloom, she saw Hay Lin and Irma squirming in the clutches of a monster!

Will gasped as she looked at the creature. It was *the* monster – the one that had acted so weird at the Halloween party the night before. A wave of fear washed over Will. That had been no kid in an ugly blue costume.

This monster was for real.

And he'd changed for the worse.

For one, he'd gotten bigger. He must have been more than seven feet tall now, and he had the girth of a refrigerator. The lumpy, rocklike bumps on his head had become full-fledged horns – sharp and threatening. His tiny teeth had turned into huge, yellow, lethal fangs.

He was effortlessly holding Hay Lin and Irma with one beefy arm. Irma kicked wildly at him with her red Hush Puppies, but she barely even connected.

"Let me go, you big ape," Irma shrieked. "If this is a joke, it's not funny."

But the monster didn't let go. In fact, it looked like he was squeezing them tighter.

"Welcome, Guardians."

Will gasped. A disembodied voice – gravelly and hissing, positively snaky – wafted over to them. Will glanced away from her struggling friends for an instant to scan the shadowy gym. Where was that voice coming from? She couldn't see anybody. But clearly, that somebody could see them. And . . . he knew who they were. He'd called them Guardians.

This *cannot* be good, Will thought in panic.

"Wh-what do you want?" she called out into the darkness. She saw Hay Lin and Irma stop kicking and grunting for a moment. This was big. This was information they needed to know.

As the horrible, reptilian voice bellowed his answer, Will felt her heart sink.

"I want to destroy you, Guardians," the voice said simply. "To destroy you and take over your world!"

Will felt as if she were drowning. She clawed at her chest, struggling for air. Finally, her lungs rescued her, making an involuntary gasp for oxygen. Will took a deep, shuddery breath, clasping her hands over her gut.

And that's when she felt something hard and warm beneath her right hand. It pulsated. In fact, it almost hurt. The thing's heat – its energy – was intense.

"By now, the Veil is weak, and without you, victory will be easy," the voice roared. "When a millennium comes to an end, the Veil's weaving loosens. Light filters through its pores, piercing through our darkness. And it is then that we see the portals that lead to your world."

"Weak?" Will whispered. The heat in her palm was searing now. It pricked at her, sending jets of energy up her arm. In fact, she felt as if the heat had entered her bloodstream. It was a feeling her body couldn't recognise. It was both awful and glorious.

Through the haze of this experience, Will heard the blue creature growl, "What shall I do with them, Master?"

"Tear open a pit and throw them in, Vathek," the voice responded.

"Help!" Hay Lin shrieked. She and Irma began screaming and squirming, trying fruitlessly to wrench themselves free from this horrible creature.

Will's mind seemed to shut down. She could hear herself breathing and feel her heart thumping slowly inside her chest. But most of all, she could feel energy shooting from her curled fist to all points of her body. Slowly, she willed her fingers to open.

And when they did, the medallion – glowing brilliantly – was resting on her palm.

"That's what it was," a voice inside Will's head said triumphantly. "The Heart of Candracar. Maybe this is the time to use it."

Her hand seemed to take over. And it knew just what to do.

"Hay Lin, Irma!" Will called, throwing the Heart of Candracar to her friends with a sweeping motion. "Water! Air!"

As the medallion soared through the air,

Will saw the glass orb that was its center seem to separate into three, vibrating, tear-shaped missiles. One became liquid and swirly. It landed in front of Irma. It hovered before her stunned eyes and then began to weave its way around her body, as if it were wrapping her in invisible ribbon.

The medallion also seemed to wrench Irma from the blue creature's grip. As she sprang away from him, he howled in rage.

The exact same thing happened to Hay Lin, except the teardrop that danced around her was almost like a vapour, a puff of shimmering air.

And finally, there was Will's teardrop. It throbbed before her eyes and turned a shocking pink. It pulsed like a beating heart.

Will felt her fear melt away. She reached out to the heart, beckoning it to come to her. And then it, too, began to swirl around her body.

Out of the corner of her eye, Will saw Hay Lin gasp with joy and throw her arms over her head. She looked as if she were feeling true freedom for the first time. Her hair came free of her goggles and began to twist around her torso like a glossy, black cyclone.

Irma's hair floated up from her scalp, and

her eyes turned sultry and mischievous. Before Will's very eyes, Irma's lips went pouty, her clothes melted away, and feathers unfurled from her back.

And that's when Will ceased to see her friends. Because she was going through her own incredible transformation. Her back arched, and her body shook, as if she were having a seizure. Will felt a wave of heat shoot through her. The energy she'd felt in her veins became stronger now. It filled her body until it seemed like her real self must have disappeared, leaving behind only a soul, floating in space.

But that wasn't possible, because Will suddenly felt her body hunch forward. She hugged her knees, curling into a ball.

This is just like the dream I had in the car, Will realised.

Then she felt a tugging on her back. Instinctively, she knew she was growing wings, just as Irma had. She was becoming the beautiful woman she'd seen in the bookshop window and in her bedroom mirror. She felt her limbs lengthening, her face changing, her muscles growing lean and strong.

Will felt a calm suffuse her as she burst out of her coiled position and leaped into a fighting stance.

With that one pouncing motion, Will accepted her fate. She was no longer just a student, just a daughter, or just a friend. She was a Guardian of the Veil, the keeper of the Heart of Candracar.

And life as she'd known it – for better or worse – had changed forever.

Will   Irma   Taranee   Cornelia   Hay Lin

The Disappearance

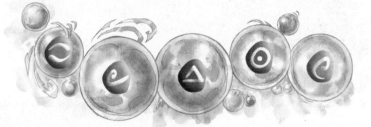

Adapted by ELIZABETH LENHARD

HarperCollins *Children's Books*

ONE

Will and her friends arrived at her apartment building just as black clouds in the sky began to roll, rumble, and spark.

As she, Cornelia, Irma, and Taranee climbed the stairs that led to the apartment she shared with her mother, Will glanced at her friends. It was hard to believe she'd known them only a few days! She already felt so familiar with Cornelia's long, blonde hair, Irma's smirk, and Taranee's raggedy fingernails. Will even knew that Taranee always gnawed on her nails when she was nervous.

In fact, Will thought, I bet I could practically read their thoughts. As she opened the door to the hallway and ushered her friends through it, she gazed at Cornelia's pale,

1

heart-shaped face. Her pink-glossed lips were pulled into a tight, tense line. Her blue eyes were steely. And she had the same expression Will got when she and her mum were having an argument.

Yup, Will thought. That's exactly how I look when I know that I'm wrong and my mum's right, but I'm not gonna admit it! And Cornelia's being just that stubborn about this whole magical powers thing. I mean, she made a vine come to life in the school courtyard. It slithered up her arm like a snake! That was magic! There's no other explanation for it. But Cornelia still refuses to say the M word.

As the girls turned a corner in the hallway, Will's eyes fell on Taranee, whose ever-clicking beaded braids were hidden under the earflaps of her big, floppy, red rain hat. Behind her little, round specs, Taranee's brown eyes were big and watery. Her chin was trembling ever so slightly.

She's wishing she was home, Will thought sympathetically. Taranee liked being tucked away in the safety of her photography dark-room or curled up in front of the fireplace.

And Irma, Will concluded as she gazed at

her, is wondering what kind of cookies I'm going to serve for our after-school snack.

As Will and her friends reached the loft door, she dug around in her pink backpack. Then she pulled out the big tangle of keys attached to the tiny rubber frog that was her key chain.

"Okay," she said, glancing at Cornelia's impatient frown, "don't laugh, you guys, but every time I try to unlock my front door, I seem to use the wrong key."

"Well, that *is* a lot of keys." Irma giggled, pointing at the crowded key chain. "Is this a home or a jail?"

"Good question," Will muttered as she fumbled through all the keys. The truth was, Will *didn't* feel as though the loft were her home – yet. She and her mum had moved to this seaside city called Heatherfield right before Halloween. They'd come here from Fadden Hills – where Will was born and raised.

Mostly, the move had been a good thing. Will had met her new friends almost immediately. And her mum seemed much happier now that she was farther away from Will's dad.

Come to think of it, Will mused with a frown, the only reason my key chain is crowded is that I can't seem to bring myself to take my old Fadden Hills house keys off it.

Will wondered what her new friends would think if they knew that she was clinging to her old keys, and her old life. They might think she was a total baby. Or that she was a little nuts.

Or, Will thought, glancing over her shoulder at Taranee's scared eyes, they might . . . understand. After all, even before we found out we had been given magical powers, we were totally bonding. Now, we share that major secret. And as everyone knows, secret-sharing is the first step towards becoming best friends.

The realisation made Will's heavy heart lift – a little. So her next thought was more of a resolution.

Okay, she told herself as she chose one of the shiny brass keys. If this key is the right one, I vow to take all my old Fadden Hills keys off this frog. Even the key to my old locker at the pool.

Will held the key up to the doorknob and bit her lip. Then she stuck the key into the lock. It fit!

And it turned! The front door swung open easily.

Will took a deep breath and thought, home, sweet home? Well, maybe . . .

Then she smiled and stepped inside. The girls crowded in behind her.

"Hello?" Taranee called out. Her voice echoed off the loft's high ceiling. Even though the apartment was lined with tall, multipaned windows, the place was dark and shadowy. The storm outside had turned the sky almost black.

"Come on in," Will said, glancing at her watch. Her mum rarely got home from her big, swanky office at Simultech early. "No one's here. My mother will be back in about an hour."

Will manoeuvred around a few cardboard boxes to hit the light switch. Naturally, she stubbed her toe on one of her own boxes filled with CDs.

"*Grrrr,*" Will mumbled, hopping up and down on one foot. Okay, she had to admit it. Another thing that might make her feel more at home in this new apartment would be finally unpacking all her stuff!

At least her friends didn't seem to mind the disheveled decor. As Cornelia unfurled the orange shawl she'd tied around her shoulders and Taranee pulled off her hat, Irma flopped back onto the comfy red couch.

"Man, I'm beat!" she said with a big sigh. "I wonder what's on TV."

Will stared at Irma for a moment. Okay, she thought, now I don't know if Irma's attitude is funny or scary. I mean, we're dealing with some heavy stuff here. She pulled off her beat-up, grey jacket and stood in front of Irma.

"You know," she began hesitantly, "with all we're going through, I'm not surprised you're tired. But aren't we taking this all a bit too lightly?"

As Irma opened one lazy, blue eye to gaze at her quizzically, Will went on.

"I mean . . ." she said, "we should be terrified. We have magical powers. Don't you realise that?"

Irma's response got an angry glare from Cornelia. But Will had to continue. "We suddenly find ourselves in the middle of something incredible, and we act like it is the most normal thing in the world," she said. "The other day we battled monsters, one of our friends has completely vanished . . . and we're here to have a nice cup of hot chocolate." Will tossed her jacket onto a chair and all but shouted, "For heaven's sake. How do you guys explain all this?"

"Hey," Irma said, propping her red shoes up on the coffee table. "Maybe we've got a few screws loose, and we never realised it before."

"Speak for yourself, Irma," Cornelia snapped. She folded her long, skinny arms over her chest.

Will threw up her hands and stomped back across the living room to the open kitchen at the far end of the loft. Taranee followed her and slouched in front of one of the tall windows.

Will grabbed the coffeepot and stuck it beneath the kitchen faucet. "There's something much bigger behind all this. I still don't really get *what*, but there is."

"As soon as Hay Lin's grandma gets better," Taranee offered, "we'll go ask her a few questions."

Will nodded. And at the same time, she cringed. The mention of Hay Lin's grandmother took her right back to that fateful moment just a few days ago. The girls had gathered – this time, for tea – in Hay Lin's apartment above her family's Chinese restaurant. The girls had been munching almond cookies and discussing their weirdly similar dreams when Hay Lin's grand-mother had stolen in and dropped a bombshell on them.

She had smiled gleefully at Will, Irma, Taranee, Cornelia, and Hay Lin (whose names happened to form the acronym W.i.t.c.h.). And then she had announced that they were Guardians of the Veil.

And what was the Veil? Well, it was a barrier that had been raised eons ago between earth and the dark world of Metamoor. It was the only thing keeping who-knew-what sorts of gruesome evildoers away from the girls' own peaceful world.

Hay Lin's grandmother had explained that when the millennium hit, the Veil had grown weak. Creatures from Metamoor were then able to travel through it, by way of portals – which were sort of cosmic doorways.

To protect the Veil, some all-knowing spirit who lived in a place called Candracar had anointed Will and her friends as its Guardians. It was now their job to make sure no bad guys breached the portals. As the Veil's protectors, four of the girls had been infused with different powers – those of earth, fire, water, and air.

And then there's me, Will thought – I'm the keeper of the Heart of Candracar.

Within Will now was a small, orb-shaped, brightly glowing medallion. And it, apparently, was the key to the four other powers.

I felt this power in the gym the other night, Will thought with a shudder. Their friend Elyon had lured Will, Hay Lin, and Irma to their school's gym. She'd told them she had a date with a cute boy she'd met, named Cedric. But when the trio had arrived, Elyon and Cedric were nowhere to be seen. In their place had been a grotesque, reptilian villain and his monstrous blue henchman, a brute named Vathek. They were just the Metamoor baddies that Hay Lin's grandmother had warned them about. They were powerful. And huge. And dangerous. In fact, the snake-man had ordered Vathek to throw the three girls into a gaping hole. That's when the Heart of Candracar had appeared in Will's hand. Somehow – instinctively – she'd channeled its power. They'd gotten amazing, beautiful outfits, changed bodies, and even sprouted wings! Not to mention the power to kick the bad guys' butts. Which they'd promptly done. Unfortunately, their fight had also started a roaring fire in the gym. The girls had skulked away while firefighters arrived to save the building. And their secret identities had been discovered by no one.

That night had been only a temporary victory. Will knew other battles awaited them. What kind of battles, or with whom, was a mystery.

And that's why she and her friends were here, trying to figure out a solution to all of this.

As if she had read Will's mind, Taranee spoke up again.

"Until we know more," she said to the group, "we'd better watch our steps and keep our eyes peeled."

Will was about to agree when a tremendous thunderclap made her jump!

Sputtter.

"There go the lights," Will said, as every lamp in the loft flickered out. She rolled her eyes.

Could this day be any creepier? she thought.

Across the room, on the couch, Irma quipped, "I'd keep my eyes peeled, but I wouldn't see anything anyway!"

A Cornelia-shaped shadow near the couch said, "The lights have gone out, Einstein."

"Don't move," Will said, feeling her way around the living room. "Somewhere around here, there should be some candles or a flashlight."

"Don't bother, Will," said Taranee's voice behind her. "I'll take care of it."

And suddenly, Will detected a bright glow dancing through the air. She spun around in time to see a tiny, orange fireball, bouncing playfully in Taranee's palm!

"Yeow!" Irma yelped in alarm.

Cornelia gaped.

And Will gulped!

But she noticed that – for perhaps the first time that afternoon – Taranee's quivery, fearful expression had melted into an easy smile.

Taranee held her hand up over her head. The fireball tipped out of her palm as gently as a soap bubble and hovered in the air a few feet above Taranee's head.

Taranee nodded and grinned. Then she held out her hand again. With a muffled *whoosh*, another fireball formed. Taranee set that one free, too.

Before the girls could catch their breath, Taranee's sizzly spheres were bobbing all around the loft, filling the space with cosy firelight. When one of the fireballs drifted by Irma's nose, she reached for it with hesitant fingers. She gasped as one fingertip pierced the fireball, then emerged unscathed.

"Wow," Irma breathed. "It doesn't burn!"

Will laughed out loud.

This magic stuff isn't *all* scary, she had to admit to herself.

With a gleam in her eye, Will walked back into the kitchen.

"Okay," she announced. "Now it's my turn to show you guys something. Anybody want a snack?"

That question got Irma off the couch. She followed Will into the kitchen with a hungry look in her eyes. Taranee and Cornelia trailed after her.

"Yeah, I do," Irma said. "Have you learned some new recipes?"

Will leaned with false casualness against the refrigerator door and said, "What can we offer my friends, James?"

"James?" Irma cried. She glanced behind

her, then peered around the rest of the kitchen. "You have a butler and you never told us?"

Suddenly, a haughty British voice rang out through the kitchen.

"There's a rather meager selection, Miss Will," the voice sniffed. "Unless someone would be so kind as to restock me."

Will watched as Irma screamed and stared at the refrigerator, particularly the ice-dispensing lever in the freezer door. Without having to look, Will knew the lever was waggling to the rhythm of James's voice. Because James, of course, was–

"The refrigerator!" Irma screeched, pointing at the ice dispenser. "The refrigerator is talking!"

As Will dissolved into a fit of giggles, James continued.

"Ahem," he said, with all the dignity a refrigerator could muster. "I should bring to your attention the fact that the cream cheese next to the pickles has long since expired."

"Sorry, James," Will said. She quickly opened the refrigerator door and whisked away the block of cream cheese. It was, indeed, green and fuzzy. Then she turned to Taranee, who was back to looking trembly and terrified, and whispered, "James has very refined tastes, you see."

"The refrigerator is talking!" Irma shrieked again.

Cornelia stared at the appliance, then blinked.

"Bizarre," she whispered.

"The refrigerator is talking!" Irma yelled once more, this time grabbing Cornelia by the shoulders and shaking her.

"All right, already," Cornelia snapped back. "I'm not deaf!"

That seemed to calm Irma down. In fact, once she was through wigging, a huge grin formed on her face.

Will grinned back. After she'd gotten used to it, she'd come to adore her talking appliances. It was, perhaps, the only aspect of this new identity that *wasn't* terrifying.

"I discovered it the other day," Will explained to her friends as they headed back into the living room. "I can talk with all the electrical appliances! I've given them each a name and they do what I tell them to. They even work without electricity."

"Now that's what I call cost-efficient!" Irma exclaimed. She went back into the living area and flopped onto the couch again. Then she turned toward the TV. "Put on channel twelve. *Boy Comet* is on. It's the hottest TV show of all time!"

Will squatted in front of the TV. It was a rickety old set that her mum refused to replace with some sleek, new, flat-screen one.

"This one works fine," Mum had said, the one time Will had begged her to update their primitive set. Of course, now that her TV could talk, Will wouldn't dream of getting rid of it. Even if it was a bit crotchety.

"*Boy Comet*, Billy?" she said to the television delicately.

"Oh, no, Will," the wheezy old television rasped. "You know I just can't stand the musical theme song of *Boy Comet*."

"B-but, but," Irma stuttered. But Billy cut her off.

"My poor speakers can't handle it!" he complained. "Whatever happened to the golden days of easy-listening music?

"Now, what do you say to a nice documentary?" Billy continued. His screen sputtered to life. A big, fat bear could be seen waddling through a field of evergreens. Some drab flute music droned in the background. "For example, this one on *Globe World* about the secret life of black bears."

Irma gasped and glared at Will indignantly.

"What can you do?" Will said with a shrug. "It's a pretty old model. . . ."

Irma grunted in frustration and stared sullenly at the black bear on Billy's screen. The entire scene was so ridiculous Will couldn't contain her giggles.

"Every day, there's something new," she snorted. "Isn't it great?"

"Just great," Irma muttered.

Irma didn't turn Billy off. In fact, *she* seemed to get sucked in to the documentary as the narrator purred, "In the winter months, the social life of larger plantigrade animals reaches decidedly low levels. . . ."

"Uh, Will?"

Will turned to see Taranee pulling a computer disk out of her cloth backpack. "Since you've found a loophole in this no-electricity thing, could I print out my science paper?"

"Sure, Taranee," Will said, grabbing the disk from her bud. "I'll handle it."

Tailed by a couple of bobbling fireballs, Taranee followed Will into her bedroom. It was just as littered with unpacked boxes as the rest of the loft. But at least Will's orange laptop and printer were all set up. That had been one of the first things she'd taken care of when she'd moved in. Will felt lost if she wasn't wired to the Web.

And, of course, now that her computer and printer had come to life, they were more entertaining than ever. Will approached her laptop and braced herself for a little griping.

"Wake up, George," she said to her computer cheerily. "There's work to be done!"

"Work, work," the computer sputtered. His voice was high-pitched and whiny, with a definite northeastern drawl. "Nothing but work. I have a right to take a break, too!"

"Aw, zip it, George!"

"*Eeep!*" Taranee squeaked in shock as the printer next to the computer started talking, too. This voice was growly and low, but decidedly female.

"If there's anyone here who has to do the

dirty work, it's me," said the printer, whom Will had named Martha.

"Is that *so?*" George retorted.

"*So* so," Martha taunted.

Taranee gaped at the bickering hardware and whispered to Will, "They're fighting?"

Will shot her friend a wry smile.

"I think they're husband and wife," she said. "I could listen to them for hours!"

And now that I'm a Guardian, she thought, with a little flutter in her stomach, I guess I'll be able to!

TWO

Taranee joined Cornelia at Will's kitchen table. Cornelia had finished pouring some drinks. She'd also pulled out a jar of cookies.

Taranee sat down and nibbled on a cookie. As she chewed, she added three spoonfuls of sugar to her cup, and she kept her eyes cast downward. Part of her wanted to block out those fireballs she'd just conjured up. She also wished she could forget that the printer in Will's bedroom wasn't running on electricity – but on *magic*.

It's all just too weird! Taranee thought. It's . . . it's not right. I mean, yeah, making those fireballs was, well, *really* cool. But having that kind of power also kind of terrifies me.

Taranee sighed and thought about her

brother, Peter. Peter was a basketball hotshot and a surfer. Foul shots or ten-foot waves – Peter faced them all with his easygoing, surfer-dude chuckle. He was afraid of nothing.

Maybe I should ask him for some pointers, Taranee thought.

Or, she realised, I guess I could just ask Irma or Cornelia.

She glanced up at Cornelia. Her blonde eye-brows were knit into a stubborn frown. Irma was still flopped on the couch, dully staring at the nature show and taking loud slurps from her mug.

Taranee knew she could really only confide in one of her friends – Will.

Will probably knows just how I feel, Taranee mused. I mean, she's also a newbie at our school, the Sheffield Institution . . . I mean, Institute. She arrived just a couple of days after I did. I'm sure she wouldn't laugh if I told her that – fireballs aside – I'm petrified of this new magical gig. I mean, who am I to save the entire world from the forces of evil? I'm just worried about passing my history test next week!

Taranee was so busy brooding she didn't notice that she'd drained her mug. That is, until

Will's voice pierced her thoughts.

"Another cup?" Will asked. When Taranee looked up, Will was standing over her.

"No thanks, Will," Taranee replied with a sigh. Cornelia didn't even bother to answer. For a moment, the only sound in the room came from the little flickers and sizzles of Taranee's floating fireballs and the droning of Irma's TV show: "And it is in the summertime that the most reprobate of the black bears are at their worst."

Finally, Cornelia broke the gloom.

"So what do you think Candracar is?" she burst out. "I mean, what do you think this place 'in the middle of infinity' is like?"

That was how Hay Lin's grandmother had described it.

"You got me," Taranee answered. "But I'm more worried thinking about the dangers we'll have to face. What is out there beyond the Veil?"

"And who," Will said, sitting down at the table with them, "were those monsters we fought?"

The three girls paused for a moment. Frustration hung in the air between them until Cornelia spoke up.

"What do you say we do a little training over the next few days?" she proposed. She took a small sip from her mug. "Sure, we have powers, but we still don't know how to use them."

"Cornelia is right," Will said. She glanced up as the sound of tires skidding through rain filled the loft. As she got to her feet to peek out the window, she added, "It would be terrible if we created some disaster just because we were inexperienced!"

"Speaking of which," Irma said, finally turning away from her bear documentary, "I wanted to tell you guys something–"

"Oh, no!" Will interrupted. She was looking through the rain-spattered window. Now she was staring in horror.

All three friends crowded behind Will.

"What's going on?" Taranee squeaked. She felt fear send little prickles down the back of her neck. "What did you see?"

"Reptile-man and the blue gorilla from the gym?" Irma asked, moving in closer behind Taranee.

"Even worse, you guys," Will groaned. "My mum's home!"

With that, Will spun around. She pointed at the dozen or so fireballs bobbing around the loft.

"The fire spheres, Taranee!" she ordered. "Hurry!"

"Right away!" Taranee quavered. Irma was flapping at the fireballs with a *TV Guide*, but the flames did not diminish. She shot Taranee a desperate look.

"*Do* something!" she hissed.

Taranee took a deep breath. She knew the fireballs were her thing. But the problem was she didn't really know how to extinguish them. In fact, she wasn't sure exactly how she'd created them! She'd just sort of closed her eyes and dreamed of dancing flames. Suddenly she had felt a burst of warmth in her palm and – ta-da!

Now that she was put on the spot, Taranee felt paralysed.

"Oh," she whispered, wringing her hands anxiously. "What to do, what to do?"

She glanced at Will, who was running through the living room like a banshee.

"Television, off!" Will ordered the TV, with a flick of her wrist. The screen immediately went black. Then she ran towards the bedroom.

Taranee took another deep breath.

Okay, she thought. Clearly, I have to learn to talk the talk. She squeezed her eyes shut and opened her mouth.

"Fire, out!" she said loudly.

When Taranee opened her eyes, she . . . could see. This was *not* a good thing. The flaming spheres were still dancing around the room!

"Out!" Taranee shouted again. She pointed at one of the fireballs in irritation. "Come on . . . extinguish! Go out! *Poof!*"

But the spheres continued to flame. Now, their playful bobbing seemed willful and taunting. Cornelia and Irma stared at Taranee in alarm.

"Hurry!" Cornelia hissed.

Almost sobbing with anxiety, Taranee finally stomped up to one of the fireballs. And before she knew exactly what she was doing, she found herself pursing her lips. She planted her face right in front of the flame and blew.

Sssszzzzzz.

The fireball disappeared, leaving nothing but a wisp of smoke.

"Cool!" Taranee breathed. Then she began

to run through the kitchen and living room, snuffing out every sphere in sight. Finally, there were just the fireballs in Will's bedroom to contend with. When Taranee ran into the room, Will was pleading with Martha.

"Printer, off!" she begged.

"Just a minute," Martha responded grouchily. "I'm still missing six lines . . . five lines . . . "

"Oooh," Taranee cried as she blew out the two fireballs hovering over Will's bed.

"Hurry!" Will shrieked.

"Four . . . " Martha was saying. "Three . . . "

"I think the coast is almost clear," Taranee said. She grabbed Will by the elbow. Together, the girls darted out of the room and dashed towards the couch, where Irma and Cornelia were already sitting. Of course, they stubbed their toes on random boxes and pieces of furniture as they went.

"I hear a key in the lock!" Irma squeaked as Will and Taranee tumbled onto the couch.

"Two . . . " Martha said in the bedroom.

"Wait a minute," Cornelia pointed out. "This looks weird, doesn't it? All of us sitting here in the dark?"

Click!

Taranee jumped. That was Mrs. Vandom's key turning in the lock! Instinctively, she reached for a fragrant candle on the coffee table and touched its wick with her fingertip. With a sizzle, the wick burst into flame.

"One!" Martha announced triumphantly from the other room. At last, the humming and whining of the printer fell silent. And a brief instant later, the front door swung open into the dimly lit loft.

"Will?" Mrs. Vandom said. She poked her head through the door apprehensively.

"Um, hi, Mum!" Will chirped nervously from the couch.

"Hiya, Mrs. Vandom," Irma said, waving at Will's mother with a big, artificial smile.

Taranee gulped. She quickly looked around the loft. Had she missed a fireball? Did Will's mum somehow know that her daughter and her friends were . . . magical?

Uh, apparently not.

"Some storm, huh?" Mrs. Vandom said. She waved hello to the girls with a friendly smile. Then she walked away to stash her raincoat in the closet.

Taranee tried to see their group through Mrs. Vandom's eyes. Yup – they really *did* look like a bunch of ordinary teenagers, gabbing by candlelight. They'd totally gotten away with their supernatural shenanigans.

And if *that's* not magic, Taranee thought with a sigh, I don't know what is!

THREE

After Hay Lin left her friends at Will's apartment building, she began to hurry home. As she walked toward the Silver Dragon – the restaurant her parents had owned ever since Hay Lin was a baby – she found herself noticing each sidewalk crack she stepped over. She stared broodingly. Then, idly, she started tapping her right toe on each crack.

Before she knew it, her left toe was tapping the sidewalk cracks, too.

A minute later, Hay Lin had only moved half a block. And that's when she realised – she was dragging her feet.

Which would have been no big deal if Hay Lin had been, like, any other teenager. But she wasn't! She was . . . Air Girl.

She was famous for skipping, not tripping. Running, not walking. She was Miss Energy. Especially since she'd learned she was magical.

But today, Hay Lin's verve was completely vacant. Her heart just wasn't in it. The reason? Her grandmother was very sick.

If Hay Lin allowed herself to think about that, her vision began to blur and her lower lip started to tremble. So she *didn't* think about it.

She couldn't however, control the sadness that kept welling up in her chest. She couldn't even bring herself to step up her pace when the thunderclouds rumbling over her head finally opened up. While raindrops spattered her long, black hair, Hay Lin simply continued to plod along.

Finally, she reached the restaurant. It was closed for the break between lunch and dinner. The empty dining room felt eerily calm.

"Anybody home?" Hay Lin called out timidly.

There was no answer. So she headed for the stairwell next to the kitchen that led up to their cosy apartment.

"Mum? Dad?" Hay Lin called as she tromped up the stairs. "Are you there?"

When she reached the top of the stairwell, she heard her father's kind, quiet voice. But he wasn't talking to her. Her father was huddled in the middle of the hallway with a silver-mustached man.

It was Grandma's physician.

"What do you think, doctor?" her dad was asking.

Hay Lin shrank against the tea-green-coloured wall and held her breath. Her dad's back was to her. He didn't know she was there. But somehow, she couldn't bring herself to interrupt the conversation.

"Last month's flu weakened her quite a bit," the doctor admitted. "She's having a hard time recovering."

"I see," her dad said. He looked at his feet.

"The medication won't be of much help," he continued. "The truth is, your mother is simply very old. She seems tired, quite frankly."

The doctor gave her dad's shoulder a sympathetic squeeze as he added, "We'll continue with all of the treatments. Stay close to her! That's what she needs most right now – her family around her."

Hay Lin felt her mouth go dry as the doctor's

words registered with her. It sounded like he was saying there was nothing he could . . . nothing that could be done.

As her dad thanked the doctor, Hay Lin realised she was gasping for breath. The sound made the doctor peek over her dad's shoulder.

"Oh," he said. "Hello, young lady."

"Hay Lin!" her dad said. He spun around and regarded his daughter. His gaze traveled from her damp, puffy, blue coat to the puddle that was quickly forming around her shoes. "You're dripping wet! Go change, before you catch something."

Hay Lin tried to catch her dad's eye. She knew that the little bit of bluster was just a cover-up. Her dad was a big softie. And Hay Lin knew he was hurting inside.

I guess he's not ready to deal, Hay Lin thought, morosely. So she simply nodded.

"Okay, Dad," she said, kicking her purple ballerina slippers into the stack next to the stairs and unzipping her coat. Then she walked down the hall toward her room.

As she tiptoed past her grandmother's room, a wispy voice wafted out towards her. It sounded a lot like the gentle chirping of a cricket.

"A warm south wind would work better than a hair dryer, little one."

"Grandma!" Hay Lin said. She peeked nervously into the sickroom. Then she walked in, slipping her coat off her shoulders.

"Go on," her grandmother said, peeking slyly into the hallway to make sure the coast was clear. "Now that your father isn't around, let me see you use your powers."

For the first time that day, Hay Lin felt a little zing of happiness shoot through her.

Her grandmother plus magic, she thought with a little giggle. I guess that's the formula.

She tossed her coat and bag onto a chair and stood at the foot of her grandmother's bed. Then she closed her eyes and concentrated.

She imagined a cool breeze skittering across her cheeks. She pictured puffs of wind fluttering her grandmother's long, white hair. Hay Lin conjured up a friendly tornado, swirling around her.

And pretty soon, she felt the familiar *whooooosh* of a *real* tornado, swirling around her body.

It's happening, Hay Lin thought with a grin. Involuntarily, she swooped her arms over her head. She squealed as her damp pigtails spiraled around her torso and her plum-coloured miniskirt fluttered in the breeze.

Now here was the part that her grandmother couldn't see – which was too bad, because it was the best part.

The feeling.

Hay Lin felt sort of like she'd swallowed a million jet-puffed marshmallows. Or she'd suddenly become a bobbling balloon, barely tethered to earth by a string. Or she was living among the clouds.

She felt weightless – as light as air.

But then, as it always did, the magic began to dissipate. And when Hay Lin felt her pigtails – dry and silky now – plop back down over her shoulders, she knew the moment was completely over.

She opened her eyes and smiled at her grandmother.

"What do you think?" she asked.

"Ha-ha!" her grandmother cried. She clapped her feeble hands together. "Splendid!"

Hay Lin dropped to her knees next to the bed and smiled as her grandmother stroked her hair. Up close, she was startled by how sick her grandmother really looked. Her hair had gone wispy and thin. Her skin was pallid with illness. And her body looked tiny and weak inside her big, quilted, green robe.

Yet the cool, dry hand on top of Hay Lin's head felt powerful. As did her grandmother's words.

"I think you'll become very good, my little Hay Lin," she pronounced. Then she moved her hand to Hay Lin's cheek and gave it a pinch. "But first, you'll have to put on a few pounds, if you don't want the northwest wind to carry you off!"

"The wind is my friend, Grandma," Hay Lin giggled. Then she felt her face grow serious.

"How do you feel today?" she asked quietly.

"*Hmph!*" her grandmother said, looking even tinier as she scrunched back into the two fluffy pillows propping her up. "Let's just say that I've seen better days."

Then, as always, her grandmother turned the focus away from herself.

"And the other Guardians of the Veil?" she asked. "Are they well?"

"They're fine, Grandma," Hay Lin said. But

she wasn't really thinking about her friends. She suddenly felt something desperate and hard well up in her throat. And she couldn't hide the fear in her voice when she asked, "But you'll get better, won't you?"

"Of course!" her grandmother said, waving her skinny hand dismissively. "I foresee great improvement. Now, help me sit up, Hay Lin. There's something beneath my pillow."

Hay Lin jumped to her feet and held her grandmother's arm as the elderly woman leaned forward. Then, when her grandmother nodded at her, Hay Lin thrust her hand beneath the pillows. Her fingers touched something smooth and powdery.

"A scroll?" Hay Lin asked. She pulled out the rolled-up piece of paper. It was raggedy at the edges and yellowed with age. It was bound by a glinty brass ring.

"This is for you and your friends," her grandmother said quietly. "Give it to Will. She'll know what to do with it."

"Wh-what is it?"

"It's a map of the twelve portals, little one," her grandmother said. She settled back against her pillows heavily. "That is the number of openings in the Veil – the twelve passages that the creatures of Metamoor will attempt to cross through to reach our world."

Gulping, Hay Lin unfurled the delicate parchment. She blinked. She turned the big piece of paper over. Then she peeked over at her grandmother. Was Grandma losing her mind as well as her health?

"There's . . . nothing written on it," she said in confusion.

"Are you sure, Hay Lin?" her grandmother replied with a glint in her eyes that scrunched her crow's-feet into . . . a *lot* of wrinkles!

Hay Lin bit her lip and took another look at the "map." And suddenly, she felt the paper do a little shimmy in her hands. With a metallic, *zwing*ing noise, shadowy lines began to form on it.

"Oh!" Hay Lin squeaked. She gaped as the shadows grew darker. They seemed to pulse and expand, growing more complex with each passing second. The lines rounded and turned corners. Shadows scuffled into place around them. And suddenly, Hay Lin found herself looking at a familiar landscape – a city fanning out from an ocean beachfront surrounded by mountains on the other side. Rather than a dry street map, this looked more like an overhead photograph. Hay Lin could see the curve of every street, the rooftop of every unique building, even the little spit of beach that housed a black-and-white–striped lighthouse – a lighthouse Hay Lin recognised.

She'd visited that tall, fishy-smelling, cylindrical building on at least three school field trips. Each time, she'd yawned her way through some tour guide's nasal explanation: "This lighthouse is the oldest structure in Heatherfield. It has averted countless ship disasters, and today serves as a welcoming beacon to visitors from *blah, blah, blah, blah*."

"This is Heatherfield!" Hay Lin exclaimed. As she spoke, the final street and building shimmered into place on the parchment. Automatically, Hay Lin's eyes sought out her part of town. And she noticed that one building on the map began to pulse. Then it started to glow, turning a glimmery pink.

"That shiny point . . . ?" she said.

"Is your school gym, where your first battle took place," Grandmother confirmed. "That was the first passageway. The flames closed it up."

Then Grandmother reached over the map and put a bony finger beneath Hay Lin's chin. She turned her granddaughter's impish face towards her own aged one. Hay Lin found herself staring into her grandmother's rheumy eyes. She could see a dozen different emotions in those eyes – love, weariness, hope, nostalgia, and, most of all, resolve. Above all, even above her illness, Hay Lin knew that her grandmother was a very strong woman. And she seemed to be making every effort to pass that strength on to her granddaughter.

That was a lucky thing. Because her grandmother's next pronouncement chilled Hay Lin to the bone.

"But the next eleven portals," her grandmother informed her, "you and the other Guardians will have to close yourselves!"

FOUR

As Hay Lin spoke with her grandmother, some-one was listening in. It was not an eavesdropping parent or one of the many microscopic, other-worldly creatures that inhabited Yan Lin's bed-room, guarding her from evil.

No, it was the Oracle – the benevolent, all-knowing being who had anointed the five Guardians of the Veil. He was gazing down upon the magical grandmother and grand-daughter from the Temple of Candracar, the mystical palace that floated in the heart of infinity. The temple was suspended in a silvery substance that was lighter than air and purer than water.

Inside the temple, the Oracle strolled along a pathway that hovered magically above a lily-studded pond. The mazelike walkways were endless, as was the distance between the pond's clear, warm waters and the temple's ceiling. The walls that enclosed the pond merely seemed to soar up into infinity. They were also covered with the colours and figures of a thousand otherworldly artists. For it was only fitting that the minister of all things good and beautiful should be surrounded, at every step, with beauty.

The Oracle paused on the walkway and clasped his hands. Then he pulled his hands back into the flowing, bell-shaped sleeves of his long robe. Tibor – the ancient, stern man who always had and always would stand guard behind the Oracle's left shoulder – stopped as well. His silver hair and beard trailed down over his own long robes.

The Oracle's face broke into a peaceful smile. As the thoughts in his head became heavier, a flickering green window appeared in the air beside him.

Finally, the Oracle and Tibor began to watch over Hay Lin and her grandmother – his messenger from the Temple of Candracar.

The Oracle felt pleasure suffuse his being as

Yan Lin informed her sprightly little grand-daughter that the Guardians must close all the portals in the Veil themselves. Hay Lin, though daunted, did not lash out in fear or hostility.

The quavering Taranee or stubborn Cornelia might have responded differently, the Oracle thought. But that knowledge didn't crease his clear brow. For he also knew that Taranee, Cornelia, and all the Guardians would soon learn to accept their fates gracefully and to master their powers. He knew, even if they didn't, that magic was in their blood and in their bones. It was their destiny – their calling.

The Oracle returned his gaze to Hay Lin, who was curious about the map.

"The map doesn't show the portals," she was saying to Yan Lin. "How can anyone use it?"

As if she were speaking the Oracle's very thoughts, Yan Lin answered, "I've already told you and your friends – with time you will learn everything."

While Hay Lin continued to gaze at her grandmother quizzically, the frail, old woman bowed her silvery head.

"Yes," the Oracle said to the old woman,

with powerful waves of telepathy. "You may tell her. Tell her, Yan Lin, your story."

With a small nod, Yan Lin looked up at her granddaughter and spoke.

"Once," she said in her reedy, whispery voice, "I, too, was a Guardian of the Veil, long before you. And once I, too, was very impatient, just as you are now."

Hay Lin gasped and perched on the edge of her grandmother's bed, setting aside the precious map of Heatherfield's twelve portals.

"You were a witch, too?" Hay Lin asked.

"Witch?" her grandmother replied with a wheezy giggle. "That's not exactly a compliment! But it certainly is funny. We aren't witches. We aren't even fairies."

Taking Hay Lin's hand in her own, Yan Lin looked into her granddaughter's eyes and said, "We are something entirely different."

Hay Lin's sparkly, almond-shaped eyes widened.

"But in any case," Yan Lin continued, lightheartedly, "I don't know anything anymore. It's your turn now, Hay Lin."

It's a portent, the Oracle thought, of things to come.

The Oracle's musings – like the conversation between the elderly Guardian and the very young one – were interrupted by Hay Lin's father. He poked his head through the old woman's bedroom door. He was holding a bottle of dark liquid. "It's time for your medicine, Mother," he said. He stepped into the room and smiled. "And please, no fussing! I've tried it myself and it's very tasty!"

"If it's so good," Yan Lin shot back, "why don't you put it on today's menu?"

"Come on," her son chided. He took Hay Lin's place on the edge of the old woman's bed. "You don't want to make a scene in front of your granddaughter."

Yan Lin grimaced.

"Once I was the one who spoon-fed you, young man," she teased. "But it never crossed my mind to force something so nasty on you!"

"Very funny," the man said, pouring some of the amber liquid into a spoon and nudging it into his mother's mouth. She swallowed the elixir and made another face.

"See," Hay Lin's father announced. "That wasn't so bad, after all."

"*Bleah!*" Yan Lin said after she swallowed.

She stuck her tongue out like a child.

The gesture, at once so funny and so poignant, brought a surge of emotion to Hay Lin's heart. And the intuitive Oracle felt the emotion in his own. It was painful and bitter-sweet. He placed a cool hand on his chest and knew that its comfort was flowing earthward, into the heart of the young girl.

It worked. She smiled at her grandmother through her tears.

"Take care, Hay Lin," Yan Lin purred with a smile. "And don't forget, eat!"

"I promise," Hay Lin whispered. She leaned over and placed one simple kiss on the old woman's cool forehead. "Goodnight, Grandma."

Hay Lin walked out of the sickroom. She tucked the map – once again bound in its brass ring – safely into her coat pocket. The Oracle had seen enough. He waved his hand through the air. The pulsing, green window into his thoughts wavered until it was no more than a cloud of vapour with the faint scent of lemon-grass and hyacinth.

Then he turned to his adviser, who bowed his gray, woolly head deferentially.

"And so," the Oracle announced, "the map

of the twelve portals has been delivered."

"Honorable Yan Lin has done truly excellent work, Oracle," Tibor responded.

"Yes," the Oracle said. "And this means her mission has been completed."

"I see."

"You know what to do, Tibor," the Oracle said. He strolled away from his adviser with a graceful gait that required no effort. "Inform the council of the congregation."

As the Oracle floated away, he pictured Yan Lin in the comfort of her soft bed, surrounded by the love of her family. After she passed away, she would rise through the heavens, effortlessly traveling through galaxies and dimensions. Eventually, she would arrive in the stadiumlike fortress of the council.

There, all the council members – from stalwart Tibor to even the volatile, wolflike Luba – would join hands and dance around Yan Lin. It would be a dance of celebration, of gratitude, of welcome.

"Yes," the Oracle murmured, as he glided through his beautiful temple. "She shall have the welcome she so greatly deserves."

FIVE

Cornelia tromped up the grassy hill, holding a stick of smoldering incense out in front of her. Its blue smoke smelled like sandalwood and sea grass. She knew the scent was supposed to be comforting, but it only made her nose itch. She put a gloved hand over her mouth to stifle a sneeze. Then she glanced behind her at her friends.

Will's and Taranee's faces looked as stricken as Cornelia felt. Will's knuckles were white as she clutched her own stick of incense. And Taranee, carrying a basket of snowy flowers, was more trembly than usual.

Even Irma, Cornelia thought, a girl who can always crack a joke, looks shaken. I guess that's because this is one of the saddest things we've ever experienced. A funeral – for Hay Lin's grandmother.

A cool autumn breeze whisked over the hill. Cornelia flicked a tear from the corner of her eye and clutched her white shawl tighter around her shoulders. Then, at last, the large crowd of mourners completed their long, slow climb up the hill to the pretty meadow where the funeral service would take place. In their all-white clothes, the people looked like a flock of somber birds.

"White is the colour of mourning in Chinese culture," Hay Lin had told Cornelia on the phone after she'd gotten the news about her grandmother. Her voice had been choked with tears. "The colour of snow."

And then Hay Lin had had to go help her parents. But before she'd hung up the phone, Hay Lin had told Cornelia something else. She'd informed her that her grandmother had also been a Guardian of the Veil in her own youth.

The news had shaken Cornelia.

So, not only, she thought, has magic suddenly invaded my life, but it's going to be a part of my life forever! I'm part of generations of Guardians. And someday, I'll have to pass the magic on to some unsuspecting teenager.

Unless you win the battle, a voice inside her said. If you conquer Metamoor's evil invaders, there will be no more need for Guardians. It's up to you, Cornelia. It's up to you . . . to you . . . to you. . . .

Cornelia tried to shake the pressure-cooker thoughts from her head and return her attention to the present. Several friends and family members were speaking to the group, saying affectionate, admiring words about Yan Lin. Out of the corner of her eye, Cornelia saw mourners' hands holding bunches of white blossoms. Others clutched ivory ribbons.

"The colour of snow," Cornelia whispered to herself.

She shivered as the funeral service neared its end.

Ribbons and flowers turning to snow, she thought. Yup, that makes about as much sense as anything else right now. I mean, how many more times will our lives change forever?

In school a couple of days earlier, everything had been normal. Well, as normal as it could be since the girls had become magical.

While the sun glinted off the tin roof of the Sheffield Institute, Cornelia had been hanging out with Will in the front courtyard. And she was enjoying the power that came with possession of a choice tidbit of gossip.

The instant Hay Lin, Irma, and Taranee had come into the courtyard, Cornelia blurted out, "Did you hear the news? It's got everyone at school talking!"

"What news?" Irma said. Cornelia couldn't help but relish – just a little bit – the envious frown on Irma's face. Irma was usually the one with all the news.

That's what comes from being a busybody, Cornelia had thought.

But what she'd said was, "The police are in the principal's office!"

Hay Lin gave a delighted shriek as the girls fell into step and headed for the front steps together.

"Poor Mrs. Knickerbocker," she'd said. "She's mean, but not *so* mean that she deserves to go to jail!"

Will snorted.

"Sorry to disappoint you, Hay Lin," Will said. "I guess that you didn't watch the news on

TV this morning, did you?"

"No, why?" Hay Lin gasped. "What did I miss?"

"It's even in the papers!" Taranee cried. "A boy from our school disappeared!"

Cornelia had sighed. Well, it looked like the gossip wasn't exactly hers to dispense, after all. But at least she could provide the missing boy's name.

"Andrew Hornby," she announced. "Do you remember him?"

"Who?" Hay Lin gasped, giving a little jump. "Do you mean that gorgeous blonde guy from the upper school?"

"Exactly," Will said. "He didn't go home for three days straight! As of last night, he's officially a missing person."

The group fell silent. Even Irma! Cornelia gave her chatterbox bud a sidelong glance. Irma didn't have one breathless remark to make? Not one clever quip?

Apparently not. In fact, Irma was looking a little freaked. Her usually rosy cheeks were sweaty and pale. She was gnawing on her full lower lip, completely wrecking her carefully applied cranberry-coloured lip gloss. Irma's silence wasn't lost on Hay Lin, either.

"Wake up, Irma!" Hay Lin said, giving her friend a nudge. She whipped a fat, felt-tip pen from the pocket of her slouchy, blue jacket and scribbled "Andrew" on her palm in purple ink. Then she held her hand before Irma's blinking blue eyes.

"Isn't that the one you're crazy about?"

"Well, yeah," Irma rasped. Then she'd skidded to a halt. The girls were in the school's foyer – still several feet away from their lockers.

"What gives?" Cornelia had sighed, glancing at her watch. "We're gonna be late for first period!"

"In any case," Irma said, her forehead furrowed with resolve, "I've been trying to tell you guys something."

As she spoke, an office door swung open behind her.

And that's not just any door, Cornelia had thought, catching her breath. That's Principal Knickerbocker's door! Taranee saw it, too.

"Look!" she'd gasped. "They're coming out!"

Dragging her friends with her, Cornelia had ducked behind a corner and peeked around it.

She saw the principal saying goodbye to two police officers. The men began to stalk away, looking heavy and official in their blue hats and bulky cop jackets.

"Thank you for everything, ma'am," one of the men said over his shoulder. "If we find out anything, we'll let you know."

"I'd appreciate that very much, Officer," Mrs. Knickerbocker said. "Good luck."

Cornelia looked down at Hay Lin with a grin.

"See?" she said. "They didn't take her away."

Hay Lin smirked.

"Maybe another time!" she said. Then she cackled mischievously.

"Hay Lin!" Mrs. Knickerbocker suddenly called out. She'd spotted Hay Lin and the others peeking around the corner! "I need to speak with you right away."

"Did she hear me?" Hay Lin asked her friends in a panicked whisper. They shrugged.

All Hay Lin could do was obey Mrs. Knickerbocker's order. Shooting her friends a terrified glance, she trudged into the principal's office. As Mrs. Knickerbocker waited inside her office door, she looked as imposing as ever. Her wispy, white beehive quivered on top of her head, and her tiny eyes looked even tinier behind her horn-rimmed glasses. As Hay Lin ducked past Mrs. Knickerbocker's bulky form, Cornelia heard her squeak, "I can explain everything, ma'am! It was only a little joke, and–"

"Sit down, Hay Lin. . . . " the principal began. Then she slammed the door shut.

What Cornelia knew now was that Hay Lin hadn't been in trouble at all. Mrs. Knickerbocker had just gotten a call from Hay Lin's father. And then, behind the closed office door, she'd had to break the terrible news to Hay Lin: her grandmother had passed away that morning.

Now, here we are, Cornelia thought sadly. While she'd been lost in her memories, Yan Lin's service had ended. The white-clad mourners began walking back down the hill. But Cornelia and her fellow Guardians lingered behind to wait for Hay Lin, who was giving her parents big, sad hugs. Hay Lin burst into tears and fell into her parents' arms.

If only we could use our magic to whisk away our pain! Cornelia thought. Then it might not be so bad having these strange powers.

Cornelia sighed and glanced at Will, Taranee, and Irma. They were standing next to her, looking miserable as they gazed at Hay Lin.

Does this magic thing freak them out as much as it does me? Cornelia had to wonder. I mean, I know Taranee is scared. And I have a feeling Will's a little weirded out that her powers are different from ours. And Irma . . . Irma is probably only as upset as she would be if they canceled *Boy Comet*.

But me, Cornelia thought, I've always had this need to have my life in control. I love that feeling of balance I get when I'm doing a perfect spiral in a skating routine. Or when my room is put together just the way I like it, even if the way I like it is in a total mess.

But now, she thought, I have control over nothing. Another round of tears welled up in her eyes. She looked down at her feet.

Everything was changing. Her best friend, Elyon, and Elyon's parents were missing. And now she was also mourning with Hay Lin for

Hay Lin's sweet, departed grandmother.

Nobody asked me if I wanted to be a Guardian of the Veil, Cornelia thought miserably. As self-pity washed over her, she saw Hay Lin approach their little group. Looking even smaller and wirier than usual, Hay Lin gave Will a tight hug.

"Thanks for coming, guys," she whispered in a raspy, small voice. "I love you all."

Cornelia opened her mouth to respond. But she couldn't think of what to say. And that distressed her, too.

I can't even be a good friend to Hay Lin, Cornelia thought, kicking angrily at a tuft of grass. Because, well . . . how can I be a good fellow Guardian when I don't even want to *be* a Guardian?

What's more, she thought with a sigh, ever since Elyon vanished without a trace, I have had nobody to talk to about all this.

Cornelia bit her lip as she thought of her best friend. Elyon had done more than vanish. Apparently, she'd also set a trap for Will, Hay Lin, and Irma. They'd been scared to death by some gruesome Metamoorian monsters!

For Cornelia, that was perhaps the most

bizarre part of all of it – that Elyon could betray her friends. Cornelia couldn't quite bring herself to believe that her best friend was capable of that.

No, she thought stubbornly. It can't be true.

As Cornelia told herself that, she became vaguely aware of Hay Lin extricating herself from her hug with Will. Hay Lin was peeking over Will's shoulder and blinking her teary eyes rapidly.

No, Cornelia thought again with a determined shake of her head. I just can't believe that Elyon's bad. Not–

"Elyon!" Hay Lin suddenly screamed.

"What?" Cornelia blurted out. She saw Hay Lin pointing to a spot down the hill. Cornelia spun around and followed her friend's gaze. She saw a knotty old tree, looming over a patch of dirt at the very edge of the cemetery. A few dried leaves rustled, and a couple of forgotten grave markers leaned against a wrought-iron fence nearby.

But Cornelia saw nobody, and certainly didn't see Elyon.

She gazed back at Hay Lin. She felt confusion and pain and dashed hopes roil in her gut.

But Hay Lin seemed still to be seeing something.

"It can't be!" Hay Lin cried. "Elyon!"

Cornelia turned to squint down the hill one final time. Again, she saw nothing. That nothingness made another round of tears flood her eyes.

It really can't be, Cornelia thought, morosely. Hay Lin must be crazy with grief – hallucinating. Nobody's there. Certainly not Elyon.

SIX

Elyon stood beneath a gnarled old tree. Under her feet, there was no grass. There was only dirt – lumpy with tree roots, bedraggled, neglected. A cold breeze rustled her straw-coloured bangs and blew her long braids this way and that.

And suddenly, Elyon realised something.

She'd never noticed the absence of cold! In Metamoor, that is, where she had been living for . . . a few days? A few weeks? Elyon blinked slowly. She didn't know anymore. And what did it matter? She was home now, in Metamoor, where she finally belonged, after years of exile here on earth.

She stopped to enjoy the rush of cool, damp wind on her face. It was good to feel the change of weather. In Metamoor, it was always beautiful. The sun shone steadily, the air smelled of sweet flowers. It was never too hot and never too cold. There was no inconvenient rain or ominous darkness. Of course, there were no thrilling thunderstorms, either. Nor was there any variety. . . .

Elyon shook her head lightly to halt her thoughts. She refused to feel nostalgia for the false life she had lived in Heatherfield. That would only give *them* what *they* wanted.

Elyon hummed a tuneless little song and closed her eyes for a moment. When she opened them, the thought was gone. She couldn't even remember what the thought had been. Only a hazy residue remained, as easy to wipe away as a day's worth of dust on a table.

She blinked her enormous blue eyes lazily and shifted in her knee-high boots. Their soles scratched loudly in the dirt. In fact, Elyon began to feel a heightened awareness of *all* the noises – beneath her feet and in the air. Caterpillars, undulating up the old tree trunk, made rustling, moaning noises that Elyon could hear distinctly. The last dewdrop of the morning – falling off a tree leaf onto Elyon's royal blue garment – landed with a heavy, audible plop.

This, Elyon knew, was her new magic. It had begun to burble up inside her.

A few moments later, all her senses – not just her hearing – began rising to extraordinary levels. The touch of a falling leaf glancing against her arm rippled through her entire body. The sun – glinting off faraway shafts of white marble – sparkled and danced in her eyes.

And that breeze! There were voices in it – the joyful call of songbirds flying hundreds of feet in the air and the soothing song of the dead beneath Elyon's feet.

Elyon was positively brimming with magic now.

And that meant it was time.

Elyon gazed up the hill. It was carpeted with a lush swath of verdant grass. She gave an-other lazy blink. Her mouth tightened into the smallest of smiles.

She didn't need to call attention to herself.

Her magic would call to *them*.

Them?

That would be her "friends" – the ones

Elyon had left behind, the ones now mourning beside an open grave. Elyon had watched impassively as Hay Lin hugged Will and said, "I love you all."

Though Hay Lin's voice was just a raspy whisper, Elyon heard it clearly. Hay Lin could have been just inches away, whispering in her ear, sharing a secret, the way she used to during science class at the Sheffield Institute.

Again, Elyon closed her eyes to the memory before it could even solidify in her head. Then she felt it leave her mind like a puff of vapour, swept away by the wind.

A good thing, too. Because Hay Lin had just spotted her. Elyon watched the skinny girl withdraw from Will's embrace and point at her.

Elyon smiled her tight, tiny smile.

"It can't be!" Hay Lin cried. "Elyon!"

A rustle of disbelief and confusion swept through the group. Elyon could feel their emotions thrumming through her own chest. She could feel Taranee clasp her hands in agitation. She could sense the buzz of confusion inside Irma's head. She felt hope lift in Cornelia's heart. And then she felt it die.

Because Elyon was no longer there.

Or, rather, she was invisible.

That was Elyon's magic at work. It had reached its height, vibrating and shimmering through her with incredible power. In fact, the magic was so strong it threatened to fly away from her, like a skittish bird.

Since she'd arrived in Metamoor, Elyon had been practising. Her mind had become increasingly supple. She'd learned to control her unwieldy magic – to catch it, mold it.

And now, her work had paid off. She had used her magic to will herself – her inconsequential body, anyway – into a state of invisibility.

Elyon was still there, of course. She felt the scratchy dirt beneath the soles of her boots, and she wiggled her nose as another breeze skipped playfully across it. But when she looked down at herself, all she saw was dirt and tree roots.

Her body was simply not there.

And that's what her *friends* were now telling Hay Lin. But Hay Lin was resisting.

"Elyon's here!" she insisted, pointing at the base of the tree.

"What do you mean?" Will asked. She

gazed down the hill, seeing right through Elyon. "Where?"

"She *was* down there," Hay Lin insisted. Her voice was still heavy with tears for her grandmother. "I saw her!"

Hay Lin ran a few steps forward and called out to her once more.

"ELYON!" she screamed.

Elyon did not answer.

Still, Hay Lin would not give up.

"She *was* there," she repeated to Will. "I swear it! She can't have hidden so quickly!" Will shrugged and glanced back at the rest of the group. "Let's go take a look," she proposed. She started down the hill after Hay Lin.

No, Elyon thought. She squinted at Will, focusing on her with all her energy.

No.

"Maybe," Will began to say, "it was only *uhhhnnn . . .* "

Suddenly, Will staggered. She squeezed her eyes shut. Her hand flew to her tousled red hair and clutched at her head.

Elyon watched Will falter. Will looked dizzy, and her face was screwed up with confusion and – perhaps – pain. Elyon felt a flicker of concern in her chest. But it was quickly extinguished. Feelings like that belonged to the old Elyon. The one who had lived in Heatherfield.

As Will took a few unsteady steps backwards, Elyon blinked with calm satisfaction. Will was moving away from Elyon's tree, away from her.

"Will, are you okay?" Taranee cried. All four friends turned to catch Will before her wave of dizziness knocked her over.

As Will's friends gathered around her, like a healing force field, Elyon watched – or did she feel? – the wooziness drain from Will's head.

Will's brown eyes slowly fluttered open. Her fingers unclenched, and she smoothed a hank of hair from her now damp forehead.

"Yeah," she muttered slowly. "I think I'm okay."

Elyon blinked again.

And Will gave Taranee a wan smile.

"Everything's fine," she sighed.

Cornelia glanced over her shoulder at the base of the craggy tree, the space still inhabited by Elyon's spirit. Cornelia sighed. And then she announced, "Let's go home, Hay Lin. You must have been mistaken. You're just upset."

The girls began to climb back up the hill, heading toward the lingering crowd of mourners. As she followed her friends, Hay Lin shot one final glance over her shoulder.

Hay Lin is a dangerous one, Elyon thought. She, more than the others, believes in that which isn't seen.

Smart girl, she thought.

Then she felt the magic burble up within her once again. This time, it gave form to that which had been formless. Her body, her pale blonde braids, her dress of rippling, silken fabric and billowing sleeves – all slowly became corporeal.

Elyon smiled. And this time, her smile was for real.

Because – in the same way that the magic had told her *their* thoughts and feelings – it now informed her that she was no longer alone.

Behind her was . . . he. Lord Cedric. Elyon didn't have to turn around to sense his presence or see his beauty. She envisioned his long, silky hair rippling in the breeze behind him. His crimson coat framed his square shoulders with perfect precision.

Cedric's sharp features were creased into a

smug smile. "Excellent, Elyon," he said, praising her.

A warmth suffused Elyon, like warm honey, like sweet satisfaction. She yearned to hear the words again.

And thus – she did.

"Truly," Cedric whispered, "excellent."

SEVEN

The day after Hay Lin's grandmother's funeral was a Sunday. And Will was relieved that she didn't have to dash off to school. There was no alarm and no panic. Sundays were for sleeping late.

But on Sunday morning, Will got up early. Why was it on the days that she could sleep late, she often woke up early?

Her mother was up as well and busy making waffles. Waffles were a good reason to get up early on a Sunday.

Not only were waffles served: so was "Mum-and-Will banter." Every time Will drowned her waffles in syrup, for instance, her mother made a crack about the high cost of maple products. Then she would suggest they move to the mountains to keep Will supplied with all the maple syrup her heart desired.

Next, Will would tease her mother about the fact that she – a grown-up! – never ate the crusts of her whole wheat toast.

And then the two would munch in silence while they read the Sunday paper. Will read the funnies and the sports section (she always checked it for any swimming news). Her mum grabbed the style section and read the front-page headlines out loud to Will.

As traditions went, Sunday breakfast was definitely not bad. In fact, Will had to admit, it was pretty nice. It was also one of the few times her mum relaxed completely, shaking off the stresses of that week's work at Simultech.

For a moment, on that particular morning, Will stopped to imagine how her mother would have reacted if she had known Will was a Guardian of the Veil.

Talk about stress! Will thought as she chewed a bite of waffle. One minute, I'm Susan Vandom's sorta slouchy daughter. I've got nothing to worry about but being the new kid at school. The next minute, I'm a magical being with the powers of the Heart of Candracar pulsing through my veins.

Will tried to imagine that as a normal thing. She saw herself putting on her jacket and heading for the door.

"See ya, Mum," she would call out. "I'm off to close another one of those pesky portals to the evil world of Metamoor."

"On a school night?!" her mum would protest.

"Well, y'know," Will would reply, "if I don't, the world as we know it will end. Total apocalypse. Kabam, kablooey, game over."

"Well . . . all right," her mum would allow with a shrug. "But as soon as you get home from saving the world, young lady, I want that biology homework done!"

As the daydream evaporated, Will realised the funny papers were crumpled in her fists. Her knuckles were white with tension.

"Whoa!" she whispered. She tossed the newspaper back onto the kitchen table.

"Has one of your comic strips taken a dramatic turn?" her mum asked with a wry smile.

Will gave a shaky laugh.

"Nah," she said, getting to her feet. "I think I might have had one too many waffles. I'm stuffed. Think I'll go for a bike ride."

"Good idea," her mum agreed. She got up from the table to clear their breakfast dishes. "Have a nice ride. I'm going to relax with a nice, postbrunch nap."

And I am going to keep my secret identity secret, Will thought as she went to her room to grab a jacket. I mean, first Mum and Dad get a divorce. Then Mum and I move to Heatherfield. Then I turn *magical*. It's way too much! The only thing that could make life more complicated right now would be Mum's knowing I'm a Guardian. She'd worry about me constantly. And probably ground me for life. Which would ruin everything.

As Will wheeled her bike out of the loft and into her building's elevator, her heart felt heavy.

The biggest bummer, she muttered to herself, is that none of this makes me care any less about being a newbie at Sheffield. Will sighed. When the elevator arrived at the lobby, she wheeled her bike out of the building. As she hopped on and started pedaling, her mind flashed to the first time she'd ever seen her magical self. She'd been riding her bike then, too. She'd seen her altered reflection in a shop window.

And her appearance had stunned her. As the keeper of the Heart of Candracar, Will had looked like an older teenager. Her usual uniform of slouchy jeans and sneakers had been replaced by striped tights, a midriff-baring purple dress, and rad, round-toed boots. But the most incredible thing had been Will's body. Not only had her back sprouted delicate, feathery wings, but all her flat planes had turned curvy. Her legs had lengthened and her waist had shrunk.

It had been the coolest.

Will steered her bike towards Heatherfield Park.

Naturally, she thought wistfully as she pedaled, there's no way anybody at Sheffield will get to see my cool alter ego. No, all they get is the real me.

Wait a minute, she thought. Before we all became magical, Taranee, Irma, Cornelia, and Hay Lin saw the *real* me. And they *liked* me.

The thought sent a happy shimmer through Will.

Then she pedaled through the arched gateway to Heatherfield Park. Almost instantly, the noise of the busy city streets disappeared, and Will was surrounded by the wonderful quiet of a Sunday. All she could hear was her bike tyres crunching through fallen leaves and joggers trotting around her.

She sighed contentedly.

Maybe, Will thought, this place isn't so bad, after all. The park is wonderful at this time of morning. The city seems so far away.

Will turned down a path and began to ride through a grove of trees. The trees were well on their way towards shedding all their leaves for the winter. The crisp, cool air smelled like mulch and wood smoke.

Suddenly, Will hit her bike brakes and skidded to a halt. In the branches of a nearby tree, she saw a group of boys.

"Uriah and his gang!" Will muttered. "What are they up to?"

Sheffield Institute's biggest bully definitely ruined the landscape Will had been enjoying. The redheaded, pimply-faced, pointy-nosed Uriah was perched on a thick branch. His thin lips were curled into a mischievous smile. He looked ready to pounce on something.

At the base of the tree were Uriah's friends – if you could call dudes who followed him around like puppies and obeyed his every order friends. Hulking, blonde Laurent was laughing his loud, donkeylike laugh and clapping his big, meaty hands together. Kurt – who was as short and tubby as Uriah was tall and skinny – rested his hands on his big belly and grinned up at the bully.

But Nigel – who had chin-length, silky brown hair and a kind face – was trying to be the voice of reason.

"I don't think this is a good idea, Uriah," he called up to the treetop.

"For the little gentleman," Uriah sneered, "nothing like this is ever a good idea. Chill out, Nigel! We're just having a little fun! If you don't try doing certain things at this age, when are you ever gonna do them?"

"Putting a dormouse in Martin's locker," Nigel retorted irritably, "is not what I'd call a 'little' fun."

Uriah's getting ready to catch a dormouse?! Oh, No! Will thought. She loved dormice almost as much as she loved frogs. The little, squirrel-like animals with the black masks over their eyes were really cute.

Will also knew that a dormouse in distress could cause some serious damage. And Martin Tubbs didn't deserve to have his locker ransacked by one, even if he was a total nerd who drove her friends crazy with his megacrush on Irma.

What was more, no dormouse deserved to be aggravated by the likes of Uriah!

Will gazed up into Uriah's tree. She could spot the little dormouse he was stalking, now. The poor thing was scampering around another tree branch, looking trapped and panicky.

Will felt her face go hot with anger. But she didn't make her presence known. Not yet. She had to act carefully. She knew Uriah was a big coward deep down. (After all, when he'd tried to vandalize Will's bike on her first day at Sheffield, one harsh stare from Cornelia had made him back down completely.) But still, there was no telling how he would react to a challenge from Will.

So she quietly walked her bike to a spot a few feet behind the gang and watched as Uriah tried to bag his prey.

"*Grrrr,*" Uriah growled as he made a grab for the little cutie. It darted easily out of his way and hopped to another branch.

"Mostly it's not fun," Uriah called down to Nigel, "because the stupid little critter won't let me catch him!"

But then, for once, Uriah came up with a clever solution. He suddenly grabbed the tree trunk and swung himself halfway around the tree. That caught the dormouse by surprise. The creature paused for an instant and flicked its bushy tail.

"Aha!" Uriah cried. "Gotcha!"

He grabbed the dormouse.

Will started to gasp. But then the dormouse slithered out of Uriah's grasp. In fact, the creature buried its sharp little teeth in Uriah's finger with a chomping sound.

"*Yaaaagggh!*" Uriah squealed. As he shook his hand wildly – with the dormouse still gnawing on his fingertip – he flailed himself right off the tree branch, and he landed loudly in a pile of leaves.

"Heh, heh, heh," Laurent giggled. "Now, this is what I call fun."

Uriah probably would have belted him if he

hadn't been so busy shrieking.

"*Aahhhh!*" he screamed again. Still lying on his back, he waved the determined little dormouse around his head. "Get it off me! Get it off me!"

Finally, Uriah gave his hand one last, mighty flail. It sent the dormouse crashing into the tree trunk! It slammed against the bark, then landed on the ground with a thud. As the little animal got to its feet, shaking its head blearily, Uriah gaped at his raw fingertip. Then he spotted a thick branch nearby.

He grabbed it.

He staggered to his feet and raised the branch over his head. All the while, he glared down at the disoriented dormouse.

"Why," he grunted, "you rotten little–"

"Don't you dare!"

The order had shot out of Will's mouth almost involuntarily! But when Uriah jumped back and dropped his weapon, Will knew she'd done the right thing.

At least, she *thought* she had. As Uriah's thugs all turned to glower at her, she started to have some second thoughts. Four to one – that was definitely a little unnerving!

Not that Will let on. She glared right back at the gang. Her fists were clenched, and her feet were planted firmly in the dirt.

"Ah, the new girl," Laurent said.

"So," Uriah sneered at Will, "what's your problem?"

"Leave the sweet thing alone," she shouted, pointing at the dormouse. The little animal was still staggering at the base of the tree.

"*Oooh*," Uriah cried in a reedy falsetto. "I'm soooo scared. Look! I'm shakin' like a leaf!"

Then Uriah's expression returned to its usual threatening sneer. He thrust his greasy nose up at Will's.

"So, whaddya wanna do about it?" he growled. "This time, Cornelia's not here to get you out of trouble."

"For the likes of you," Will shot back, "I'm enough!"

"Oh, yeah?"

Uriah clenched his fists. Will clenched hers. And then, suddenly, she realised something.

She meant it! And she wasn't scared of this gang of guys anymore.

Why should I be? she asked herself as she took a threatening step toward them. I've got magical powers. I could kick all their butts with one wing tied behind my back!

Before Will could test the theory, Nigel stepped between her and Uriah.

"Hey . . . " he murmured. He put a firm hand on Uriah's shoulder and gave him a long look. It was half-placating, half-pleading.

And, at last, Uriah backed off. He pointed at Will and growled, "I'm not through with you!"

But even as he said it, he was scurrying toward the path. Naturally, his cronies fell into step behind him.

Idiots, Will thought. They get all tough with girls and defenseless animals. I swear I'll teach them a thing or two!

Rrrrrrrr.

The muffled whimper made Will jump. She'd almost forgotten about the true victim here – the dormouse! Will ran to the tree and crouched down next to the trembling critter. As she stroked its silky fur and tickled it comfortingly beneath the chin, she felt her anger melt away.

"So," she cooed to the sweet little dormouse, "how do you feel?"

The dormouse chittered again and blinked

its hazy, black eyes. Then it opened its mouth wide.

Aw, Will thought. It's yawning! Poor little thing must be exhaust–

Chomp!

"Ow!" Will squealed.

She wrenched her pinkie from the dormouse's needlelike teeth and clutched it painfully.

Or maybe it's just hungry, she thought with a groan. Then she gaped down at the dizzy dormouse.

"Hey!" she said. "Ungrateful little thing! I rescue you and this is the thanks I get?"

The dormouse, of course, ignored her and staggered a few steps away. But someone was listening. Someone in baggy red cords and big, boyish basketball shoes.

"Need a hand?" the boy's voice said playfully.

"You again!" Will said. She didn't bother to look up. She was too busy examining her sore pinkie and scowling.

I can't believe it! she thought as she grimaced through the pain in her finger. Uriah just doesn't know when to give up! Well, maybe *this* will help him see the light!

"I can manage, thanks!" she said. Then she slammed her fist down hard on the boy's big, sneaker-clad toe!

"Ow!" he cried. "What's your problem?!"

Will finally looked up at her tormentor.

Then she gulped.

The boy painfully clutching his foot was not Uriah.

In fact, he was a cute boy.

A *really* cute boy.

A really cute boy that Will recognised! He was Matt Olsen, the lead singer in an amazing band called Cobalt Blue. Will had seen him sing at the Halloween party only a few nights ago. He was a total hottie *and* a complete Infielder (as in, in with the most popular crowd at Sheffield Institute).

"Omigosh!" Will screamed. "Sorry! Sorry! Sorry! I . . . made a mistake! I . . . I thought you were someone else."

Matt painfully lowered his foot and glanced from the little dormouse to Will. Will smoothed her hair and staggered to her feet. She felt her cheeks flush bright red. Then she smoothed her hair back – again.

Real smooth, spaz, Will told herself. Now focus! He's talking to you!

"Dormice have a mean side to them," Matt said with a wry smile, "but you're pretty tough yourself!"

Okay, Will thought. This is *not* a good beginning. She decided to ignore Matt's teasing and . . . and what?! What should she say?!

Will imagined Cornelia rolling her eyes and dryly suggesting, "You could start by introducing yourself!"

"You're Matt, right?" Will said with a nervous smile. "I really liked you at the concert on Halloween."

Oh . . . my . . . God, Will thought desperately. Why don't you just come out and *tell* him you've been crushing on him ever since his concert. That would be *really* cool!

"That is," Will gulped, "I mean . . . I liked your singing!"

"Gee, thanks!" Matt said. He smiled again. But this time, it wasn't a wry smile. Or a sly smile. It was just . . . a sweet smile.

A really, really, cute smile, Will thought dreamily. She gazed up at Matt, who was tall and lanky and had a superstrong jaw dotted by just the right amount of scruffiness. He had perfectly tousled brown hair and a cool fisherman's cap and really nice hands. . . .

Oh yeah, Will remembered. I'm supposed to be introducing myself here.

"My name's Will," she said.

Matt gave Will a little nod – so cute! – and then pointed at the dormouse. He'd just stumbled into a tree root and fallen over with a tiny thud.

"And this is your pet, huh, Will?" Matt said. He crouched down to stroke the critter's fluffy tail. "Looks like it came out of hibernation a bit too early. Look how out of it the poor thing is!"

The dormouse chittered wanly and looked around in confusion.

"It's still stunned," Matt continued. "And cold and hungry, too." Will peered over Matt's shoulder at the animal.

Matt pulled out a woolly, orange sweater from his messenger bag.

"Here, it'll feel better with this," Matt said. In one deft motion, he scooped the dormouse into the sweater and rolled the wool up in a ball. In an instant, the critter was completely swaddled. Only its face poked out of the end of the bundled sweater. And that face looked very contented.

"It'll snuggle up inside," Matt said, getting to his feet with the dormouse in his sweater cradled in his arms. "And every once in a while, when it feels like it, it'll pop out to eat something."

Will gazed up at Matt's still smiling face.

His eyes are such a pretty brown, she was thinking. He smells like cedar. And . . . whoops, it's time for me to say something now!

"Um, looks like you know all about this stuff," Will said, nodding at the cosy little dormouse.

"My grandpa has a pet shop," Matt explained. "But don't ask me to take it over there! He's busy enough with all the animals he already has!"

With that, Matt held the dormouse out for Will to take.

That finally brought Will back to earth.

Wait a minute, she thought. Is Matt expecting me to take the dormouse home? Without authorisation from Mum? Does our new building even allow pets?!

"Hold on!" Will cried. "I can't keep it!"

"Are you kidding?" Matt said. "You two were obviously made for each other."

Will gazed into the little creature's eyes. The mischief in them had been replaced by a sleepy sweetness.

Rrrrrr, the dormouse chittered.

Then Matt placed the animal in her arms. And Will felt something melt inside her. Despite herself, she began cooing to the dormouse.

Between this little guy and Matt, she thought dreamily, soon there's gonna be nothing left of me but a big puddle of mush. Ooh, right, Matt's talking to me again!

"See you at school," he was saying. When Will looked up, she felt a little zing travel through her. He was also writing something on a little card! Something that had to be . . .

"Here's my number," he said, handing the card to her. "If you need any advice on the dormouse . . . "

Will took the card. She looked at Matt. And then she blinked.

Here's the part, now, Will told herself, where you say, "Thanks!" Then you do something flirty or sassy. Something Irma-esque.

But Will's throat was too dry for her to talk. She merely smiled tremulously as he began to walk away. Before he got too far, he turned back around. He shot her another one of those really cute smiles. Finally, Will found her voice. Well, sort of.

"Bye!" she squeaked. Then she waved.

As Matt ambled off down the path, Will took a deep, long breath. Then she glanced down at the bundle of dormouse in her arms.

Rrrrooon, the critter cooed.

Finally, Will allowed herself to melt completely.

"Yes," Will whispered to the little dormouse. "I'm starting to like this city a lot!"

EIGHT

Irma sighed as she gazed into her bedroom closet. It was Monday morning – a crucial day in Sheffield Institute's social order. And what determined someone's standing in this complex system?

The outfit, of course.

But Monday's dress code wasn't as simple as wearing something supercool or stylish. No . . . that would be too easy. (And besides, supercool clothes were for Wednesdays, when everyone was making plans for the weekend.)

On Mondays, you had to dress with a weary air. Slouchy clothes meant you were tired. And *that* meant you'd been out all weekend, having fun. Maybe you'd had a date. Or you had gone to a bunch of parties. Or you had stayed out way past curfew at a concert.

If that was the case, you could lean against your locker Monday morning and say things like, "What a weekend. I'm exhausted!"

But you can't go overboard, Irma thought as she flipped listlessly through her clothes. If your outfit is *too* sloppy, you doom yourself to the dreaded "blending in." Nobody notices you. And by Tuesday, you're a nonperson. A totally unpopular Outfielder!

The thought made Irma shudder.

But only a little bit.

I can't believe, she thought, that only a week or so ago, *this* was my biggest worry. Now I have to, like, save the world from big blue monsters and stuff. Plus, I *really* have to tell my friends about–

"Irmaaaaa!"

Irma jumped. Could her dad's bellowing be any louder?

"You're late!"

"Coming! Coming!" she called. She turned back to her closet.

Finally, Irma shrugged and closed her eyes. She thrust both hands into the closet and grabbed two hangers. And when she opened her eyes, she was holding her favourite jeans and a pink sweater with a keyhole collar.

"Hey!" she whispered. "I should choose my outfits this way more often. This is the perfect cas-yet-cool Monday morning ensemble."

She hopped into the jeans and yanked the sweater over her head. Then she stepped into some funky, charcoal-gray clogs and grabbed a handful of hair bobs. As she hurried down the stairs, she whipped her hair into two pigtails and expertly pinned back a few tousled strands with some tiny blue barrettes.

Finally, she arrived in the kitchen. Her mum was just putting a carton of milk on the table next to a box of Irma's favourite cereal. And her dad was shrugging himself into his police sergeant's jacket and cap.

"Your breakfast, sweetheart," her mum said, retying the belt on her favourite orange bathrobe and smiling at her daughter.

Her dad, of course, was his usual Mr. Gruff self.

"Why aren't you ready?" he grumbled. "Why can't you ever manage to be on time?"

"But I *am* on time!" Irma declared, tilting her face up at her dad.

"Sure, it's the rest of the world that's early!" her dad said. He rolled his eyes and threw up his hands.

Irma rolled her eyes, too. But she couldn't help giggling at the same time. Driving her dad crazy was as much a part of her morning routine as brushing her teeth.

"Now drink your milk," her dad ordered, "and get out of here, on the double!"

Irma plopped down at the breakfast table and filled her bowl with Frosty Oats. Then she glanced at the milk carton. The sight of it made her cringe.

On the side of the carton was a picture of Andrew Hornby – glinting white smile, floppy shock of hair, cleft chin, and all. The words beneath the picture almost made Irma lose her appetite altogether: "Have you seen this boy? Blonde hair, green eyes . . . "

Irma shot a timid look at her dad as she poured some milk into her cereal.

"Any word about this boy? At the police station?" she asked in a small voice. Then she took a little bite of cereal.

"Not yet," her dad said. He buckled his holster around his thick waist. "But there's other news! Sergeant Sommer just told me a moment ago – the police in Aubry found the car of your friend Elyon's parents."

Her mum, who was standing at the sink, stopped drying the dish in her hand.

"Really?" she asked.

"Yep," her dad replied. "But there's still no trace of the girl or her family. Vanished into thin air!"

Her mum frowned while Irma gasped. Her cereal had suddenly turned to paste in her mouth. She could barely bring herself to swallow the mouthful.

"Aubry is pretty far from here," her mum said. "What were they doing all the way over there?"

"I'll let you know when I've read the report from the patrolman who found the car," her dad said. He pulled his cap more firmly over his brushy, blonde hair. Then he grinned at Irma and his wife and said, "See you later, ladies!"

"Be careful, Tom," her mum called.

Irma merely waved as her dad whisked out the door.

She took another bite of cereal and stared at Andrew's picture on the milk carton.

The plot thickens, she thought. Andrew's picture blurred as Irma began musing anxiously.

What *had* happened to Elyon? she wondered. Irma had no idea, but she knew it had to have something to do with the big, scaly meanies who had attacked her, Will, and Hay Lin in the gym.

If only her dad had known what she knew. He'd be searching for clues in science-fiction novels instead of police reports. But there was no way she could clue him in. He'd freak! Plus, he'd never believe her.

Irma and the other girls were on their own.

Which meant they needed to know this latest bit of information! Not to mention the *other* thing. The news Irma had been trying to reveal for days.

The thought of telling her friends her secret chilled Irma to the bone. But what choice did she have? She needed help – desperately. And her fellow Guardians were the only ones she could go to.

Twenty minutes later, Irma was walking with the four other Guardians into the school cafeteria. A couple of years ago, some seniors had converted a corner of the cafeteria into a coffeehouse. They even had a cappuccino machine! It was a great place to hang out, do homework, flirt with some hotties, and, of course, get your all-important caffeine fix.

But coffee was the last thing Irma needed today. She was jumpy enough. As the girls ducked through the cafeteria doors, Irma told them what she'd heard that morning.

"Aubry, huh?" Taranee said. "That's so wild! Do you think they were running away?"

"Could be," Hay Lin piped up. "But from what?"

"Who knows?" Cornelia said. "Even though we were in the same class together for three years, Elyon never told me much about her family."

Irma bit her lip as the group headed for a table near the window. Her friends were as clueless as she was! She slumped into a chair dejectedly. All this mystery was making her weary.

Will had the cure for that! The next thing she said made Irma jump.

"Maybe Elyon's disappearance and the dis-appearance of that boy are connected," Will proposed. "What do you all think?"

"That's a possibility!" Hay Lin said. She plopped down into the chair next to Irma.

"No, it's not a possibility!" Irma blurted.

She felt four pairs of eyes swing toward her.

"How can you be so sure?" Cornelia asked.

Irma felt a wave of nervousness flutter through her stomach. It was finally time to tell her friends what she knew. *Ugh* – why had she eaten two bowls of cereal? Her stomach was doing flips. This was going to be harder than she thought.

"I've been trying to tell you guys something for a few days now," Irma said. She heard her voice shaking a little. "But I really don't know how to explain it."

The girls blinked at her expectantly.

"I . . . I . . . know what happened to Andrew Hornby!" Irma cried.

"Whaaaat?!" Hay Lin squealed.

"So, why didn't you tell us before?" Cornelia demanded with a stern expression. Normally, this would have totally annoyed Irma. Cornelia was always criticising her.

But in this case, Irma thought guiltily, I deserve Cornelia's scorn.

"I didn't tell you," Irma admitted in a small,

squeaky voice, "because I was the one who made him disappear! But I didn't mean to. That is, I was going to undo everything!"

"Oh, no, Irma!" Cornelia said, rolling her eyes. "What kind of mess have you gotten yourself into this time?!"

"I really liked him – Andrew, you know – and he never even looked at me," Irma explained. She felt her skin crawl as her friends gazed at her in alarm. "And so . . . "

"And so?" Will prompted.

Irma heaved a big sigh.

"Well, it all happened around a week ago," she began. "Do you know the Zot, that disco near the square?"

Cornelia nodded. Of course, she'd been there. Cornelia had been *everywhere*. Irma tried to shake off her annoyance with Cornelia and continued.

"Well, they threw this big party," she said. "I knew Andrew was going. It was my chance to get him to notice me. And so . . . "

Will suddenly slapped her hands over her ears and beseeched Irma, "Don't say it. *Please* don't say it!"

"I transformed myself," Irma blurted. Then

she slumped over miserably, dropping her fore-head on the cafeteria table.

"She said it!" Will cried.

Irma felt awful.

Why, why, why, she wondered, is the right decision so clear in hindsight? At the time, it seemed like no biggie at all.

In fact . . . it had been fun.

"My parents had been asleep for awhile," she told her gaping friends. "All I had to do was think about it, and I changed my appearance."

Irma couldn't help feeling an electric thrill tingle down her spine as she remembered her second transformation into her magical self.

She'd simply stood at the foot of her bed and looked down at her slightly plump, short legs, her slouchy sweater, and the choppy ends of her wayward hairdo. Then she'd wished them all away. Instantly, she'd been surrounded by a whirl of magical energy. It had been so power-ful it had whisked her clothes away. Irma had thrown her arms into the air as her body grew lean and willowy. She'd felt her flower-petal wings emerge from her back. The entire trans-formation gave her an enormous sense of power. And freedom.

Because there was no denying it. The magical Irma was gorgeous. Her blue eyes had gotten bigger and they winked coyly. Her hair was silky and arranged in a perfectly sleek do. And her figure was lithe and completely curvy.

"I hid my wings under a shawl," Irma said, "and I sneaked into the party."

She felt less guilty with each word. She just couldn't forget how thrilling it had been. And how fun!

"You should have seen it," she said breath-lessly. "I was the center of attention!"

"Including Andrew's?" Cornelia asked.

"Especially his!" Irma said. "We talked and danced all night. It was fantastic!"

Hay Lin – never known for her boy-craziness – huffed in exasperation. "I can't believe it!" she sputtered. "You used your pow-ers for a party?!"

"I didn't think I was doing anything wrong," Irma protested.

"And then?" Will sighed. "Get to the point, Irma!"

"Right," Irma said. She felt her face redden and her breath quicken. Here came the really awful part!

"So, in the end, Andrew offered me a ride home in his car and I accepted," she explained. "But he wanted to pull a fast one! He parked the car in a dark place and he tried to kiss me!"

"And you?" all four friends cried at once.

"You really want to know?" Irma squeaked. "I . . . uh . . . turned him into a toad!"

Irma still felt panicky as she remembered Andrew's sudden transformation. Make that transformations. First he'd gone from sweet, cute, boyfriend material into a leering, lecherous guy. And then he'd gotten a funny, bug-eyed look on his face. He'd uttered one final word: *"Ribbit!"* Then he'd morphed into a green, warty, springy-legged toad.

"He got scared, jumped out the window, and disappeared," Irma confessed. "I followed him! I looked for him. But it was useless!"

There! Irma's shameless story was out on the table. Her friends could commence hating and ostracising her now.

Irma sighed and hung her head, awaiting her fate.

Pffffftt.

Huh? Irma looked up at Hay Lin. She was covering her mouth with her hand. Her eyes were a little watery and *very* smiley.

Snorrt!

This time it was Will who was covering her mouth. She was definitely trying to suppress a giggle.

But it was Cornelia who finally threw her head back and started laughing. That, of course, set off a chain reaction.

"Waaaah-ha-ha-ha!" Hay Lin finally gasped.

Taranee and Will collapsed onto the table in uncontrollable, heaving giggles.

Well, this is unexpected, Irma thought. And . . . totally wrong!

"What are you laughing about!" she gasped. "This is serious! I feel terrible! It's a tragedy! A catastrophe!"

That, of course, only made her friends cackle even harder. Cornelia was wiping tears from her scrunched-up blue eyes, and Taranee looked as if she were having trouble breathing.

Okay, somehow this is *not* making me feel any better, Irma thought, crossing her arms irritably over her chest. In fact, the only thing that could make this whole scene any *more* annoying would be – Martin Tubbs.

And, of course, there he was – Martin

Tubbs. Geek extraordinaire. And madly in love with Irma. Martin always seemed to show up at the precise moment that Irma did *not* want to see him. Which was, well, pretty much always.

But *especially* now, when her friends were making fun of her in the biggest way.

She glanced at Martin. He was looking even more dorky than usual in a backwards baseball cap, V-necked sweater, and his usual Coke-bottle glasses.

"Martin," she growled, "disappe–"

"NO!" screamed her friends suddenly. Will and Taranee leaped across the table to restrain her, while Hay Lin slapped her hand over Irma's mouth.

Oh yeah, Irma thought, remembering the toad issue at hand.

As lovely as it might be to make Martin Tubbs *really* disappear, that would only add to her magical problems.

So Irma composed herself. She shook off her friends and turned to Martin with a big, sugary, and totally fake smile.

"Um, would you be so kind," she said, "as to shove off?"

Martin grinned.

"Your wish is my command, sweet thing," he said. Then he trotted off to class.

Close call, Irma thought. She felt weariness suffuse her being once again. And I thought being magical was going to make life easier!

NINE

Taranee walked with her friends towards the cafeteria exit. She couldn't stop staring at Irma. She didn't know what she found more amazing – the fact that Irma had used her magic to turn a boy into a toad, *or* that she'd had the courage to whip herself into her magical form and go to a disco, all by herself!

The idea of it catapulted Taranee into shivers of shyness.

But then, as she watched Irma plow through the cafeteria's double doors, another thought suddenly occurred to her.

Hey, she thought. Why *couldn't* I do that? After all, I'm just as magical as Irma. I can whip fire out of thin air! If I can do that, I can certainly take my magical self to a party.

Taranee tried to imagine herself in her magical uniform – tight, striped leggings and slim halter top, her beaded braids transformed into an awesome updo. She pictured herself making friends with a crowd of cool kids she'd never met, dancing confidently to the music, telling jokes that sent everyone in the room into gales of laughter.

Then she pictured her glasses flying off as she spun around the dance floor. After that, she would trip blindly over a chair and spill soda all over her Guardian clothes!

Taranee cringed. Then she couldn't help giggling at the image.

"Hee, hee," she whispered to herself. "Okay, I guess I still have a ways to go. And banding together with my friends on this Elyon/Andrew mystery is as good a place to start as any."

Taranee returned to the conversation.

"And so?" Irma was asking as the group tromped into the courtyard. They had to cut across the square to get to Sheffield's main building for class. "What do we do?"

"Simple," Will said. "We have to find Andrew right away and . . . *uhnnn!*"

Taranee gasped. Will was clenching her forehead and staggering blindly. Taranee caught Will's trembling arm before she could tumble into the grass.

"Will!" she cried. "Are you having that funny feeling again? Should we start worrying?"

Will looked as pale and trembly as she had after Hay Lin's grandmother's funeral. She blinked with heavy eyelids and breathed, "It's like a shiver. Dizziness. Like I'm falling into nothingness!"

"No!" Hay Lin suddenly said.

Taranee spun around in surprise. That was kind of harsh! Then she realised Hay Lin wasn't talking to Will. She was pointing to a pink stucco wall at the far end of the courtyard.

"Hay Lin?" Cornelia said.

"Look!" Hay Lin screamed. She pointed wildly at the wall. "This time it's not my imagi-nation!"

Taranee and the others looked at the wall. Collectively they gasped.

"Elyon!" Cornelia cried.

Hay Lin was right. This time it *wasn't* her imagination. Taranee could see Elyon clearly. She was dressed in a royal-blue suit with a fluffy, grey, cowl neck. She had one hand propped casually on the wall. But her face was anything but casual. She was staring at the girls coldly.

And then she did something – magical.

"Omigosh!" Hay Lin cried. "She's going right through that wall. She's a ghost!"

Taranee squeaked as her gaze shifted from Elyon's cold glare to her arm. Elyon did indeed seem to be half-disappearing into the hard, stucco wall!

And Elyon didn't stop there. Now she was shifting sideways. The entire right side of her body melted into the wall. Taranee held her breath. What was going to happen next?!

Then Elyon's face began to look desperate. She lifted her hand toward the girls. And then, she disappeared through the wall entirely.

Taranee started breathing again – make that hyperventilating – while her friend sprang into action.

"It's like she's calling to us," Will said. "Maybe she wants to tell us something!"

"Let's follow her," Cornelia yelled.

Will, Hay Lin, and Irma didn't hesitate. They began to rush across the courtyard to the wall where Elyon had disappeared.

"W-w-we can't just leave!" Taranee found herself whining. "We still have classes!"

"Oh, puh-leeze!" Irma said. She was grinning as she dashed across the grass.

"Seriously," Taranee said as she chased after her friends. "If Mrs. Knickerbocker catches us, there's going to be trouble!"

Taranee could just picture her no-nonsense mum learning that Taranee had skipped out on school. Somehow, Taranee didn't think she'd believe her excuse: "Oh, Mum, I just *had* to ditch class. The ghost of my friend Elyon stopped by the school yard!"

Taranee rolled her eyes and looked longingly over her shoulder at the crowd of kids streaming into Sheffield for the day.

Then Cornelia's voice made her jump.

"The principal will never find out," she assured her. Then she spoke to the group. "Step aside, ladies. I'll open an emergency door."

Cornelia gritted her teeth and thrust her palm toward the wall. Suddenly, her hand began shaking.

And glowing!

Green, vibrating rings of energy began pulsing out of her palms. Taranee didn't know how Cornelia was wielding this power any more than she understood her own sudden ability to conjure up fire.

All she did know was – it worked!

A huge, circular hole suddenly appeared in the thick, stone-and-stucco wall.

"Whoa!" Taranee gasped as the girls began to scramble through the opening. After she herself had clambered through the hole, she asked Cornelia, "And do you know how to close the emergency door?"

"Sure," Cornelia said with a shrug. "It's all a question of concentration. All you have to do is think about it really hard and–"

Cornelia closed her eyes and tried to zap the wall shut again with her magic vibes.

But when she opened her eyes, the hole was still there! In fact, now it was more than just a hole! It was a jaggedy gash that extended all the way to the top of the wall! An absolute chasm!

Cornelia cringed. Then she shrugged and grinned at her friends.

"Okay," she tittered. "So I still need a little more practise."

"We're in for it," Taranee said, rolling her eyes.

"And on top of that," Hay Lin observed as she looked up and down the street, "we've lost Elyon, too."

Will shook her head.

"Let's go," she said. "There's only one place where we can hope to find her. And that place is her house!"

Cornelia nodded in agreement, and they began to hurry down the street toward Elyon's house. But Taranee hesitated for a moment. She peered back through the hole in the wall, scanning the school yard for a sign of Principal Knickerbocker's bouncing white beehive. The courtyard was empty and it looked as though they really had escaped without notice.

We *are* the Guardians of the Veil, Taranee thought desperately. We *have* to go look for Elyon. She's part of this whole battle between good and evil.

"And, hey," she whispered to herself as another thought suddenly occurred to her. "Maybe someone in Candracar could write me an excuse note!"

The idea made Taranee giggle again. Then

she began dashing down the sidewalk after her friends.

"Wait for me," she called.

Ten minutes later, the girls were tiptoeing across Elyon's lawn. Her big, grey house looked utterly abandoned. Every window was dark, and the grass was already becoming long and unruly. Irma led the girls around to the back-yard.

"This way," she said in a hushed voice. "It looks like the backdoor is open!"

Without even hesitating, Irma, Cornelia, Hay Lin, and Will ducked through the door. Yet Taranee couldn't bring herself to step over the threshold. As the girls made their way into the kitchen, Taranee clung to the doorjamb.

"Are we really sure of what we're doing?" Taranee asked. "This is called unlawful entry. My mother is a judge, and my father is a lawyer, and I know for sure that the people who do these things get locked up!"

"If you don't feel up to it," Cornelia said slyly, "no one's forcing you. Wait for us out here."

Taranee blinked at Cornelia. Then she

glanced over her shoulder at the windswept, and very empty, backyard.

"You want me to stay out there all alone?" she squeaked. "Forget it!"

Cornelia giggled.

Great, Taranee thought as she shoved the backdoor closed with her foot. Cornelia's totally manipulating me into breaking and entering. Let's just hope she can manipulate me out of trouble if we get caught.

She followed her friends through the kitchen and into the living room.

"Wow!" Hay Lin breathed. Taranee gasped, too. The place was sort of creepy. The ceiling seemed to loom several stories over their heads. It was dotted with ornate chandeliers with red crystals. Underfoot was a sumptuous Oriental rug. And covering the windows were heavily swagging red velvet curtains.

"It looks so much smaller from the outside," Hay Lin said.

"Which way do we go?" Will wondered aloud.

Frup, frup, frup, frup.

What's that sound? Taranee asked herself. Then she saw Will pointing at the ground.

"Look!" she screamed. "Footprints!"

That's exactly what that sound is, Taranee thought. Then she gasped as she actually saw the footprints scurrying across the hardwood floor. She could see the imprint of invisible shoes scuffing the floor. She could even see little billows of dust rise with each step.

The only thing Taranee couldn't see were the feet that were making the footprints. Those were invisible!

The footprints weren't just appearing randomly. They were walking with a purpose.

Right toward a door beneath the staircase.

"Looks like a clear invitation to me," Will announced, following right on the footprints' heels. Will opened the door. It swung open with an eerie *creeeeaak*.

"It's the basement," Will told the others.

Naturally, Taranee thought dryly, the footprints would take us to the creepiest part of the house.

Will peered into the gloom of the basement. Taranee peeked over her shoulder. But she couldn't see a thing.

"Give us some light, Taranee," Will said.

"With pleasure," Taranee replied.

She closed her eyes and cupped her hands out in front of her. Then she felt something warm form in her hands. In fact, the warmth extended all the way up her arms, settling finally in her chest.

The feeling was so lovely Taranee had to smile. Then she opened her eyes. When she did, she saw a huge swirl of fire curling out of her hands. The fireball floated upwards until it stopped just beneath the basement ceiling.

The room – a big, empty, circular cavern of a space – was completely illuminated.

And for the first time since she'd arrived at school that morning, Taranee forgot to feel scared. For the first time, she realised something: her magical powers were just that – powers!

The thought filled Taranee with determination. And this realisation made it just a little easier for her to square her shoulders and follow her friends down the stairs into Elyon's mysterious basement.

TEN

As the fireball floated out of Taranee's palm, Cornelia stared into the basement.

There was no sign of the footprints any-where. No, it was just Elyon's same old, loom-ing basement. Whenever Cornelia had spent the night at Elyon's house in the past, she'd avoided the basement. It was creepy. It looked like the inside of a giant tin can. The walls were gunmetal grey and perfectly curved. The floor was stubbly cement. And except for a few boxes scattered next to the curving staircase, the high-ceilinged room was perfectly empty.

Now Cornelia drifted down the stairs in a haze. As she walked, she sifted through her memories, trying to remember each time she'd come over to Elyon's house.

Had she ever noticed a glimmer of magic there before?

Cornelia pictured wan, wispy-haired Elyon and her sweet, ordinary parents. Nothing about them seemed magical or sinister. Elyon's parents didn't even seem that interesting. (But that was kinda normal, too. They *were* parents, after all.)

No, Cornelia decided. If Elyon was magical, like Cornelia and the other Guardians, she must have been as oblivious to it as they'd once been.

Cornelia shrugged sadly.

Then again, she thought, what difference does it make? Elyon's gone now, anyway.

The thought filled Cornelia with emptiness as she reached the basement floor with the rest of the girls. They all began gazing around the basement in confusion.

"There's no sign of the footprints," Irma said.

"And this basement has no doors," Will added. "Where were they trying to lead us?"

An echoey, ghostly voice came from behind them.

"To me, girls."

Cornelia gasped and spun around. It was

Elyon! She was pressed against the far wall of the basement. Her eyes were wide and soulless, and her arms were outstretched.

"Come to me," she intoned.

Will took one halting step forward while Irma and Taranee cringed behind her. She peered at Elyon, who stared back at her blankly.

"Elyon!" Will said hesitantly. "Can . . . can you hear us?"

Elyon's only reply was the same monotone phrase.

"Come to me," she said. "Come to me."

As she spoke, Elyon's body began to melt into the wall behind her! She drifted through the wall, the way smoke disappears into the air. Cornelia barely realised Elyon was melting away until Elyon was almost gone! In a few seconds, only her face and her outstretched arm were visible.

"Come to me," she whispered one more time.

And then she disappeared.

Cornelia ran to the wall and banged her fist against it angrily. The thump made a hollow, metallic *dong*ing sound.

"Another wall!" she said. "This is becoming a habit." She could hear a desperate catch in her own voice. She hated the sound of it! And – for a moment, anyway – she hated Elyon for making her feel so confused. And helpless. And . . . sad.

Where had Elyon *gone*?

Cornelia tapped on the wall some more. It was clearly some kind of metal. The wall was made of huge panels of metal, wedged together with rough seams.

"Let me take a look," Irma offered. She stole up next to Cornelia. She began scratching at the seam next to the spot where Elyon had melted away.

"Hey," she said. "It's not solid, after all. I can see . . . there's a door behind all this."

Cornelia peered over Irma's shoulder. Irma was right. Cornelia could see the edges of an entryway between the metal plates.

A doorknob, or a way to get beyond the plates, was nowhere to be seen.

"Looks like it's sealed," Irma said. "There's no way to open it!"

Cornelia jumped. She could open it. She had the powers of the earth within her! She could manipulate matter with nothing more than an impulse and her new magic.

Cornelia couldn't help remembering her gaffe in the school yard only a few minutes before. While blasting a huge hole in the wall had been a cinch, closing it up had been a disaster. She'd ended up destroying half the wall.

She had laughed it off at the time, but deep down, the mistake had filled her with panic.

Cornelia was used to getting good grades at school. Her ice-skating routines were precise and perfect. She almost never fell. And as for her look – she made sure she never had a blonde hair out of place. She liked being in control.

And now, she was far from in control. Her magic felt like a skittish horse that she hadn't tamed yet. If it failed Cornelia again, Elyon might drift farther away still.

And the mysteries facing the Guardians would only deepen.

I want some answers! she thought. And I think Elyon knows something.

Feeling confidence rise within her again like bolts of energy, Cornelia said to Irma, "No need for opening the door. All we have to do is – step aside, Irma!"

She didn't have to ask Irma twice. As Cornelia reared back, feeling green bursts of magic build up in her fingertips, Irma scurried out of the way.

Cornelia gritted her teeth.

She focused every ounce of her mental strength upon the metal plate.

And then, she gave it a magical *zap*!

Just as she'd hoped, the huge, heavy plate toppled toward her with a creaky roar. As Cornelia jumped nimbly out of the way, the plate crashed to the cement floor with a thunderous *briiingggg*!

There was now a gaping hole in the wall.

"Whoa!" Hay Lin cried. She scampered over the plate and jumped through the hole. The rest of the girls followed. As Cornelia walked over the fallen slab of metal, stamping her feet for emphasis, she saw that there was a green hieroglyphic on the door.

"Huh?" she said, gazing at it curiously. It was a green circle with a slice cut out of the center in the shape of a backward *C*. On top of the circle was a long, thin triangle. Beneath it was another triangle. But this one was short and squat.

Cornelia shrugged and hopped through the opening she'd made in the wall.

"Whoa!" she heard Hay Lin say again. But this time, she spoke in an awed whisper.

They had entered an enormous, endless cavern!

Actually, it wasn't really a cavern, since it was clearly manmade. (Or creature-made, Cornelia thought, with a shudder.) The long, shadowy tunnel was paved with slabs of marble and lined with pale bricks. Hanging from the walls were yellow lightbulbs, all of which were faintly, eerily glowing. Over the girls' heads were successive arches made of dark, red brick. And beneath their feet was the same green symbol Cornelia had noticed on the door. Except this time, it was about twenty feet long!

This sort of feels like a big, long throat, Cornelia thought, right down to that funky, moist smell in the air. It's like a combination of mold and stagnant pond water. *Ew!* Now I know what it's like to be swallowed by a whale!

"What is this place?" Will wondered aloud.

"If it's a broom closet," Hay Lin whispered, "it's the weirdest one I've ever seen."

As Hay Lin gazed over her head in wonder,

she didn't seem to notice – as Cornelia did – that something *very* odd was happening in Hay Lin's jacket pocket. It looked . . . it looked as if flames were shooting out of the pocket! But there was no scent of smoke in the air, and Hay Lin's blue jacket didn't seem to be burning.

Before Cornelia could cry out, Taranee grabbed Hay Lin. Fire, after all, was her turf.

"Your jacket!" she shrieked.

"*Aagh!*" Hay Lin cried. But then she closed her mouth and nodded her head.

"Oh, yeah," she muttered. Fearlessly, she plunged her hand into her pocket. When her hand emerged, the flames had disappeared. Instead, Hay Lin was holding a folded piece of paper. It looked aged and yellowed. Its edges were roughened, and the paper was so worn it was practically transparent.

"Whew!" Hay Lin breathed as she unfolded the paper into a huge square. "What a relief. It's my grandmother's map. The chart of the twelve portals!"

"Where did that come from?" Will exclaimed, looking at the map. "And why didn't you tell us about it?"

"I was going to, but with everything that's

happened, it completely slipped my mind," Hay Lin said.

The girls crowded around her to peer at the paper. Cornelia could see the familiar shape of Heatherfield's beach. Drawings of two big buildings not far from the beach were pink and glowing.

"It's a map of the city," Taranee said, realising what the map was showing. "And these shiny points . . . ?"

"They're the passageways leading to Metamoor," Hay Lin explained. "The portals that we have to close. The first was the one in the gym."

"And this other one?" Will piped up, pointing at the other glowing building. It was a few blocks away from Sheffield on the map.

As soon as Will asked the question, Cornelia knew the answer. She recognised the glowing house on the map. And as she did, her heart sank and an oppressive buzz began to fill her head.

She felt as if she were suddenly moving in slow motion as she watched the realisation dawn on the faces of her friends.

Only Will had the strength to say the truth

out loud. "It's Elyon's house!" she cried, pointing at the shiny point of the map. She looked at her friends desperately. "We're inside the portal!"

The moment the words left Will's mouth, the dank, scary passageway filled with a low rumbling – a rumbling that quickly morphed into a roar.

The floor began to shake beneath the girls' feet. Puffs of dust sifted down from the vibrating brick ceiling.

And then – with a horrible, wrenching boom – something erupted out of the floor! It was a new wall! It unfurled from the marble tiles like a hard-edged snake. Then it shot up towards the ceiling until it hit the top of the tunnel with a slam. Next, the wall widened, expanding until it struck one side of the tunnel, and then the other.

In an instant, the wall had sealed the tunnel shut.

"It's a trap!" Will screamed.

That's exactly what it is, Cornelia thought. She looked around wildly, searching for a solution, for a way out, for . . .

For Hay Lin.

Cornelia saw Will pounding on the fresh, new brick wall. She saw Taranee wringing her hands in terror. And she saw Irma spinning around in confusion.

But Hay Lin was nowhere to be seen.

That's because, Cornelia realised in alarm, she's caught behind the wall!

Will, Irma, and Taranee all seemed to realise it at the same time Cornelia did. And all three of them turned to her for a solution.

"Cornelia!" Irma shrieked at her. "Do something!"

Cornelia gazed at the wall. It was imposing, impenetrable, and made of solid brick! It would be much harder to crack than Sheffield's stucco walls or even the metal plates in Elyon's basement. She felt her breath coming in short, shallow gasps.

She didn't understand any of this.

Was Elyon trapped behind the wall, too? Or was Elyon the one who'd created the wall?

Had she been taken away from them?

Or had she betrayed them?

The only thing that Cornelia *did* know was – Elyon was not the friend Cornelia had thought she'd been.

Hay Lin, on the other hand, was a part of W.i.t.c.h. And a true friend.

There's no way I'm going to lose *her*, Cornelia thought. I've *got* to save Hay Lin. And I'm going to do it with my magic.

And for the first time since she'd gotten them, Cornelia felt grateful for her magical powers. She felt energized by them. And, yes, in control of them.

Without hesitating for another instant, she stalked over to the wall and thrust her arms out before her.

"Move back!" she barked to her friends. "I'm going to knock this wall down!"

ELEVEN

Hay Lin screamed as the brick wall suddenly burst up through the floor.

She felt her grandmother's map slip from her trembling fingers. And she watched the stunned faces of her friends – all four of them – disappear.

Trembling, Hay Lin gazed up. She watched the wall connect to the brick ceiling with a dusty groan. She screamed again and began running to her right. But it was no use – the wall had hurtled outward as well as up. It sealed the tunnel shut. On both sides.

There was no way around it.

Hay Lin was trapped.

Alone.

Drawing in a deep, shuddery breath, Hay Lin screamed one last time.

"*Aaaaaah!*" she cried, throwing herself against the wall. The bricks were cold and smooth, like a reptile's scales. But they were also hard, unyielding, impenetrable. Hay Lin couldn't hear a single sound from the other side of the wall. It was as if her friends had suddenly just been swallowed up.

Then Hay Lin realised something – it was actually the other way around. *She* was the one who had been snatched away, who had disappeared.

The face of her grandmother suddenly flashed through Hay Lin's mind.

But her grandmother's face was quickly replaced by the sight of red spots. She was so afraid, she was becoming half-blind!

Hay Lin squeezed her eyes shut and pounded on the wall, sobbing.

"Get me out of here!" she shrieked.

"What are you afraid of, Hay Lin?"

The voice – Elyon's voice – was right behind her. Hay Lin felt beads of sweat break out on her forehead.

She hadn't thought anything could be worse

than being trapped in this brick-lined crypt by herself. But she'd been wrong.

Sharing this dank, forbidding space with the ghost of Elyon was much, much worse.

Barely able to breathe now, Hay Lin refused to turn around and face Elyon's creepy, blank stare. She clawed at the bricks in the new wall. The rough mortar tore bloody gashes in her palms and sliced through her fingernails. But Hay Lin didn't care. She only wanted to get out. Out. Out!

"Follow me! Come with me to the other side," Elyon was saying to Hay Lin's back. "I'm your friend!"

That made Hay Lin stop sobbing, stop screaming, stop clawing. She breathed in ragged gasps. Weakly, she let her forehead rest against the brick wall.

You're not my friend, she thought. She couldn't say the words out loud because her throat was too choked with fear. But she could think them. And, silently, she shouted at the girl lurking behind her.

You're *not* Elyon, Hay Lin thought. Elyon was my friend. And a friend wouldn't have lured me into this weird, terrifying place. A friend wouldn't beg me – *force* me – to leave behind my home, my family, my world!

Again, her grandmother's face popped into Hay Lin's mind. She imagined her grandmother saying to her, "I think you'll become very good, my little Hay Lin."

A fresh round of sobs racked Hay Lin's thin body. She wanted to be good. She wanted to be strong! She wanted to fight off this new, evil version of Elyon.

That's what Grandma would have done, Hay Lin thought. For an instant, she tried to imagine her elderly, tiny grandmother as a sprightly young Guardian of the Veil. And that's when Hay Lin felt herself weakened by a stab of grief.

She collapsed to the floor – overcome with sadness. She was never going to see her sweet, loving grandmother again. She knew that. But now she wondered if she'd ever see her *parents* again! Would Elyon take her away from them forever?

Weakly, Hay Lin shook her head. She couldn't let that happen!

"No . . . " she moaned. She finally turned towards Elyon. And she found the courage –

somehow – to say her thoughts out loud: "You're not real. And this is only a nightmare."

Her words seemed only to make Elyon more determined. She shook her ghostly head slowly. Then she grinned a malevolent grin. And then the wall behind her – another looming bank of bricks and mortar – began to undulate. It was as if the stony bricks had suddenly turned to jelly.

Next, just above Elyon's blonde, shaggy head, a blue circle began forming in the bricks. It shimmered like mercury and swirled like clouds.

The glowing circle began to grow. It shivered and rumbled as it expanded into a writhing, growling . . .

Portal! Hay Lin thought desperately. That's the tunnel to Metamoor! Just like the one that erupted in the gym! I have to close it or be sucked in myself!

Before Hay Lin could even contemplate a way to close this enormous, terrifying chasm, something appeared within it.

It was a creature.

The creature was as broad as a refrigerator. Its head was covered with lumpy, rocklike protuberances, and it had bared, spiky teeth.

And its skin was bright blue.

It was Vathek – the creature who'd tried to hurt Hay Lin, Irma, and Will in the gym. Now he'd come to finish the job!

"Yes, little girl! It's all true!" the creature growled at her. His voice was choked and gurgly, as deep as a black hole. "But this time, you can't escape."

Hay Lin scrabbled backwards on the floor until she hit the wall behind her with a thud. She threw her arms over her head, preparing herself for the pain of Vathek's talons.

She imagined Elyon's treacherous hands, yanking her into the portal.

And then she pictured her grandmother's face, one last time.

"*Aaaaaagggh!*" Hay Lin screamed.

TWELVE

Will watched Cornelia stalk up to the wall that had just sprung out of the floor. She felt as though she were watching a movie she didn't quite understand. It was all happening so fast!

As Will watched Cornelia stare at the wall in determination, the facts finally sank in.

They had *definitely* found the second portal to the place Hay Lin's grandmother had told them about.

And that portal *definitely* didn't want to be found. That's why a brick wall had suddenly erupted right before their eyes, blocking them from the rest of the tunnel.

And here was the other thing Will knew.

The wall had separated them. Four of

the Guardians were in this main chamber.

Hay Lin was gone – trapped on the other side of that evil, animate wall.

And she was in extreme danger.

Who knows what else is lurking behind the wall, Will thought. Creatures of Metamoor? Some sort of vacuum cleaner that could suck Hay Lin into a new dimension?

All those unknowns filled Will with fear. But, more important, they filled her with deter-mination! She looked from Irma to Taranee to Cornelia and felt invisible bonds stretching among them.

It's the magic bonding us together, Will said to herself. That's what I'm feeling. And that's what's going to get us out of this mess. Starting with Cornelia and her power over all earthly substances!

Will watched Cornelia plant her feet and grit her teeth. Then Cornelia pressed her hands to the dark, brooding bricks of the wall. She squeezed her eyes shut.

Will could practically see the magic coursing through Cornelia. Her slender body vibrated with power. Her arms pulsed with it. And out of her palms emanated the now familiar green rings of cosmic energy.

A hole began to form in the brick wall. It was small. And inside of it, Will could see only blackness.

It's just beginning, Will thought. She almost smiled in anticipation. Then she felt her back stiffen and her eyes squeeze shut. She was bracing herself for a shower of brick shards and shattered mortar bits. Her muscles tensed, ready to pounce through the large opening Cornelia's magic was about to drill through the wall.

Then Will heard a loud noise.

Whhuuump!

The sound was like a monster taking a huge bite out of something. Or a vacuum cleaner swallowing up something solid.

It did not sound like magic breaking effortlessly through a brick wall.

With a sinking heart, Will opened her eyes. And then she screamed in alarm.

The wall had changed all right. But the little hole that Will had seen within it hadn't widened. Instead, it extended itself into a tall tower. A sort of tentacle, made entirely of bricks, had grown out of the wall, shooting at Cornelia with the precision of a frog's tongue.

With one gulp, the tentacle swallowed up both of Cornelia's hands. The bricks swirled around her hands, binding them together as effectively as a pair of handcuffs might have done.

The tentacle grew and grew. Now it was swallowing Cornelia's wrists. Next, it moved up to her elbows! Then the tube of bricks began jerking back and forth, dragging Cornelia to and fro.

Cornelia didn't – or couldn't – scream. She merely looked over her shoulder in terror. And – with her large, frightened eyes – she begged Will for help.

"The house is alive!" Will cried to Irma and Taranee. "Let's stick together."

As the girls clung to each of her arms, Will tried to patch a plan together in her mind.

Okay, she thought desperately, we just have to–

Braaaaaaaaammm!

–get out of the way! Will thought. Another wall was barreling up through the floor!

Will jumped backwards. Then she found herself gazing in shock at an enormous tower of bricks.

This new wall was not a horizontal blockade

like the one that had trapped Hay Lin. Instead, it was a circular stack of bricks. As it grew, like Jack's bean stalk on a rampage, it plunged right between Will, Taranee, and Irma.

Will stumbled backwards.

Taranee leaped to one side.

And Irma jumped away so fast she landed on her backside, directly opposite Will.

"Holy cow!" she screamed.

Almost instantly, another wall rose up in front of Irma, completely blocking her from Will's view. From what Will could see, there'd been only a few feet between the side of their original tunnel and the new wall. Which meant Irma was now trapped in a claustrophobic cell of bricks!

Will spun around to look for Taranee. She almost sobbed with relief when she realised that she could still see her.

Quickly Will's relief turned to horror as Taranee was attacked by a brick wall. This time, the wall took the shape of a cylinder, whirling around Taranee's feet. Then, the bricks began stacking around her legs, her waist, her chest. . . .

Before Will could react, Taranee was

encased in a cylinder of bricks. It was as if she had fallen into a smokestack. Only her head poked out of the top.

Will started to run to her friend.

And that's when the walls turned on her.

A solid slab of concrete erupted only inches from her toes. It hurtled a dozen feet into the air and took Will with it! She found herself hanging from the top of the wall by her fingertips. Her feet scrabbled on the wall's smooth, slablike surface. There was no toehold.

It wasn't long before her fingers started loosening.

Will glanced down over her shoulder. Maybe the stone floor wasn't too far away. Maybe if she let go, she could escape with little more than a sprained ankle or a couple of cuts and bruises.

But when Will was able to focus on what was beneath her, she saw no floor.

It had disappeared.

She was teetering over a black, bottomless abyss!

"No!" Will cried. She pumped her legs, kicking at the wall, trying desperately to climb over it. Even as she struggled, she realised some other horrible entity could be lurking on the other side of the wall – a fate even worse than the endless abyss below her.

"N-no!" she cried.

As if that would have done any good.

This evil is too much for us, Will thought. I don't know how to fight it. Not without my friends by my side!

Will could feel her fingers, still clutching the top of the wall, loosen further.

She could feel her resolve weakening.

She wasn't going to make it!

"I'm sorry," she whispered, hoping the other girls could somehow hear her.

And then she froze.

Because, deep in the back of her mind, she could hear something answering.

Someone answering.

And that someone was Elyon!

Will stopped struggling and merely clung to the top of the wall. She pressed her cheek against one of the cold, clammy bricks.

Her breathing slowed. Her heart stopped pounding so loudly. And Will was able to focus all her magical energies on listening. Just listening.

Before she knew it, she was hearing the

thoughts of her fellow Guardians.

Will didn't know how that could have been happening, or how she knew that that was what was happening. All she knew was that – for an instant, at least – her own thoughts somehow abandoned her and she found herself floating inside the consciousness of Cornelia.

The proof came when Elyon psychically spoke to Cornelia directly – and Will heard the message as plain as day.

"Don't struggle, Cornelia," Elyon's wispy, ghostly voice said inside her mind. "Metamoor is waiting for you."

Will felt Cornelia's indignation. Her anger. And finally . . . a tiny bit of . . . intrigue.

Before Will could communicate, "Don't do it! Don't give up" to Cornelia, she felt herself being swept into Taranee's head.

"It's pointless to fight back, Taranee," Elyon whispered.

"*Aaaaah!*" Taranee screamed. Her mind was filled with a searing red terror. And a yearning for comfort. And a . . . weariness.

She's weakening, Will thought. Taranee, don't–

Will was swept into Irma's head before she

could finish the thought. She felt the claustrophobia of Irma's little cell. She also felt Irma's despair.

"It's pointless to fight back," Elyon said again, this time addressing Irma directly. Will distinctly felt Irma's mind fill with conviction. She believed Elyon. She was sure she was doomed.

Will tried, silently, to scream out to Irma, "You can do it! Don't give in!"

Will was swept out of Irma's mind, as inexplicably as she had entered it. She was back in her own body. And she was clinging to survival by her very fingernails.

The wall from which she was hanging began to shudder and rumble. It was trying to shake her off. Elyon and the powerful force wanted her and her friends. It would stop at nothing to steal them away.

"No!" Will screamed one final time. And as she did, a burst of physical strength surged through her. She gave her legs one mighty kick, imagining herself bounding out of a swimming pool, as lithe and powerful as a dolphin. Then, somehow, she heaved herself up to the top of the wall!

She hooked one arm, and then the other, over the top of the wall. Letting both of her elbows hang down, she balanced on her chest.

At last, she stopped flailing with her feet. She unclenched her scuffed fingers. She was safe from the abyss – for the moment.

Now she could come up with a plan.

Something made her stop plotting almost as soon as she'd begun. It was a familiar surge of heat in her right palm. She extended her fist out, away from the evil wall, and closed her eyes. She felt jets of electricity shooting up her arm, zapping her mind and body with energy.

Next, she felt power jolt through her entire being, accompanied by an exquisite stab of pain. Her mind was humming with magic.

The first time she'd had this feeling, Will had been bewildered and terrified. But now, she knew exactly what was happening. She pried her eyes open and let conscious thought reenter her mind.

"We have to fight," she told herself. "It can't end like this. Our only chance lies in the Heart of Candracar and in our powers at their very strongest!"

And then, with a combination of extreme

strength and desperate determination, she uncurled her fingers, prying her fist open. A blast of blinding pink light shot out of her hand. But Will blinked through it.

And then she grinned.

Floating just above her outstretched hand was a medallion. It was a swirling glass orb, cradled by a gleaming curlicue of shimmering metal.

It was the Heart of Candracar.

It was their salvation.

Will watched the Heart throb and thrum before her. And then, the orb began to divide. Four shimmering teardrops separated from the medallion and hovered in its orbit. The first was blue and glimmery, swirling with barely contained power.

The next teardrop was filled with orange swirls. It danced like a flickering candle flame.

Then there was a burst of green; a sudden scent of grass and earth.

And finally, a white-edged wisp of wind.

Water.

Fire.

Earth.

And air.

Will watched the teardrops – each a distillation of the Guardians' powers – soar away. The orange teardrop shot toward Taranee's tower-like prison. The watery orb whisked into Irma's dim cell. The green one connected with Cornelia as she continued to pull desperately at her trapped arms.

The wispy teardrop of air vanished from Will's view. But she hoped it was somehow penetrating Hay Lin's wall and infusing her with magic.

Finally, Will's eyes focused on her own orb – the flaring, flashing, pink Heart of Candracar. It seared her eyes and filled her heart with joy. Power. Heat.

Will felt her body convulse. Swirls of energy wrapped around her like a shawl, whisking away her clothes.

Then, with an involuntary spasm, Will curled up into a ball. One kernel of survival instinct in her subconscious helped her cling to the wall as she transformed from girl . . . to Guardian.

When Will felt delicate wings separate from her back, and felt her limbs extend to lanky leanness, she finally allowed her body to untense. She looked down at herself.

She had changed completely. She was wearing her Guardian uniform of striped leggings, purple boots, and a tiny skirt whose waistband curled and coiled around her navel.

Yes! Will thought.

She pushed off from the wall. She hovered in the air for a moment, and then she landed.

On the floor.

Somehow, her magic had restored this tunnel back to its original state.

Gazing around her wildly, Will saw Taranee suddenly burst forth from her cylindrical fortress. Her hair fluttered around her head in shimmery tendrils, and her newly pumped biceps were flexed.

"Free!" she cried.

"Strong!" Cornelia answered from the opposite side of the room. Will turned just in time to see Cornelia bat the brick tentacle off her arms like a pesky bug. The bricks flew in all directions, and she was completely freed. She strode up to Will and Taranee, unfettered and triumphant. Her blonde locks had grown longer and silkier. Beneath her body-skimming cropped top billowed a dramatically long, purple skirt.

Next, Will turned to the wall that was trapping Irma. Irma was punching her way through it effortlessly. In a few seconds, she reduced the wall to rubble. Stepping through the dust, she strode over to join her friends. She was cocking one beautiful, arched eyebrow.

"And I'm angry!" she added boldly with a curled lip.

The girls stood for a moment, blinking at one another's splendidly transformed bodies. Then they looked at Hay Lin's wall expectantly.

But nothing happened.

Uh-oh, Will thought. Something's wrong. Why isn't Hay Lin breaking out of her prison?

There was no time to search for the answer. All Will knew was, if Hay Lin hadn't broken through the wall herself, she needed their help!

Will sprang into action. She gave Taranee, Cornelia, and Irma determined glances. They had to get ready to work together.

"Everything okay?" she said.

Taranee was gazing down at her endless, muscled legs.

"It's incredible," she cried. "I'm . . . I'm different!"

Cornelia, too, was gasping with delight. Will

had forgotten that this was the first time they'd all been together in their magical forms.

Irma, of course, was an expert at it by now.

"Cool, isn't it?" she asked. She cocked one of her hips sassily. "And that's not the best part!"

"Oh?" Taranee said.

Will watched Irma curl her hands into powerful fists. Then her huge blue eyes squinted at Hay Lin's wall.

She, like Will, was ready to use their magic to crash through the wall and rescue Hay Lin – the final link in the Power of Five.

Their fellow Guardian.

Their friend.

And as the four girls lined up, Will felt those invisible, magical bonds stretching among them again.

If we work together, she told herself, there's nothing we can't fight. There's nothing we can't accomplish.

At least, that's what Will had to believe – if she was going to save the world.

Will   Irma   Taranee   Cornelia   Hay Lin

Finding Meridian

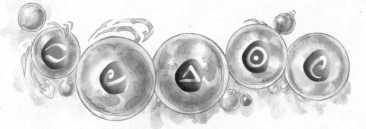

Adapted by **ELIZABETH LENHARD**

HarperCollins *Children's Books*

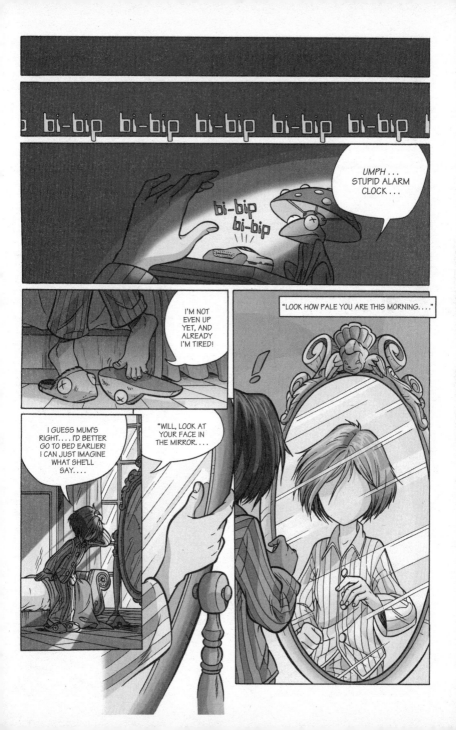

ONE

I wonder if I'll *ever* get used to this? Will thought.

She felt the familiar quickening of her heartbeat. *Thump-thump-thumpity-thump.*

Then her mouth got dry. Her palms got wet. And finally, Will's vision went blurry. But when she blinked the haze away, she found that she was still witnessing the same incredible scene. Her friend, Hay Lin, had just snapped a huge cement pillar in two. The chunk of rock must have weighed five hundred pounds!

How had skinny little Hay Lin done it?

Simple – magic.

Yup, Will thought. She gazed at all four of her friends, scattered around the abandoned construction site. We're all magic – every one of us. I still can't quite wrap my brain around it.

Judging from her friends' expressions, they were a bit weirded-out as well. Taranee was gripping her pink satchel with clenched fists. It was white knuckles, trembling fingers time, all the way.

Irma was Taranee's complete opposite. She was giggling so hard that her shaggy, honey-coloured pigtails were practically dancing.

Hay Lin's almond-shaped eyes were twinkling with a mixture of mischief and sheer determination.

And Cornelia was sticking out her bottom lip – she was all skepticism and sulkiness.

That about sums it up, Will thought, as she took in her friends' wild range of emotions. These magical powers are both fabulous and awful, thrilling and scary. They're dividing us, but they're also bringing us together.

Magic was what Will and her friends were all about these days. When they'd planned to hang out today, for instance, it hadn't been to lounge around a coffeehouse, chowing down on scones and gossiping about the cutest boys at their school, the Sheffield Institute.

No, instead, they were hiding behind this

construction site's tall, wooden fence, practising their magic.

It was clear that Hay Lin, at least, was getting pretty good at it! Not only had she just cracked that chunk of cement off its base as if she were plucking a leaf from a tree, she'd also whipped the huge, craggy block into the sky on a mystical swirl of air. Finally, she'd plunked the block down onto a slab of stone with a tremendous *crunch*.

Then Cornelia had stepped in. She'd stared at the block, her arms outstretched and her blue eyes steely.

With waves of power that were almost palpable, Cornelia had cracked the stone slab on which the cement block rested. It splintered like a thin sheet of ice. Ropy vines poked through the cracks like mischievous green snakes. In the blink of an eye, they coiled their way completely around the block.

Then Cornelia's eyes got even squintier. Her mouth twisted into a stiff smile. She concentrated so hard her long, silky, blonde hair stood on end. And then – *skrump*! The ropy vines squeezed the cement block into smithereens! Shards of rock flew in every direction.

Taranee jumped, her round spectacles going askew on her nose. Hay Lin scowled. Cornelia had totally one-upped her. And Irma, who was always clashing with Cornelia, simply rolled her eyes and pretended to be bored.

Meanwhile, Cornelia just folded her slender arms across her chest and smirked.

"I bet you can't do that," she said to her friends.

Will shuddered at the memory.

The crazy thing, she thought, is that we can *all* do that. Or something like it.

Will looked around at her new friends. She'd only known them for a little while. She'd met them on her first day at the Sheffield Institute, right after she and her Mum had moved to this breezy seaside city called Heatherfield. The girls' friendship had started normally enough. They'd gabbed about crushes, complained about history homework, and commiserated about pain-in-the-butt siblings. But it hadn't been long before the five girls had discovered that they were anything but normal.

Cornelia could control the earth (as was obvious from the shattered cement block). Hay Lin – who was so tiny she looked as if the wind could carry her away – had the powers of air. Wishy-washy Irma was all about water. And Taranee could hold fire in the palm of her hand.

And me, Will thought with a shrug, well, that's the craziest part. I somehow ended up as the leader of our whole crew – Will, Irma, Taranee, Cornelia, Hay Lin. Otherwise known as W.i.t.c.h.

She glanced with irritation at the heavens. That's where she imagined the mystical beings who'd given them their powers resided.

Nice work, Will thought. I can't believe you made me – awkward, frog-collecting Will Vandom – the leader of these girls.

But before Will could get too deep into an angstfest, Irma interrupted her thoughts. She was offering her opinion on Cornelia's feat of shattering the pillar.

"Oh, that's just *amazing*, Cornelia," she said sarcastically. "Actually, I've never seen anything so silly in my entire life."

Cornelia sniffed and turned her back on Irma.

Then Irma sniffed and turned her back on Cornelia.

And then Taranee looked expectantly at Will.

Uh, right, Will thought. I guess it's leadership time!

She stepped forward and eyed Irma and Cornelia nervously.

"Oh, come on," she said with a nervous laugh. "Would you two stop bickering? We're here to practise, not fight!"

"Will's right," Taranee agreed. "We should help each other. We're a team now. . . ."

"I guess you're right, Taranee," Hay Lin piped up. She was now sitting pensively on top of another cement block nearby. "But we don't know how our powers work yet! If only Grandma had told us something more before she . . . passed away."

Hay Lin's reedy, mournful voice trailed off. Will cringed for her friend. Yan Lin's death was still fresh for them all. And what was worse, Hay Lin's tiny, mysterious grandmother had died before the girls could ask her everything they yearned to know about their magical new powers.

Yan Lin would have been able to explain everything, Will thought. After all, she was magical once, too. She was the one who informed us of our magical destiny.

Will was still trying to grasp the things that Yan Lin had told them over tea and cookies in Hay Lin's cosy kitchen.

For starters, Yan Lin told them about worlds that existed somewhere in the universe, far away from earth.

In Candracar – which was a sort of other-worldly temple – benevolent, mystical beings kept watch over all things good and just.

Then there was the land of Metamoor. Evil creatures from Metamoor wanted to take over the world. And only one thing was stopping them – the Veil. The Veil was a supernatural barrier, placed around the earth to keep bad things out.

There was just one catch, Yan Lin had told the girls. The dawn of the millennium had weakened the Veil. Twelve portals had opened in its invisible fabric. And now, terrifying, evil creatures from Metamoor were beginning to break through those portals into Heatherfield.

One of the girls' friends, Elyon, had even gone through the portal. Elyon had been miss-ing for a while now. Just before she'd disappeared, she'd asked Will, Hay Lin, and Irma to accompany her on a date at the school gym. But when the three girls had arrived, Elyon had been nowhere to be seen. There *were* however, a couple of murderous creatures waiting for the girls. And they'd almost managed to toss the girls into a bottomless chasm!

Later, Elyon – or some evil ghost of Elyon – had drawn all five girls into the basement of her abandoned house. There she'd tried to pull Hay Lin into a portal that had opened up in the basement wall.

Both times, the girls had been transformed into Guardians of the Veil. It had started with the Heart of Candracar – a shimmering, magical orb that Yan Lin had given to Will. The orb lay inside Will's body. Usually, it was dormant. But if Will and her friends needed it for any reason, Will could call the Heart. Then it would appear in her palm. Its power transformed the girls into their magical selves – young women with long legs, mature faces and bodies, and fabulous outfits.

And, best of all, Will thought with a giggle, we have magical powers and strength enough to kick any bad guy's butt!

Still, the girls had far from mastered their magic. Will didn't know how much power they were capable of.

She also didn't know how much they'd need. The girls had fought off a hulking, blue lug of a creature and a vengeful, dark-voiced snake man in the gym. In Elyon's basement, they had conquered brick walls that had come to life and tried to bury them alive.

But Will had a feeling that she and her friends hadn't yet seen the worst of Metamoor's evil soldiers.

And *that's* why they were at this construction site, training for battle.

And arguing.

Will turned to Hay Lin. Her face – usually so sunny – was clouded with grief for her grandmother.

"We'll have to do this without her," Will said to Hay Lin softly. "That's all."

"Do you really think that's enough?" Cornelia broke in. She kicked a cement shard across the grass.

"I mean," she continued angrily, "look around you! We can do magic! We can transfigure things! We can command water, air, earth, and fire. But we don't know why!"

"Well," Hay Lin said wanly, "we're the Guardians of the Veil."

"I know that," Cornelia snapped. "But why? Why us?!"

Irma's scowl turned into a flirty smile. She cocked one round hip and wiggled her eyebrows.

"Because we're so pretty," she cooed. "Don't you think?"

"I'm not joking, Irma," Cornelia said with a glower. Then she turned her back on Irma, Hay Lin, and Taranee and glared straight at Will. "Our lives have changed, Will. But we didn't choose it."

"You're right," Will responded with a shrug. "But I don't know. I'm as confused as you are."

Cornelia's hands scrunched up into frustrated fists.

"I thought our *leader* always had the right answer," she said. Her voice was full of sullen bitterness. Full of challenge.

Will's temper flared. Normally, she was a bit deferential to Cornelia. After all – Cornelia was the *true* leader in the group. She was tall and willowy and effortlessly popular. She had megaconfidence and she was usually pretty nice, to boot.

But now she was being unfair. And Will wasn't going to let her get away with it.

"Well, you know what, Cornelia? I *don't* have the answers," she blurted out. "As a matter of fact, I'm not even sure I'm meant to be your leader. As you said, Cornelia, we didn't choose this!"

Hay Lin huffed in frustration and grabbed her pink-and-purple backpack. She'd stashed it next to the cement block she was using as a stool.

Unzipping the pack, she pulled out a weighty, dusty, blue book. They'd found the book in Elyon's basement, right after they had chased Elyon and her Metamoorian thug back through the portal.

"I'm sure the solution to all our problems is in this book," Hay Lin said. She held it in her lap and gazed at her friends hopefully.

"You're wrong, Hay Lin," Cornelia said with a sneer. "This book is just another of the problems."

Taranee gave Cornelia a furtive glance and then joined Hay Lin in examining the book.

The edges of its pages were scuffed and ragged. But its spine? That was unbroken.

"Did you manage to get it open?" Taranee asked Hay Lin.

"Not yet," Hay Lin sighed. "And I tried everything!" To demonstrate, she grabbed the front and back covers of the book and yanked at them with all her strength. But the book remained firmly closed.

As Hay Lin struggled with the book, Will felt the back of her neck prickle in a familiar way. Then a wave of dizziness washed over her. She could almost feel her freckled cheeks go pale. And when she lifted a hand to her forehead, her fingers were trembling.

"There's . . . there's a spell on that book," Will gasped, staggering away from Hay Lin. "Put it away!"

TWO

Irma ran over to Will. The sight of her friend all pale and shaky made her feel a little fluttery herself.

"Do you have that strange sensation again?" Irma cried.

Will nodded fuzzily. Out of the corner of her eye, Irma saw Hay Lin scurry to zip the mysterious blue book back into her backpack. Instantly, Will's shakes began to lessen. She blinked slowly. Then she raised her head and looked Irma in the eyes.

Irma tried to flash Will a reassuring grin, but inside her gut was an uneasy rumbling. Sort of like the feeling she got after eating one too many bowls of Fizzing Frosted Corn Pops.

This isn't the first time Will's had an attack like this, Irma mused nervously. Will had also gone limp and trembly at the Halloween party, right before all sorts of sci-fi craziness had broken loose. And it had happened again after Yan Lin's funeral, when Hay Lin had first seen the ghostly Elyon.

And now, Irma thought, our leader's been hit again – by that annoying old book.

"Ugh," Will sighed. "It's really strange. I feel dizzy. . . . I have butterflies in my stomach. . . ."

Then she tried to smile.

"I guess I'll get used to it in the end," she offered.

Irma sighed with relief. She really wanted Will to be okay – for Will's sake, but also for her own peace of mind.

I mean, Irma thought, if the keeper of the Heart of Candracar loses it, what'll happen to the rest of us?!

Irma could never say anything like that out loud. Talk about dragging down a party. So instead, she responded in her usual fashion – with a quip.

"Maybe," she said to Will, "this dizzy spell

is all about something you had for breakfast!"

"I don't think so," Will laughed. "It doesn't last long. . . . And it's so difficult to describe. I mean . . . I feel the same way every time our maths teacher calls me up to the blackboard!"

"Ah!" Hay Lin said with a glint in her eyes. "That just means you're scared."

"Wait a minute!" Irma said, her eyes getting wide again. "Maybe Will gets that particular feeling for a reason. Do you think our maths teacher could be a creature from Metamoor?"

"Mrs. Rudolph?" Taranee said with a gulp. "But she's such a nice old lady!"

Irma walked over to Taranee and slung an arm over her shoulders.

"Things aren't always what they seem, Taranee," she said. "Devoting your entire life to maths is simply *not* human."

Taranee guffawed, and Irma smiled with satisfaction. It took a lot of talent to make Taranee laugh these days. But when Irma glanced from Taranee to Will, her smirk faded. Will was wiping a sheen of cold sweat off her upper lip and looking seriously freaked out. Irma's stomach swooped back to its nervous fluttering.

Wouldn't it be cool, she thought wistfully, if our maths teacher *were* our biggest enemy? I would *so* prefer a pop quiz to another fight with Metamoorian ghouls. Irma pictured the giant blue monster who'd almost tossed her into a pit that first night at the gym. She shuddered. But before she could imagine herself in a full-blown horrorfest, Will recovered and got back on track.

"All right, then," she said, trying to sound bright and cheerful. "The break's over. Shall we start?"

"Sure!" Hay Lin said. She pulled her knee up beneath her pointy chin. "I'd like to experiment with a little combined action. C'mon, let's try! I wonder what happens if we combine . . . let's see . . . the powers of water and earth."

"Maybe you'll get the power of . . . mud?" Irma giggled. She glanced around at her friends, expecting a laugh in return. Everyone gave her one – except, of course, Cornelia. *She* merely glared.

Irma sucked in her breath quickly.

Could Cornelia *be* any more annoying? she wondered. When she's not being all magicker-than-thou, she's supersour!

Not that Irma wasn't used to Cornelia's well-crafted pout. They'd always been at odds with each other.

Face it, Irma told herself. If we were music, I'd be grunge and Cornelia would be techno. I'm a softie, and Cornelia's Miss Right Angle. We are brunette and blonde, night and day.

And that had always worked fine when they were just two normal girls. But now they were Guardians of the Veil – fighting off evil and saving the world together!

Ugh! Irma thought. If only I could save the world with Will, Taranee, Hay Lin, and a couple of cute boys! She shot a glare of her own at Cornelia. Then she rubbed her hands together. She'd show her! It was time for a little magic.

But of course, the oh-so-on-top-of-it-all Cornelia had been thinking the same thing.

"I'll go first!" she said.

"No," Irma retorted, "*I'll* go first."

She whirled around to face the empty stretch of grass behind the construction site. She raised her hands out in front of her. Almost immediately, she felt her magic begin to bubble up within her. She wasn't even sure what she intended to do. But she knew it would be spectacular. And it would definitely be wet!

Irma's vision went blurry, the way it did when she opened her eyes under water. She felt weightless – no, buoyant. And her outstretched hands began to take on a bluish cast. Irma's fingers were trembling. Her pigtails trembled. Even the frayed threads dangling from the hem of her denim skirt shook!

Finally, she gasped, as a cool rush of power surged through her. At the same time, a swirly, blue swoosh of magic flew out of her hands! It looped the loop through the air toward the center of the lawn.

Irma watched in awe as the magic – *her* magic – danced through the air.

Of course, her moment of singular glory didn't last long. When Irma glanced Cornelia's way, her arms were thrust out before her, too. Cornelia's long hair began to dance and flutter behind her back. Her blue eyes darkened to a mossy green. And then, a whoosh of emerald-coloured magic rushed out of *her* palms. It arced neatly over Irma's squiggly, blue stream.

Fwoooooom!

Both magical rays landed on the same spot. Irma gulped, and all five girls froze, waiting to see what would happen next.

They didn't have to wait long.

The earth beneath their feet begin to quake. And rumble. It practically growled!

And then – it erupted.

FWOOOOOOOOOSSHHH! A massive geyser of water shot straight out of the earth, bubbling high into the air! Irma and Cornelia, who were standing only a few feet away from the instant Old Faithful, were knocked off their feet.

"Aaagh!" they shrieked. The plume sent bits of dirt, grass, and rock flying all around them. Then the geyser reached its peak – and fell. Torrents of water began to rain down upon the girls.

Irma cringed as the cold water hit her. But her discomfort didn't last more than an instant. After all, water was Irma's best friend. Even when she was wearing one of her favourite out-fits, she never really minded a downpour.

And here's the other thing, Irma thought gleefully. We're being spattered with drops of water. *Not* clods of dirt. Water has totally trumped earth! I've won! My magic has kicked Cornelia's magic's butt. And don't think she doesn't know it!

Cornelia was scowling down at her own

soaked sweater and sopping hair. Then she turned on Irma in a rage.

"See what you did!" she yelled.

"Poor girl," Irma taunted. "You're gonna need a barrel of hair conditioner to fix that mop!"

Irma laughed and put her wet hands on her wet hips. Then she got ready for Cornelia to hurl a zinger back at her. Irma knew the drill. This was the part where Cornelia said something snide.

Then Irma would respond with something snotty.

Cornelia would make a retort. And then Irma . . . it was the law of the universe, or at least, of Sheffield Institute.

Night and day, Irma thought again.

But when she glanced through the sudden, magical rain shower at her pals, her grin faded. Hay Lin and Taranee were bewildered. And Will was looking seriously stressed. Will looked from Cornelia to Irma to the geyser. She chewed on her lip. She crossed her arms over her skinny stomach. Her shoulders hunched up so high they almost touched her ears!

Somehow, Irma knew just what Will was

thinking. She was thinking of Metamoor.

And monsters.

And huge, nasty portals ready to gobble them all up.

And then she was thinking about Saturday morning TV stuff – like cooperation and compassion and hard work. She was thinking that if the Guardians didn't work together, they were going to fail. The world would be doomed.

How did Irma know Will was thinking about all these things? She knew because she was sort of thinking along the same lines.

But it was Will who decided to *do* something about it. Suddenly, she flung her arms out in front of her. They pulsated with the Heart of Candracar's pink-tinted magic. And then Will screamed, "*Stop!*"

Blub, blub, blub, blub . . .

Irma gasped and returned her gaze to her giant plume of water. It had obeyed Will's order and completely petered out. In just a few seconds, it had drained itself to a mere trickle. Then the last whiffs of her and Cornelia's magic evaporated with a fizzle.

Irma, along with the other Guardians, turned back to gaze at Will. In the aftermath of her big power surge, Will was looking more shy and sheepish than ever. She glanced at her four friends and giggled self-consciously. She shuffled one sneaker through the damp grass. And then she shrugged and smoothed back her dripping hair.

Oh, brother, Irma thought wearily. Cornelia and I are at war. Taranee's a total scaredy-cat. Hay Lin's mega-sad. And Will's totally embarrassed about being the leader. And *we're* gonna save the world? This I've gotta see!

THREE

It was Monday morning. Maths class. Twenty-four entire hours since Irma's magic had completely trounced Cornelia's at the abandoned construction site.

But Cornelia was still seething. In fact, she was clenching her pencil so hard, it started to splinter in her hand. *That* made Cornelia catch her breath.

I've got to chill! she thought. What am I so stressed about? I am *so* going to get this magic thing down. I just have to look at it as a challenge. Like the jumps I've been trying to land at skating practise. Next time Irma and I face off, I'm totally going to win. I can feel it.

The thought brought a stiff little smile to Cornelia's face. But it didn't succeed in making her shoulders relax or her jaw unclench.

Face it, Cornelia thought with a sigh. Winning a magic contest isn't going to make me happy. What would make me happy is withdrawing from this battle altogether! Did I ask for these powers? No! Do I want them? Not much.

But even as those thoughts darted around her head – the way they did about once an hour those days – Cornelia knew they weren't *completely* true.

The fact was, the idea of having magical powers that nobody else had (well, except for her fellow Guardians) made Cornelia shiver with delight.

So, what was the damage, really?

It was the fact that she couldn't control her new power. She *hated* being a newbie at anything! That was why she studied so hard and spent so many hours at the ice rink. If Cornelia was going to do anything, she wanted to do it well.

She even cared about excelling in maths, a feat that was especially hard to pull off today. On Mondays, Cornelia's maths class was two whole hours long. And not just any two hours. They were the last – and the sleepiest – two hours of the school day.

Mrs. Rudolph was sitting at the front of the classroom, droning on about binomials. Cornelia was dutifully taking notes. In between jottings, she glanced around the classroom. Her gaze froze on Will, who was sitting a few desks ahead of Cornelia. Even from her seat behind Will's, Cornelia could tell that her friend was conked out. Her chin was resting on top of her hands and her back was lifting in deep, regular breaths.

Apparently, Cornelia wasn't the only one who'd noticed.

"Will!" Mrs. Rudolph said suddenly. She folded her hands smugly on top on her desk. "Would you like to join in on the subject we were discussing?"

Will lifted her head woozily.

"Huh . . . ?" she muttered.

Uh-oh, Cornelia thought. A fellow witch is in trouble. In fact, she's in danger of completely humiliating herself!

Will jumped out of her chair and stood at attention in the aisle. She looked around and blinked blearily. Then she turned back to Mrs. Rudolph, whose plump face looked quite amused behind her big, tinted glasses.

"Sorry, ma'am," Will squeaked in a shaky voice. "I didn't get what you asked. I . . . I wasn't listening."

"That's why I asked you," Mrs. Rudolph said. She stood up and stepped out from behind her desk. She folded her hands behind her wide back and gazed at Will with a mixture of sternness and amusement. "You must know your lesson really well, since you can afford not to listen. We were reviewing Ruffini's theorem. Would you like to complete my explanation?"

Mrs. Rudolph tossed Will a piece of chalk. Will caught it with a gulp. A flush of scarlet surged to her cheeks.

"Uh . . . well . . . of course," Will stammered. "The theorem of . . . what's his name?"

Mrs. Rudolph sank back into her desk chair and gave Will a dry look.

"Ruffini, Will," she said in her deep, throaty voice. "Maths, you know . . . binomials . . . polynomials . . . x squared . . ."

"Oh sure, I got it," Will said with a nervous giggle. Her shoulders hunched up to her ears, the way they always did when she wanted to sink into the floor. She shuffled up to the black-board and held her chalk an inch away from the blackboard. Her other hand fluttered up to her chin. She glanced at the ceiling, as if she hoped the correct answer might drop through it and smack her on the head. She muttered, "Well . . . Ruffini's theorem . . . let me see. . . . hmm– . . ."

Cornelia knew Will was panicking. Cornelia was also bored stiff with the cruel game that Mrs. Rudolph was playing.

"Take your time," the maths teacher was saying to Will. "We're in no hurry. We have a good fifteen minutes before the end of the class."

That's when Cornelia knew what she was going to do. All it took was a flick of her right index finger. A swirl of barely-there, celery-green magic flowed out of her fingertip. Cornelia narrowed her eyes, focusing on the magical wisp. She watched it float up toward the ceiling, then bobble its way toward the classroom door.

She smirked as the magic curled like a woolly scarf around the bell that hung just over the doorway.

Fifteen minutes can be a long, long time, my friend, Cornelia thought, glancing at the still-paralysed Will. But you know what they say – time flies when you're having fun!

Brrrrrinnnng! The bell began to ring loudly. Cornelia's smile grew a bit wider and she nodded with satisfaction as her filament of green magic melted into the air.

Will's eyes widened in confusion.

Mrs. Rudolph's mouth popped open in surprise.

The rest of the kids in the class didn't seem to care that the bell was early. They were too busy shaking the sleepy fog from their heads and jumping giddily out of their chairs. They bounded towards the door, waving to Mrs. Rudolph in elation.

"See you, Mrs. Rudolph!" they called, pulling on their backpacks and rushing from the classroom.

"But . . . wait a minute!" the flummoxed teacher cried. "Where are you going?"

As Cornelia grabbed her messenger bag, she heard Mrs. Rudolph mutter, "I can't believe that! The bell rang earlier than usual today."

Cornelia waited by the door as Will hurried back to her desk to stuff her notebook and maths textbook into her pink backpack.

"Saved by the bell, huh?" Cornelia whispered.

"Thanks," Will breathed back.

"You owe me one!"

Cornelia grinned and began to flounce out of the classroom. Will was right on her heels.

"All right, then," Will called out to Mrs. Rudolph happily. "Good-bye, ma'am!"

"Wait a minute, Will," Mrs. Rudolph called out to her. Cornelia gulped and stopped to hover just outside the classroom door. Did Mrs. Rudolph think Will was responsible for the early bell? Was she going to get in trouble?

Cornelia cocked her head anxiously and eavesdropped on the sudden student-teacher confab.

"You hadn't done your homework, had you?" Mrs. Rudolph asked Will.

"It's . . . it's just that theorem," Will protested. "I tried – not much, that's true. But I did try! I really don't understand it!"

Mrs. Rudolph led Will out into the hall. Cornelia tailed them as they walked towards the school's front door.

"How are you getting along in Heatherfield, Will?" Mrs. Rudolph asked. "I mean . . . you've been here for a little while. Everything all right?"

Cornelia raised her eyebrows. Who knew maths teachers had an ounce of sympathy in them? she thought. Or maybe even two.

"Everything's fine," Will said, flashing a grateful grin at the teacher. "Why do you ask?"

"I know maths isn't much fun," Mrs. Rudolph said, patting Will on the shoulder. "But I've noticed . . . you always look so pensive and absentminded."

"Things aren't so easy for me right now," Will admitted.

You can say *that* again, Cornelia thought.

"But I'm fine," Will assured Mrs. Rudolph.

"I'm glad to hear that," the teacher replied. They'd reached the sidewalk in front of the school. Mrs. Rudolph paused and faced Will. "By the way, I could help you with that theorem if you like. I don't usually do private tutoring, but I'll make an exception for you. If that can help you be more attentive during my class, that is. . . ."

"I– " Will stammered. "Thank you so much, Mrs. Rudolph!"

"Any afternoon would do," the maths teacher said kindly. "What do you think? I'm sure an hour or so will be enough."

"Great," Will said. "You choose the day."

"Why don't I call you to let you know?" Mrs. Rudolph proposed. While Will wrote her cell phone number down for the teacher, Taranee walked up to Cornelia's side. She raised her eyebrows as Mrs. Rudolph slipped Will's number into her purse and walked away. Then Will joined Taranee and Cornelia.

"Will!" Taranee giggled. "Since when have you been *friends* with our maths teacher?!"

"She was so nice to me," Will said with a befuddled look on her face. "I totally expected to get an F!"

"And you certainly would have gotten one," Cornelia smirked, "if *someone* hadn't saved you."

As Will flashed Cornelia another grateful smile, Cornelia felt a sense of peace wash over her. Maybe she *was* finally getting a handle on her magic. It was about time! She breathed in a big gulp of crisp autumn air and glanced across the street. Maybe she'd actually enjoy the afternoon now. She could start with a smoothie from the restaurant on the corner. Lots of people from Heatherfield hung out there. It was the best place to hang out after school or work.

Cornelia peered over towards the sidewalk café to see if there were a table available in the sun.

Darn, she thought. Looks as if every seat's taken. I wonder if anyone is about to lea–

"Oh!" Cornelia blurted out.

She blinked and shook her head. Was she seeing what she thought she was seeing?

"What?" Will said, looking at Cornelia quizzically.

"Uh, it looks like making friends with the Sheffield teachers must be a family hobby," Cornelia said. "That looks just like your mother, having a 'meeting' with our history teacher!"

She tried to sound breezy. But as she watched Will's face go white, she felt a little pang of sadness for her. It had to be awful for Will. Not only were her parents divorced, but now Will's mum was hanging out with Mr. Collins. Yuck!

Taranee sent Will a sympathetic look, too, but Will didn't notice. She stood frozen on the curb, staring across the street.

The scene did not look good.

Not only were Ms. Vandom and Mr. Collins

making eyes at each other over their meal, they were also *sharing*! As Mr. Collins handed a fork to Ms. Vandom, Cornelia was sure she saw his hand linger on top of hers.

Cornelia glanced at Will. She must have seen that, too. She was holding her breath, and tears had already begun sparkling in her eyes. And when Ms. Vandom gave Mr. Collins's hand a squeeze, Will gasped out loud. Then she spun around and began running down the side-walk, her loafers pounding the cement angrily.

Cornelia saw Ms. Vandom's head turn towards the sound. Will's mother jumped out of her seat in alarm.

"Will!" she cried, rushing out of the café. Ms. Vandom crossed the street to chase after her daughter.

"Go away," Will shouted at her mum over her shoulder. "Leave me alone!"

But Ms. Vandom didn't listen. She caught up to Will and grabbed her hand.

"Will!" she gasped. "What's the matter with you?"

"I . . . I saw you sitting out there with him," Will spat. "You embarrassed me in front of my friends!"

That made Cornelia give Taranee a guilty glance. Taranee motioned in the opposite direction. Let's get out of here, her expression said.

Good idea, Cornelia thought. It's time to get out of earshot before things get more mortifying for all of us.

As she and Taranee tiptoed away from the scene, Cornelia couldn't help but overhear the end of the fight.

"What do you mean?" Ms. Vandom was saying to Will. "Dean's just a friend."

"Dean!" Will shrieked. "You're already calling him by his first name?"

"It's you who are embarrassing me, now," Ms. Vandom said in exasperation. "This was just a business meeting. Your school and Simultech are– "

"Oh, come on!" Will accused. "You were holding his hand. I saw you!"

With that, Will burst into tears. She turned to run away again. That time, Ms. Vandom let her go. When Cornelia peeked back at Will's mother, her face was anguished.

Mr. Collins stole up behind her and put his hands on her shoulders.

"Susan," he said apologetically.

"Oh, Dean," Ms. Vandom sighed. "What'll I do?"

Whoa, Cornelia thought as she finally slunk around the corner, trailing Taranee by several feet. Talk about a trauma.

She grimaced in sympathy for Will. She couldn't imagine what it must be like to have a broken family. To see your mother holding hands with a stranger.

And on top of that, to have to be the keeper of the Heart of Candracar.

Something in Cornelia's chest tightened, just a bit.

Hmmm, she thought grimly. I guess we'll just have to wait and see if Will can handle drama on the home front *and* lead W.i.t.c.h at the same time!

FOUR

Will took the steps to her loft two at a time, her heart pounding. If she didn't get behind a closed door immediately, she would die!

Okay, she *might not* die. But she would definitely humiliate herself – by blubbering in public. And she'd already had all the mortification she could possibly stand today.

Finally, Will reached her floor in the old building where she and her mum lived. Will could hear her feet hitting the cement floor with echoey thuds as she raced down the hall.

She gasped with relief as she made it to her door. She unlocked it and slumped inside.

Then, at last, she let go.

Flopping back against the door, she let her face crumple. Her tears finally spilled out of her eyes and streamed down her cheeks. Her breath came in big, sobbing gasps.

As she cried, the scene played itself over and over in her mind: she'd actually seen her mum making goo-goo eyes at her *history teacher*.

She'd seen their hands touch.

She'd seen her mum giggle like a little girl.

And then, Mum had denied the whole thing. She'd lied to her own daughter!

The thought launched Will into a fresh round of sobs. Stumbling into the kitchen, she grabbed a paper towel and blew her nose loudly. She wiped away the new flood of tears.

Finally, she was all cried out. Sniffling listlessly, she slumped to the kitchen pantry. She pulled out a loaf of soft, fluffy, white bread and a jar of chocolate-hazelnut spread. She flopped down at the kitchen table with a plate, pulled out three slices of bread, and smeared them with the gooey chocolate spread.

"Bread and chocolate," she muttered. "The perfect food for despair."

But when she lifted one of the fragrant slices to her lips, she found she was too despondent even to take a bite. In disgust, she tossed the snack back onto her plate. Then she shoved the plate away and folded her arms on the table. She rested her chin on top of her folded hands and sighed.

She tried hard to remember what life had been like when she'd lived in Fadden Hills. Her parents had been happy together. She'd been a typical, oblivious kid racing from school to swim practise to sleepover parties without a care in the world.

Those days were *so* over.

"Are you okay, Miss Will?"

Will glanced at the refrigerator. The ice lever in the door was waggling and a clipped British voice was rumbling out of the water spout.

I rest my case, Will sighed. Appliances that talk? Definitely not normal.

Still, she couldn't help but smile. She had to admit, being able to communicate with her fridge, TV, and computer *did* make her apartment feel less lonely!

"I'm fine, James," she said quietly.

"Are you sure?" James the fridge continued. "Usually, when you open that jar, it means you're sad."

"Well," Will said with a sigh, "today I'd

need a whole barrel of chocolate to make me feel better."

Swirling her butter knife idly through the chocolate spread, she felt her eyes begin to tear up again.

If only I could have a normal family like my friends. A family where people just love each other, she thought.

Propping her head on her hand, she thought of Cornelia's picture-perfect family – a mother, a father, and two daughters, all living happily in a glamorous penthouse apartment. She pictured Cornelia and her little sister, Lilian, bopping each other with pillows and jumping on the bed. They laughed hysterically while their mum smiled at them from the bedroom doorway.

A family just like all the others . . . Will day-dreamed. Without any secrets. Without any mysteries.

Cornelia and her giggly sister shimmered away and Will's mind filled with the image of Taranee hanging at home. Her shy friend was sitting on a couch, reading a book, while her big brother, Peter, loped through the living room, carrying his surfboard. Peter would be on his way to the beach, braving the cold to catch the last good waves of the day.

Will could almost feel the comfort Taranee got from her brash big brother. Where Taranee was shy, Peter was all confidence and kindness. Will knew Peter made Taranee feel safe. But who did she have to make her feel safe?

And what would it be like to have a family like Hay Lin's? Will wondered sadly.

She pictured Hay Lin's parents, sitting down to an early dinner before their Chinese restaurant started to fill up with hungry customers. In their warm, cluttered kitchen – a cosy, pistachio-green room directly upstairs from the Silver Dragon's dining room – Hay Lin's pretty mother would be cupping a bowl of steaming seafood soup in her palm. Her husband might be scooping up a mouthful of rice with his red chopsticks.

When Hay Lin got home, a warm dinner would be waiting for her. Along with the smiles of her two parents.

"*Mmmmm,*" Will sighed wistfully. She slowly screwed the lid back onto her jar of chocolate and tossed the cold loaf of bread back into the pantry. "A family without any lies. Must be nice."

FIVE

I can't believe my parents bought my lie, Hay Lin thought.

What's more, Hay Lin couldn't believe she'd *told* the lie. She'd just called home from the school pay phone. And she'd made sure to call at just the moment her mum would be putting dinner on the table. She had put on a breezy voice and told her mother, "I'm at the library with Irma. I'll be home later."

Hay Lin *was* with Irma – but they weren't at the library. In fact, they were loitering outside of Mrs. Rudolph's house, a few blocks away from school. Hay Lin cringed with guilt as she pictured her parents at home. Right now, they'd be starting their meal, with soup served in Hay Lin's favourite pink-and-white bowls.

Maybe it was her favourite soup, too – sizzling rice. The thought of the crunchy clusters of rice and the crispy vegetables in her grandmother's famous soup recipe made her mouth water.

Then she imagined her dad looking in confusion at her empty chair.

"Is Hay Lin not coming home for dinner?" her dad would ask as her mum placed a tray of warm food in front of him.

"She called five minutes ago," her mum would say. "She's in the library, doing homework with Irma."

"She always calls at the last minute," her dad would say with a scowl. "Hay Lin must learn – this is not a restaurant!"

"But dear," her mum would say with a placid little smile. "This *is* a restaurant."

Hay Lin couldn't help but giggle at that part. That was her mum. Straightforward and honest to a fault.

Not like Hay Lin.

She cringed again and pictured her dad's disapproving frown. She knew he wasn't as trusting as Mum. There was definitely going to be an interrogation when Hay Lin got home.

And who knew when *that* was happening?

Rumble-rumble-rumble. Irma looked at Hay Lin.

"What was that sound?" she asked with wide eyes.

"It was my stomach," Hay Lin whined. "I'm starving. It's late! Let's go home."

Irma shook her head stubbornly.

"I want to find out Mrs. Rudolph's secrets first," she insisted.

That was why she and Hay Lin had been camped out behind their maths teacher's, ever since school had let out.

Hay Lin rolled her eyes as she remembered how Irma had dragged her there. School had just let out. In fact, the bell had rung fifteen minutes early! Hay Lin was psyched. She'd skipped out of Sheffield and run into Irma at their usual meeting spot at the base of the west steps.

"School's out early!" Hay Lin had announced. "It's a sign!"

"A sign of what?" Irma had asked. She was only half-listening as she peered at something across the courtyard.

"A sign that we should go do something!"

Hay Lin had said, dancing in a little circle around her friend.

"We have fifteen extra minutes in our lives," she continued. "We can use them to make a quick trip to Baubles."

"Why do you want to go there?" Irma said, rolling her eyes. "There's an art-supply store right near your apartment."

"Yeah, but Baubles is the best," Hay Lin whined. "They have the most amazing oil paints – every colour you can imagine. And beads! Scads and scads of beads. Maybe we could go and grab some beads. I could make you a necklace."

That idea caught Irma's attention. She fingered the glittery choker that was already strung around her neck and looked at Hay Lin with a defiant pout.

"I don't know, Hay Lin," she said. "I have something else in mind. . . ."

With that, Irma began to drift across the courtyard. Hay Lin sighed. Irma was very stubborn. But she was also the most fun friend Hay Lin had. So she'd shrugged and followed Irma toward the sidewalk. The girls hid behind a pillar and watched the scene – Will was talking to

Mrs. Rudolph, and Cornelia and Taranee were standing nearby.

"Oooh," Hay Lin breathed in Irma's ear. "Scandal. Mrs. Rudolph is talking to Will about . . . *maths homework!"*

Irma had giggled. Then she'd stared at Mrs. Rudolph again.

"Why would Mrs. Rudolph take such an interest in Will?" she wondered out loud.

"Uh, I don't know," Hay Lin said sarcastically. "Because Will's in her algebra class, perhaps?"

"Or maybe because Mrs. Rudolph really *is* a creature from Metamoor," Irma said, rubbing her hands together. Hay Lin saw little sparks of watery blue magic shoot out from between Irma's palms.

"Hello?" Hay Lin said. "May I remind you what a creature from Metamoor looks like? We're talking eight-foot-tall, lumpy, blue hulks. Or red-eyed serpents. They're not grandmas who teach algebra. They're bad guys who pop out of portals. Or have you forgotten?"

Hay Lin shuddered. There was no way she could forget how horrible the Metamoorian creatures were. She'd only recently come face-to-face with an enormous blue one in Elyon's basement. She still remembered his yellow fangs and the stony lumps on his head. How could she forget the venom in his beady little eyes as he'd lunged at Hay Lin, trying to drag her into the portal? She would have been a goner if her friends hadn't transformed themselves into their magical forms and slammed in to rescue her.

Hay Lin shook herself out of the memory and gave Mrs. Rudolph another look. The lady was petite and plump, with a wobbly double chin and giant, tinted glasses. She wore a green scarf pinned with a little brooch. She looked as harmless as a house cat.

The teacher smiled warmly as Will handed her a slip of paper. Then she began walking plumply down the sidewalk.

"Let's follow her!" Irma blurted. She ducked around the pillar and began slinking down the sidewalk, half a block behind the maths teacher. Hay Lin trotted along behind Irma.

"I can't believe we're spying on a *maths teacher*, when we could be on our way to the store," she complained.

"Have you forgotten who you are?" Irma

said, giving Hay Lin a sneaky smile. "You're a Guardian of the Veil. Spying on aliens from another world is totally part of the job description."

Hay Lin huffed indignantly. But, as she was sure Irma had known she would, she acquiesced.

"Have it your way, spy girl," she'd said.

The two girls crept along the sidewalk, being careful to stay several paces behind Mrs. Rudolph. Irma ducked behind a tree, looking over her shoulder with exaggerated furtiveness.

Hay Lin giggled and somersaulted to a crouching position behind a garbage can. Two can play at this "spy game," she thought.

"The coast is clear," Irma hissed. Then the two girls began stealing up the sidewalk again.

This feels just like when we were little, Hay Lin thought with a grin. We'd play Spy, Detective, Policewoman – anything that gave us an excuse to sneak around Heatherfield and duck into places we shouldn't be.

Part of Hay Lin wanted to think of this as just another one of those little-kid games. Something fun. Something light.

But deep down in the pit of her stomach,

she'd known this was serious. Irma might have been joking about Mrs. Rudolph, but the truth was, bad guys from Metamoor *were* out there! Hay Lin had seen them. And now, her old fear-lessness was history.

The realisation made Hay Lin shiver. Her stomach growled again and she returned to the present. She was still standing, hungry and miserable, outside Mrs. Rudolph's big pink-granite house. Hay Lin glanced at her watch. They'd been standing there for the past two hours, peering into the maths teacher's window. It had been the most boring two hours of her entire life.

"You want to know Mrs. Rudolph's secrets?" Hay Lin said to Irma in exasperation. "She spends the whole afternoon grading maths tests! Why can't you admit you were wrong?"

Irma shrugged.

"Maybe I will," she said. "But first, I want to check one more time."

"Whatever . . ." Hay Lin muttered.

"I've got an idea," Irma said suddenly. "Are you free tomorrow morning?"

"We are *supposed* to be in school tomorrow morning," Hay Lin said irritably. She started walking away from Mrs. Rudolph's – and towards her apartment.

"Oh," Irma scoffed, falling into step beside Hay Lin. "We'll spend almost twenty years of our life in a classroom. We can take one little day off!"

"Irma!" Hay Lin gasped. "You're terrible. When I get flunked, I'll know who I have to thank."

"What if that woman really is a monster?" Irma protested. "Don't be selfish, Hay Lin. You have a chance to save the world."

"No, no, no," Hay Lin chanted. But inside, she could feel her resistance crumbling. Irma was pressing every one of her buttons – her sense of adventure . . . her hunger to save the world . . . her desire to get out of school whenever she could.

"I don't want to," Hay Lin said weakly.

"Are you *really* going to change your mind?" Irma said, staring at Hay Lin tauntingly.

"Oh, for Pete's sake," Hay Lin sputtered. "You know what? Okay!"

The next morning, there they were, once again holed up behind the wall outside Mrs.

Rudolph's house, surveying the scene.

I cannot *believe* I okayed this, Hay Lin thought miserably.

She and Irma had had to sneak past the school to get here. They'd jumped as the early-morning bell rang. Then they'd skittered nervously down the alleys behind the buildings, hoping not to be spotted by any grown-ups.

And now, they were holding their breath and waiting for Mrs. Rudolph to emerge.

Suddenly, the front door of the pink house opened.

Their target was in sight!

Mrs. Rudolph stepped out onto the porch, wearing a bright pink coat and her woolly green scarf. She locked the front door and slipped the key beneath a pot of pink flowers at the top of the porch steps.

Hay Lin and Irma stood perfectly still as Mrs. Rudolph lumbered down the steps and through the front gate. Then she walked down the block and disappeared around the corner.

"All clear?" Irma whispered to Hay Lin.

Hay Lin gulped. There was still time to make it back to Sheffield. She'd simply get a tardy demerit – no biggie. But one look at

Irma's determined blue eyes and Hay Lin knew there was no backing out now.

"Nobody around," she whispered resignedly.

Irma hopped lightly onto a garbage can and pulled herself up to the top of the wall. As she dropped to the lawn on the other side of the fence, Hay Lin clambered after her.

"I'm sweating," Hay Lin hissed.

"This is the warmest autumn we've had in twenty-five years," Irma said as she started across the lawn. "I heard it on TV."

"You know what I mean," Hay Lin said, pointing a cranky finger at her friend.

"Don't worry!" Irma scoffed. "We'll just do a tiny bit of poking around."

"What'll we do if Mrs. Rudolph comes back?" Hay Lin asked as the girls climbed the steps to the front porch.

"Mrs. Rudolph's at school," Irma assured Hay Lin. "She won't be back for the whole day."

With that, Irma pulled a plastic card out of her jeans pocket. Hay Lin recognised it as her friend's phone card. Irma's dad insisted she carry one with her in case she ever needed to make an emergency call. Being a police sergeant, Mr. Lair was a total worrier.

Irma must have picked up tips about break-ing and entering from her dad, too! Hay Lin gaped as Irma slipped the phone card into the cranny between the door and the doorjamb. She started jiggling the card around, trying to unlock the door.

"What are you doing?" Hay Lin asked. "Why don't you just use the key under the flowerpot?"

"This way, we won't have to touch any-thing," Irma whispered. "We won't leave any trace. It always works in the movies. Look . . ."

Irma jiggled the card some more. She shifted it up and down. Then she scowled and bent the card back and forth.

Craaaccckk!

"Oh, no!" Irma cried. Oh, yes. The phone card had snapped in two. She stared at it in horror.

"May I?" Hay Lin said, rolling her eyes. She went to the flowerpot at the edge of the porch and swiped the key out from underneath it. Then she nudged Irma aside, unlocked Mrs. Rudolph's door, and stepped into the house. The foyer was dim, but grand, with a little

Oriental rug, a dramatic, green-carpeted staircase, and a brass chandelier.

"You first!" Hay Lin said, motioning Irma inside.

"But . . . but . . ." Irma stood on the porch, stuttering nervously. Finally, she stepped into the middle of the foyer.

Hay Lin was feeling more confident now. She could *totally* handle this mission. She could even make sure Mrs. Rudolph wouldn't suspect a thing!

While Irma poked timidly around the foyer, Hay Lin used the key to lock the door from the inside. Then she went to a window next to the door and slid it open.

"And now, just a light breeze," she said playfully. She held the key on her palm. Then she felt her magic well up within her, like a cool gust of wind.

Pursing her lips, Hay Lin blew on the key. Her breath came out as a silvery wisp of magic! It carried the key out the window on a pillow of air. Then it lifted the flowerpot as if it had weighed no more than a pebble. Finally, it slid the key back underneath.

"There!" Hay Lin announced, turning to

Irma triumphantly. "The key is back in place."

"Bright idea!" Irma said. But her tone of voice wasn't exactly nice. In fact, she was scowling at Hay Lin. "Now you've locked us in!"

Oh. Uh, Irma had a point there. Hay Lin's shoulders sagged.

So, I was a *little* impetuous, she thought guiltily. That's just what Dad said to me last night when I finally got home from the stakeout Irma and I had. Maybe I oughtta work on that a bit.

But there was no time to start fixing that now. There was way too much snooping to do. Hay Lin started to follow Irma into Mrs. Rudolph's living room.

"You just stay here," Irma said, holding up her hand. "You've done enough already."

"Okay, okay," Hay Lin said with a grin. She knew Irma couldn't stay mad at her for long. She gave a salute and added, "I'll stand guard. But, hurry up, sir!"

Hay Lin peeked out the front window. As Irma shuffled around in the living room, then the kitchen, she called out, "If only we knew what we were looking for."

"I know," Hay Lin agreed. "It seems like a perfectly ordinary house. So, you're not finding anything?"

"Nothing," Irma said, coming back to the foyer after a few minutes. "Let's try upstairs."

Irma trotted up the stairs with Hay Lin following her.

"Aha!" Irma cried triumphantly as she ducked into a bedroom. When Hay Lin peeked in, she saw a big, comfy-looking bed, an wardrobe, a lot of little pictures on the walls, and other ordinary bedroom stuff.

"Uh, Irma," Hay Lin said dryly. "There's nothing in here."

"I wouldn't call that wardrobe nothing," Irma declared. "Or that chest!"

She pointed to a big trunk at the foot of the bed. Then, with a sneaky smile on her face, she walked over to the wardrobe. In one swift motion, she threw its doors open and began rifling through Mrs. Rudolph's cardigan sweaters and voluminous dresses.

"Irma!" Hay Lin gasped. "What are you doing? You promised we wouldn't touch anything."

"Well . . . I changed my mind," Irma

declared. "C'mon. Help me."

Hay Lin shook her head. She didn't want to stick her nose into Mrs. Rudolph's closet. It smelled like lavender and something else in there. Yuck. Instead, she drifted over to the bedroom window.

Idly, she gazed out over the street below. Adults were strolling busily down the sidewalk. There were businessmen in suits with briefcases, mums with strollers, delivery guys. . . .

So, this is what Heatherfield looks like during school hours, Hay Lin mused. No bicycles, no Rollerbladers, no kids, no . . . way!

"Eeeek!" Hay Lin shrieked.

"Aha!" Irma cried, running over to join her at the window. "Did you find something?"

"No, but someone's going to find us!"

Hay Lin pointed with a trembling finger at the house's front gate. Mrs. Rudolph was walking right through it!

SIX

Irma gasped. She pressed her hands to the window and stared at the woman hauling two heavy shopping bags up the front walk.

"Mrs. Rudolph!" she shrieked. "Wh – what is she doing here? She was supposed to be in school!"

"It's all your fault!" Hay Lin yelled back at her. Then she turned on her heel, dashed out of the bedroom, and sped down the stairs.

Irma careened after her.

"Don't panic! Just don't panic," Irma cried. "I have an emergency plan."

The girls skidded to a halt in the living room. Hay Lin spun around to face Irma.

"What plan?" she demanded. Then she gasped and looked at the front door.

Thump. Thump. Thump. That was the sound of Mrs. Rudolph's heavy feet tromping up the stairs to the porch.

Thump. Thump. Thump. That was the sound of Irma's heart slamming in her chest.

Irma bit her lip.

What plan, indeed? She had no plan! In fact, it had never even occurred to her that they could be caught. Now, for the first time, something else struck Irma.

Could Mrs. Rudolph *really* be a creature from Metamoor who had somehow sensed the presence of the Guardians in her house?

Were Irma and Hay Lin in actual danger?

Irma couldn't believe it. Really, she'd meant for the whole outing to be an adventure, a magical and fun adventure. Once again, being magical had turned out to be nothing but a big bummer!

Her magic wasn't going to get her out of this fix. No, Irma was going to have to rely on something very, very basic.

"Let's hide!" she whispered. She ran across the living room and threw open a door. Behind it was a small closet cluttered with a few boxes, brooms, and dustpans.

As Mrs. Rudolph's key began to click in the

lock, Hay Lin unleashed a terrified squeak and zipped across the room after Irma. The girls dove into the closet and pulled the door shut. An instant later, Mrs. Rudolph stepped inside the house.

Irma squeezed one eye shut and pressed the other to the closet door. She could just see Mrs. Rudolph through the narrow slit between the door and doorjamb. The teacher's short, straight, blonde hair was sticking to her damp forehead. She dragged her heavy grocery bags over to the coffee table and thunked them down with a moan.

"Ooof," she said, letting go of the heavy bags and straightening up painfully. She pressed her hands to her back.

"*Ouch, ouch, ouch,*" she complained. "Oh dear, my back. It's time I start using the super-market's delivery service."

Wow, Irma thought, Mrs. Rudolph must be even older than she looks.

Hay Lin was not impressed.

"Here she is," she whispered to Irma taunt-ingly. "Your *evil* creature from Metamoor. Looks like she's got a bad case of arthritis."

"*Shhh,*" Irma hissed. She peeked through

the door again. "She's making a phone call."

"*Oooh*," Hay Lin said, wiggling her fingers at Irma. "I'm *so-o-o-o* scared. Maybe she's going to ask a few monsters to tea."

Irma whipped around and glared at Hay Lin.

"Should I pinch you?" she whispered. "Do you want me to pinch you?"

Before Hay Lin could answer, they heard Mrs. Rudolph's voice.

"Hello, Will?" she was saying.

Irma caught her breath and returned to her spying. Mrs. Rudolph was perched on the arm of a chair near the telephone table. "This is Mrs. Rudolph. Do you have a minute?"

Irma glanced at Hay Lin, who looked startled. Then they continued eavesdropping.

"Why don't you come by this afternoon for that tutoring," Mrs. Rudolph said. "Today's my day off. . . . So I'll be waiting for you after school, then?"

After a pause, Mrs. Rudolph nodded.

"Perfect. See you later," she said to Will. Then she hung up.

"Very good," Mrs. Rudolph said, pulling herself to her feet. She went to the coffee table and rifled through one of her grocery bags.

"That means I've got some time to relax," she murmured. "I'll have a nice snack and read a book."

Irma huffed in frustration as she watched Mrs. Rudolph pull a pineapple out of the grocery sack.

That phone call to Will was totally innocent, she thought. And now, we're going to have to sit here in the closet while Mrs. Rudolph reads and eats a healthy fruit snack. At the very least, she could do something funny, like eating peanut butter out of the jar with her fingers. Or jumping around on the bed. Or something else you couldn't *ever* imagine a teacher doing.

Irma almost giggled. But she stopped herself when something else caught her eye through the crack in the closet door. She pressed her face back to the door for a closer look.

Irma's eyes widened. A hot rush of fear washed through her.

Mrs. Rudolph *was* doing something strange. And it was definitely something Irma couldn't imagine a teacher doing.

Their sweet, portly maths teacher was holding her pineapple in her hand. It seemed innocent enough. But instead of going to the kitchen to slice it up, she simply looked at it hungrily and opened her mouth wide.

Her teeth! Irma thought in alarm. Her teeth are as pointy and jagged as a shark's. They're . . . fangs!

Mrs. Rudolph's pointy choppers were sharp enough to rip right through a pineapple's rough skin. And that's just what they did: the teacher took a huge bite right out of the unpeeled fruit.

"Hmmm," Mrs. Rudolph muttered with her mouth full of pineapple chunks. "Very tasty!"

"Oh, no," Irma whispered. She couldn't quite believe what she'd just seen!

"What?" Hay Lin whispered. "What did you see?"

Irma shook her head. She couldn't speak. She wished she were somewhere else – at home, trading jokes with her dad. Or in the bathtub. Or even at school!

Anywhere but here.

Feeling as if she were in a trance, Irma pressed her eye to the crack in the door again.

Mrs. Rudolph had finished devouring her pineapple. Now she was lowering herself painfully down onto a red-velvet armchair. She plunked one of her feet onto a footstool in front of the chair and pulled her high-heeled shoe off.

"These things are killing me," she murmured.

Irma frowned in confusion.

Wait a minute, she thought. Now Mrs. Rudolph looks totally normal. She actually looks like somebody's grandmother in that awful gray skirt and brown sweater.

Was Irma's mind playing tricks on her? Had she imagined the fangs? She watched Mrs. Rudolph settle back into her chair and pick up a book from the table.

Then Mrs. Rudolph started to read.

Irma shrugged.

Huh, she thought. Okay, so it was a false alarm. I'm completely making up stories. But I'm just going to keep spying for a little bit. There's nothing else to do, after all.

Irma continued to peek out at Mrs. Rudolph. A moment later, she uttered a tiny gasp. She *hadn't* been imagining the teacher's pointy teeth. Because now the rest of her was changing, too!

At first, the changes were so subtle Irma almost didn't catch them. But then they became unmistakable – Mrs. Rudolph's feet were morphing from a woman's feet into . . . paws! Monstrous paws, with three floppy toes and thumblike digits sprouting from the heels. They reminded Irma of a sloth she'd seen once in the zoo.

Next, Mrs. Rudolph's hands thickened into horny claws.

Her skin turned green and brown. It looked as leathery as an armadillo's shell.

Most horrifying of all was Mrs. Rudolph's plump face. It made an awful crunching noise as it widened and bulged. The teacher's nose shortened into a snout. Her eyes turned bulgy and bright red. Her ears became long and floppy, almost like soft antlers. And thick, red, dreadlock-type things sprouted from her head. Most grotesque of all was the column of stubby red horns that suddenly jutted from her meaty neck.

Mrs. Rudolph wasn't just a creature from Metamoor. She was an enormous and *disgusting* creature from Metamoor!

Irma felt her hands turn icy. Cold sweat popped out on her forehead. She felt she was going to be sick! Or she might just . . .

"Faint," Irma whispered woozily. "I'm going to faint. . . . Help me, Hay Lin!"

Irma's eyelids fluttered as she collapsed on the floor. She heard her body hit the hard wood with a soft thump. Then she saw Hay Lin's face – pale and anxious – hovering above hers.

"Irma," she whispered. Irma could hear the panic in Hay Lin's voice. She knew all her friend wanted to do was run. And so did Irma! But she was too weak. She could barely keep her eyes open. . . .

"Irma!" Hay Lin begged again. "Wake up!"

All Irma could do was open her mouth in a wordless, soundless scream as she looked over Hay Lin's shoulder. The closet door was slowly opening. And looming in the doorway was the creature formerly known as Mrs. Rudolph. She was as big around as a tree trunk. Her red eyes were sparking with anger.

"May I help you ladies?" the creature growled.

Hay Lin jumped and glanced over her shoulder. Her hand tightened on Irma's arm. Her mouth snapped open in horror. And the last thing Irma heard before everything went black was Hay Lin's squeaky scream: *"He-e-e-e-elp!"*

SEVEN

Will trudged slowly up the sidewalk toward the address Mrs. Rudolph had given her. She was feeling totally torn. On one hand, she dreaded spending the next hour on maths. On the other, she was grateful to Mrs. Rudolph for taking an interest in her.

"I guess at least *some* grown-ups care about what I think," she muttered to herself.

And then again, some *don't*, she added in her mind. She was thinking, of course, about her mother. Last night had been decidedly uncomfortable. When her mum had gotten back from work, she'd tried to pull Will into a heart-to-heart about "Dean." Before she'd even taken off her coat, she'd come into the kitchen, where Will was still brooding, still not eating her bread and chocolate.

"Honey," her mum had said, reaching for Will's shoulder.

Will had sighed and squirmed out of her mother's reach. So her mum had simply sat down next to her. Morosely, she'd picked up one of Will's slices of bread and opened her mouth to take a bite. But then, just as her daughter had, she'd tossed it back onto the plate.

"I don't know what to say, Will. I've told you the truth," she said.

"Let's just not talk about it," Will muttered through gritted teeth.

"I want you to know," her mum said. "It *was* just a business meeting. But, well . . . after we talked for a while, maybe it did become a little more social."

"Stop!" Will cried, slapping her hands over her ears in disgust.

That had made her mum go all stern and scowly.

"Listen, I'm sorry if I surprised you today," she said. "I'm sorry about everything – all the changes. But the fact is, I'm going to have to move on with my life eventually. And so are you."

Will had given her mother one withering glare and stomped off to her room. She'd slammed the door and flopped onto her bed. Her dormouse scrambled up to perch on top of her stomach. He sniffed at her chin and looked at her quizzically. Will patted the animal's head idly as she fumed.

"*I'm* going to have to move on with my life?" she complained. "If only my mum knew how *much* I've moved on. I've been morphing into this strange magical thing; fighting off ugly bad guys from some unknown world; searching for Elyon; trying to pass maths! And she wants me to move on? Ha! My mother is completely out of touch."

The dormouse had cocked his twitchy little head, then pounced onto her foot to gnaw on her sock. Will had sighed. And, then, she'd stayed in her bedroom, avoiding her mum, for the rest of the night.

This morning, she'd merely waved good-bye to her mother before heading off to school. Her attitude had been so chilly, Will had half-expected icicles to sprout from the loft floor.

The image made Will shiver – from sadness more than cold. Will had thought she could count on her mum through anything. They were supposed to be a team. A team of two. Not two, plus one mustachioed history teacher. He was *not* part of the Heatherfield plan.

Of course, flunking maths isn't part of the plan either, Will thought. So she continued to trudge toward Mrs. Rudolph's big, pink house. She walked up the front steps. It was time to make her entrance.

"Oh, it's you, Will."

Mrs. Rudolph opened the door with a warm smile.

"Please come in, dear," she said. Will thanked her and walked through the foyer into the living room.

Pretty nice house for a maths teacher, Will thought. I wonder where Mrs. Rudolph is fr–

Thuuump!

Will jumped! The closet door had just flown open. And inside was–

"Irma!" Will screamed.

Irma was sitting on the floor of the closet. Her legs were tied with ropes and her hands were bound behind her back. A white handkerchief was bound tightly around her mouth. Behind her, Hay Lin huddled against the closet wall. She was bound and gagged, too.

No force could keep Irma quiet for long. As Will stood in the middle of the living room – frozen in fear and confusion – Irma shook her head back and forth. Finally, she squirmed enough to edge the handkerchief out of her mouth. Then she shouted at Will, "It's a trap!"

Will spun around to face Mrs. Rudolph, who was clasping and unclasping her hands nervously before her chest.

"Mrs. Rudolph," Will gasped desperately. "What's going on?"

"I . . . I . . ." the teacher stuttered, "I can explain everything, Will!"

She started to come toward her, her arms outstretched. But Irma screamed again.

"Watch out, Will," she warned. "She's a monster from Metamoor!"

Will was trying to wrap her brain around this bizarre scene. Her two friends were tied up in the closet. And her maths teacher was . . . an alien?

If so, she was an alien who was getting a little too close for comfort. Mrs. Rudolph was making her way across the living room, her face contorted with fear and regret.

Will gazed at her maths teacher. Before she could figure out whether to choose fight or flight, Will's head started to spin. She clutched it with both hands.

She was feeling that familiar dizziness.

And the unpleasant prickles in her skin.

And the cold sweat.

Uhhnnn, Will moaned inwardly. Not again! There's something in this house! Or . . . some-one . . .

Suddenly, her vision cleared. Mrs. Rudolph was almost upon her! Will's instincts took over.

"Stay away!" she shouted at the trembling woman. She waved her arm at Mrs. Rudolph and unleashed a flurry of pink-tinted magic.

With a metallic clang, the magic formed a sort of glowing screen in the air. It stopped Mrs. Rudolph in her tracks.

"*Aaaahh!*" the woman cried in pain and sur-prise.

"Quick!" Irma shouted from behind Will. "Untie us!"

With one last angry glance at Mrs. Rudolph, Will spun around and ran to the closet. She dropped to her knees and unknotted the ropes coiled around Irma. Then she freed Hay Lin.

"Okay!" she said, hopping to her feet. Her mind was racing. "Now what?"

There are three of us, she thought. And only one of Mrs. Rudolph. We're smaller and quicker than she is. I bet we could make a break for it and get to the door.

Will spun around, preparing to dash. But then, she saw something that stopped *her* in her tracks.

"*Aaagh!*" she gasped.

O-kay, she thought. Change of plans.

Mrs. Rudolph had disappeared.

In her place was one of the most grotesque creatures Will had even seen. And lately, she'd seen quite a few.

The creature was as big around as it was tall. It had red eyes and red dreadlocks. Its body reminded Will of a scaly turtle and its floppy feet made her think of space aliens. Its voice was growly and burbly and . . . female.

"This is how I really look," the creature said, holding out its stubby, scaly arms imploringly. "But please don't be afraid. I won't harm you!"

The creature pointed one of her claws – as yellowed and hard as a horse's hoof – at Will and added, "You're the keeper of the Heart of Candracar. You're the new Guardians of the Veil!"

So, Will thought shakily, who *hasn't* heard about our crazy new identities? And another thing . . .

"Where's Mrs. Rudolph?" she demanded. "What have you done to her?"

Hay Lin grabbed Will by the elbow.

"Wake up, Will!" she screeched. "She *is* Mrs. Rudolph!"

"And she's getting away!" Irma cried.

It was true. The creature, or Mrs. Rudolph, was making a break for it. She was running up the stairs at a surprisingly swift waddle.

"Don't let her get away!" Irma cried, dashing after the monster. Effortlessly, she plunged past Will. All three girls began chasing Mrs. Rudolph up the stairs.

"Why don't you understand?" the creature called over her shoulder. "This is not what it seems! You've spoiled everything!" She reached the top of the staircase and disappeared around a corner.

"After her!" Irma cried.

The girls finished barreling up the stairs and

ran down the hallway – just in time to see Mrs. Rudolph yank open a hatch in the ceiling. She pulled a ladder down to the floor. The ladder made a few complaining creaks as the creature locked it into place, then groaned under her weight as she scrambled awkwardly up the steps.

"She's holed up in the attic," Hay Lin cried.

"Now we've got her," Irma declared.

Will leaped onto the ladder and climbed into the attic, her friends at her heels. She watched Mrs. Rudolph pound across the room, dodging old furniture, dusty boxes, and broken lamps. It looked like any other attic of a big old house.

But as Will had learned by now – looks are often deceiving.

When Mrs. Rudolph reached the far end of the attic, she extended her arms. The wall began to undulate. And shimmer. It danced between solidity and nothingness.

And then, with a great *fwooooosh*, a tunnel formed in the wall. It seemed to be composed of clouds. Or water. Or roiling earth. It seemed like a little bit of everything.

Only one thing was clear. It was formed by magic.

"It's a portal!" Irma screamed as she ran up behind Will. Mrs. Rudolph turned away from the pulsating hole in the wall and gazed at the girls sadly.

"I thought I'd never pass through this portal again," she growled softly. "It seems I was wrong after all. Good-bye, girls."

"Mrs. Rudolph!" Will called out in bewilderment.

But the woman-turned-monster merely stepped through the portal.

"I'm coming back, Metamoor!" she cried.

Then she was gone.

"What are we going to do, Will?" Hay Lin cried.

A short time ago, Will wouldn't have known what to do.

Or she would have racked her brain for a solution.

But now, the magic within her took over. She lifted her hand. It was already humming with power, spewing jets of pink magic through the dusky attic.

She felt her body contract as strength suffused her arms, then her legs, and finally her mind.

Then Will unclasped her fist. The Heart of Candracar was hovering over her palm, glowing brilliantly.

The sight of the shimmery glass orb, cradled in its swirly, silver prongs, made Will gasp out loud with delight. The Heart sent a silvery, round teardrop of magic over to Hay Lin.

Next, it let fly a bobbling blue orb toward Irma.

Each girl experienced a breathless transformation. They were swooped up in a swirl of magic – magic that elongated their limbs and smoothed out their knobby knees and angular elbows. Their faces grew more beautiful, more knowing. Their hair bounced into shiny, perfect waves around their high cheekbones.

And soon, they were standing tall in their purple-and-turquoise uniforms, their opalescent wings fluttering angrily behind them.

Irma peered into the portal. Mrs. Rudolph was still visible. She was running through the tunnel, but the girls' transformation had happened so quickly she hadn't gotten very far.

"Let's move!" Irma cried. "She's getting away."

Will started to comply. But then, an image

of Hay Lin's grandmother flashed in her mind. Will almost felt as if Yan Lin were speaking to her from some ethereal place. Perhaps it was Candracar, the fortress of magic that had given the girls their power. Or maybe the place was just Will's memory.

All Will knew was that somehow, Yan Lin was reminding her of something important: guarding the Veil meant closing the portals and keeping invaders out. The fleeing monster wasn't nearly as important as the tunnel through which she was escaping.

Will called out to Irma.

"Let her go," she ordered. "Let's focus on the portal instead. At my signal . . ."

Will glanced at Hay Lin and Irma out of the corners of her eyes. They were raising their arms in front of them. Silvery sparks of Hay Lin's airy magic were already flashing from her fingernails. And Irma's hands were blurred by her watery power.

"Hit!" Will yelled.

Esssaaaaak!

Will watched a jolt of pink magic shoot from the center of her palms. At the same time, Irma unleashed a stream of blue magic, and Hay Lin a stream of silver. The three separate bands danced and coiled around each other until they had combined to create one vivid, purple mass – a veritable freight train of magic.

It hit the portal with a tremendous boom – as loud as a thunderclap.

The portal entrance was engulfed by a cloud of smoke. After an instant of stunned silence, the cloud began rumbling. Gushes of purple magic started to spew from its center. Then the cloud seemed to gather in on itself, pulling as much air from the attic as it could.

Uh-oh, Will thought desperately. It's gonna *blow*!

Fwooooommmm!

Will squeezed her eyes shut as the exploding portal hurled her through the air. She flew backwards.

Then she fell to the floor with a thud.

"Ooof!" Will grunted.

She pressed her forehead to the floor for a moment, her entire body shaking from the impact – not to mention the wonder – of what she'd just experienced.

She peeked around the attic.

The portal had disappeared! The dusty

beams and mottled-wood paneling of Mrs. Rudolph's attic wall were completely restored.

Will looked at her hands. The graceful, tapered fingers of her other self were gone! Will's own small, short-nailed hands had returned, as had the overalls and sporty pink pullover she'd been wearing when she'd shown up at Mrs. Rudolph's.

Peeking over her shoulder, Will saw Hay Lin's flailing legs – in her flared jeans and her loafers – poking out of an old trunk. And Irma had collapsed on an old chaise lounge and was batting dust out of her blue jacket.

They were back to normal.

And all previous evidence of a portal to Metamoor – not to mention their maths teacher–turned–Metamoorian monster – was gone.

"Phew," Will breathed, blowing a hank of red hair out of her eyes and gazing incredulously at her friends. "Um . . . don't know if you're busy this afternoon, but we've *got* to call an emergency W.i.t.c.h. meeting."

EIGHT

Taranee was sitting on the edge of Cornelia's bed. Like everything else in her friend's penthouse apartment, the bed was plush. Its headboard and footboard were antiques – carved wood accented with splashes of gold. The duvet was soft and fluffy. The pillows, fluffy and numerous.

But Taranee was far from comfortable. In fact, she couldn't even begin to enjoy those cushy digs. Like everything else in her life, that seemingly normal bedroom felt deceptive. Danger could be lurking in the dustless corners, in the well-stocked closet, even in the innocent-looking backpacks on the floor.

Am I just being paranoid? Taranee thought, gazing at her friends' faces. Hay Lin, Irma, and

Will looked decidedly relaxed. Which was weird, because they'd called this emergency meeting at Cornelia's house right after they'd seen their maths teacher morph into some sort of creature from the Metamoorian lagoon. *And* they'd closed a portal that had sprung up in Mrs. Rudolph's attic.

Those twisted tunnels to Metamoor popped up in the most unassuming places. The school gym. Elyon's basement.

Where's the next one gonna be? Taranee wondered. Maybe right here in Cornelia's bedroom! Maybe in my parents' kitchen! At this point, anything's possible.

Which meant Taranee could feel secure nowhere.

She didn't even completely trust herself! After all, she was still learning her way around her magical power. What if she accidentally set her bedroom on fire while she slept? Or inadvertently torched the next homework assignment that gave her grief? Or worse?

Taranee shook her head in frustration.

Now is not the time to get all freaked out, she told herself. Focus on the meeting.

She sat on her fire-starting fingers and

tuned back in. Irma and Hay Lin were just finishing the story of their crazy day at Mrs. Rudolph's. Will was sitting cross-legged on Cornelia's rug, listening with a bemused smile. Cornelia was pacing in front of the window, scowling as she listened.

"And then, the portal went *poof*, and we went flying!" Irma was saying with a laugh. "When we came to our senses, we weren't magical anymore. But the portal wasn't there anymore, either."

"We are *such* a kick-butt crew!" Hay Lin crowed.

Suddenly, a squeaky little voice filled the room.

"What'd ya do? Rob a candy store?"

The five girls gasped. They turned toward the voice. It had come from Cornelia's bedroom door.

"Lilian!" Cornelia barked.

Taranee covered her mouth with her hand as Cornelia stormed over to her baby sister, who was giggling and peeking around the door. Had Lilian heard anything?

"Get *out*!" Cornelia yelled at the little girl.

"Why can't I stay?" Lilian demanded with a

scowl. She planted her plump little fists on her hips.

"Because you can't!" Cornelia told her. She scooped Lilian up and pushed her out the door with one sweep of her long, slender arms. "Now, go away!"

Lilian stomped out into the hall.

"I bet you're talking about boys," she yelled tauntingly over her shoulder. "I'm gonna tell Mum!"

"What's up?"

Mrs. Hale's voice sounded in the hall now. She must have just come up the stairs.

Great, Taranee thought. I can't believe we have to save the world *and* dodge our parents! Give me a break!

She crowded behind Irma and Hay Lin at the bedroom door to see what would happen next.

What would happen next was some pretty smooth lying. Cornelia was *good*.

"We're doing our homework, Mum," she said breezily as she nudged her sister over to her mother. "Could you lock this little monkey in her cage, please?"

Irma guffawed and Will giggled. But Lilian

stuck out her lower lip and climbed into Mrs. Hale's arms.

"Oh," Cornelia's mum said to the rest of the girls. "They squabble all the time, but they love each other very much. Don't they?" she asked, looking directly at Cornelia.

"I'll love her even more if she can stay away from my bedroom all afternoon," Cornelia replied. Then she waved good-bye to Lilian and pushed her door decisively shut.

"Come on, Lilian," Taranee heard Mrs. Hale say from the hall. "Your sister and her friends have to do their homework. Why don't *we* bake some cookies?"

"*Wheee!*" Lilian cried.

"Phew," Cornelia said, turning back to her friends. "Now, where were we?"

Will walked over to Hay Lin's backpack, which was lying on the floor next to the bed.

"You know," she said, reaching into the pack and pulling out the mysterious blue book they'd found in Elyon's basement. "I have a feeling this book can tell us a lot."

Irma nodded vigorously.

"I think it's time to find out what this whole thing is about," she declared.

The idea made Taranee's knees feel a bit wobbly. She wasn't sure she *wanted* to know what was inside that book. She propped herself weakly against the footboard of Cornelia's bed.

But the other girls gathered around Will with eager faces.

"Even if we don't know our enemies specifically," Taranee said, "one thing is totally obvious. The creatures from Metamoor are among us. We don't know them, but it's clear they know us!" She felt her heart start to beat faster. "So, I'll say it again: We need to keep our eyes open, okay?"

"*Not* okay," Cornelia said, stamping her foot. She was wearing ballet slippers, so it didn't make much of a thump. But Taranee could still feel Cornelia's indignation. "Let me tell you something – I don't want to go on just 'keeping our eyes open.' I need to know!"

Cornelia started pacing again.

"Who are we supposed to be fighting?" she asked. "Who are these monsters? What do they want from us? The Veil . . . Candracar . . . Metamoor . . . they're just names to me. And these magical powers of ours– "

"We'll need them to open this book," Will

said, clutching the book to her chest.

Hay Lin shook her head and adjusted the pink goggles resting on top of her head.

"It's impossible, Will," she said. "I've already tried."

Will sank to her knees and put the book on the floor in front of her. Taranee joined Cornelia, Irma, and Hay Lin as they formed a circle around the tome.

"You tried on your own," Will pointed out to Hay Lin. "This time, we'll try together. Put your hands on it. . . ."

Will rested her palm on top of the book. But before anyone else could touch it, too, something strange happened.

Will's head dropped forward. She cocked an ear, listening to something. Then she spoke softly, her eyes closed.

"Why are you asking?" she said to no one in particular. "Of course, I don't."

Taranee looked at Cornelia. They exchanged a surprised, questioning look. Was Will hearing voices?

Apparently so. And those voices had told Will something. She came out of her trance and spoke to her friends.

"This book's protected by a magic halo," she reported. "Let's release some of our energy and see what happens."

Cornelia shook her head.

"Destroy my bedroom and you'll see what happens!" she said. Taranee knew what they were all thinking: What choice do we have?

If they didn't take a risk, they'd never know anything.

So Cornelia placed a reluctant hand on the book next to Will's hand. Next, Irma put her fingertips on the book. Then, Hay Lin.

Finally, they all looked expectantly at Taranee.

She felt her stomach flutter. Part of her wanted to run away and go home. She wanted to be where it was safe, where her brother would be rocking out to the same surfer-punk music he always listened to, where her mother would be reviewing cases from court and her dad would be getting dinner started in the kitchen.

Okay, if I'm feeling nostalgic for Dad's home cooking, Taranee thought wryly, something's *definitely* wrong.

Taranee shook thoughts of home from her

head and looked, instead, at her new friends. She took in Will's strong, determined face, Hay Lin's excited smile, and Irma's sly smirk, and felt a little better. Even Cornelia's defiant sneer was somehow comforting.

Maybe, Taranee realised suddenly, I'm not as far from home as I think.

So, with a shy smile, she placed her own trembling fingertips on the book.

Almost immediately, a jolt of green magic began to form between the girls' hands. It traveled from finger to finger until a faintly glowing ring hung over the book, like a halo.

Then . . . the book began to tremble.

And then, it did more than tremble. It levitated – floating right off the floor.

Taranee squeaked in surprise. But nobody let go of the book, so she didn't either.

"That's it," Will whispered. "Be careful now. Don't worry . . ."

Of course, that's exactly when something worrisome happened. The green halo swirling around the book started to swirl a little faster. Then even faster.

In fact, Taranee thought, you could definitely call that a whirl. A *sparking* whirl.

It was true – jolts of starry light were shooting out of the halo. Staticky, zapping noises filled the room.

Next, the green circle began to turn conical. It was a miniature tornado. It carried the book right out of the girls' reach, lifting it toward the ceiling.

"It worked!" Hay Lin breathed. "Something's happening."

"Oh," Taranee gasped, unable to say much else.

For a moment, the girls just stared up at the book as it hovered beneath Cornelia's ceiling. Their mouths hung open. Taranee was sure she could hear the thumping of five hearts in the room. But maybe that was just her own heart, beating five times as hard as usual.

And then, Irma pointed at the trembling tome.

"It's opening!" she cried.

Will jumped to her feet, but Cornelia grabbed her.

"Don't get too close," she warned.

As if Cornelia had predicted it, the book began to sink back towards them. At the same time, the cover continued to open. A few pages flipped back. And then, the book alighted in front of the girls' frightened faces, assaulting them with a surge of acid-green light.

"Aaah!" Will cried. Taranee recoiled in terror.

A moment later – when the girls realised none of them had been vapourised, or even burnt, by the tremendous flash – they peered at the book more curiously. The light subsided a bit. And then it died down to a gentle glow.

Taranee blinked the spots out of her eyes and looked at the volume.

"Look at that!" Cornelia exclaimed. "It's not a real book!"

She was right. The book was a container of sorts.

On its right-hand side, where there should have been pages, there was merely a cushion with a cavity cut out of its middle. Nestled inside that cavity was an object.

It looked like a piece of jewelry – a big pendant or pin. The body of the pendant was glazed with brilliant paint – half of the circle was green, the other half white. On top of the circle was a tall, skinny triangle. And on the bottom, a slightly smaller triangle.

It was clearly some kind of symbol. It also

looked . . . awfully familiar.

Suddenly, Taranee recognised it.

That design had been on the floor of Elyon's basement, she realised. It was on the pathway to the portal!

Then Taranee noticed something on the left-hand side of the book. Filling the top half of the page was a series of strange shapes. They were pictures or hieroglyphics or . . .

Taranee leaned in closer. She felt her fear melt away from her, like a fever that had suddenly broken. Now she was merely curious. Those strange letters were intriguing. . . . She *had* to get a closer look.

"There's an inscription here," she murmured to her friends. "A mysterious alphabet . . ."

Taranee leaned in even closer.

"Don't touch it!"

That was Cornelia, warning Taranee away from the inscription. But the warning merely echoed around Taranee's head and disappeared with a poof.

She couldn't help herself. She had to reach out and . . .

Ding . . .

"She touched it," Cornelia said, incredulous.

Taranee barely heard her. Her head was too full of the ghostly music that had erupted the moment she touched the book. Actually, it wasn't quite music. It was clangs and chimes and drums and cymbals that had somehow been warped and distorted.

The music subsided quickly – to make way for a voice. A man's voice.

"Fear the name of the prince of Metamoor," the deep voice said. "Kneel down before his shadow."

"Oh!" Taranee cried. She looked up at the ceiling, then glanced wildly around the room. Who was speaking?

"This is the Seal of Phobos," the disembodied voice boomed. Taranee's eyes bulged in fear. But even more frightening was the casual reaction of her friends. They were still staring at the book with expressions of calm curiosity.

"Didn't you hear that?" Taranee gasped. "That voice!"

"What voice?" Hay Lin asked with a shrug.

Taranee felt her head start to spin.

"*That* voice," she said, pointing to the

strange amulet nestled in the book. "The book talked to me. That's the Seal of Phobos."

The other girls blinked at Taranee with blank expressions on their faces. Then Irma made a sudden grab for the amulet.

"I have no idea who this 'Fabius,' is," she said, "but I'd be happy to take care of him now!"

As Irma started to lift the Seal from the book, the voice boomed again in Taranee's head. This time it was so loud she was sure her eyeballs jangled back and forth as a result.

"Phobos!" it roared.

"Ow!" Irma cried at the same time. She yanked her hand away from the Seal. "It burned me!"

Next, the Seal did more than that. It erupted from the book with a puff of smoke and began to shoot towards the ceiling. It floated in a bubble of blackness.

"Uh-oh," Irma said tremulously as the girls cowered beneath the pulsing amulet. "Did I do something wrong?"

"I knew it!" Cornelia yelled. "That thing is going to destroy my room."

And it is going to take us right along with it, Taranee thought in terror.

That's when the Seal of Phobos began to spew forth a torrent of sludgy, black clouds. The gunky-looking stuff began to creep across the ceiling, as if it were gathering strength for an attack.

Whoooooosh!

The black stuff was on the verge of exploding! It quickly doubled in volume, covering the ceiling. Then it hurtled downwards, ready to consume the five girls. It was going to smother them!

"*Eeeek!*" Taranee heard Irma cry.

And then, Will spoke. But her order did *not* inspire a whole lot of confidence.

"Duck!" she screamed!

NINE

Duck, Will thought. Did I really say that? Great. *Brilliant* idea, Will.

Nevertheless, she *did* duck, falling to the floor and covering her head with her hands.

Just a few hours ago, she'd had this same feeling. She'd had a hard time believing that Mrs. Rudolph had turned into a turtlelike ghoul, even though the evidence had been right before her eyes.

Will's mind was grappling with the *current* chain of events. A pretty pendant – a harmless-looking geometric bauble with a green-and-white center – had suddenly sprung to life.

But it can't *really* be spewing black gunk all over Cornelia's bedroom, Will said to herself. Can it?

Fearfully, she peered up at the ceiling through her splayed fingers.

Um, that would be a yes, she thought. This is really happening!

The Seal of Phobos was hurling forth clouds of inky sludge. The stuff was like night air that had become three-dimensional, darkness that had come to life.

And it was clearly evil.

For a moment, all five girls simply stared – stunned – at the roiling, expanding blackness.

But that moment didn't last long. As the blackness began to creep down toward them, Hay Lin screamed. Then she cowered on the floor, crying, "I never thought I'd miss those boring afternoons when we really *were* doing homework!"

Meanwhile, Cornelia dashed across the room. She grabbed the doorknob with both hands and began pulling on it.

"The door's stuck," she cried. "We're locked in!"

"What *is* this stuff?" Taranee wailed.

As Will watched the darkness undulate, growing inkier and denser by the second, a number of possible answers flashed through her mind.

It's evil that's taken form, she thought. It's out to get us.

Or it's some bizarre new baddie from Metamoor that's out to get us.

Or maybe it's our fear. Our fear has become something real, something solid, something that's out to get us.

Will shook her head. Why was she even trying? She didn't have a clue as to what the sludgy stuff was. But she was right about one thing. It was definitely out to get them!

And it was encroaching fast. While Will had been racking her brains for an explanation, the dark gunk had tumbled down the walls and crept across Cornelia's floor. The furniture had become cloaked in it. The girls' feet were lost in it.

Before they knew it, the stuff had climbed up to their waists. It would take only a minute for the blackness to engulf them completely!

As the blackness swirled around her torso, Will watched Hay Lin scream and claw at the wall, trying to escape. But the tarlike darkness wouldn't let her go. Taranee's hands seemed to be caught in the stuff. No matter how hard she pulled, they wouldn't come out. She was stuck!

"Will!" she screamed.

The sound of her name, spoken so desperately by her friend, brought a surge of energy to Will's limbs. She tried to jump out of the sludge. She could feel her leg muscles strain. She could feel her toes stretch and spring.

Will couldn't move. The blackness was up to her rib cage by now and it had her in its grip. In fact, it seemed to be pulling at her with greedy, sucking gulps. Will shook her head back and forth as she struggled to move through the darkness. But that only made things worse! The blackness grabbed her flailing arms and pulled them down to her sides. It had her pinned.

She was helpless.

She was no leader.

As if to prove her point, the blackness suddenly flung itself over her head. It covered her face like a gauzy, oppressive scarf. It draped itself over her eyes. It filled her head.

Will couldn't see Cornelia's room anymore. She couldn't see her own hands, pinned to her sides.

And more importantly, she couldn't see her friends. They'd been swallowed by the inky evil. They'd as good as disappeared.

Will let out a choked sob and wilted. The strength drained from her legs. Her lungs quit their panicked heaving. Her head hung in defeat.

It was all too much.

I can't fight anymore, she thought. I can't do this alone.

Will could think of nothing else until . . . she felt something move in her hand!

At first, it felt like almost nothing – a twitching muscle, or a slight shifting of the sludge.

But then, the thing grew more insistent. It forced Will's fingers to fight the blackness and close into a fist. She felt a sort of warm, pulsing pressure shoot through her entire hand. By the time she sensed jolts of energy shooting up her arm, she knew what had happened.

It was the Heart of Candracar! It was speaking to her from inside her body. And now, it was emerging from her palm. It was reminding Will of her power, her magic.

"Heart of Candracar," Will said suddenly. Her voice made no sound. The moment it left her mouth, it was swallowed up in the blackness. Will persisted.

"We're in danger," she told the Heart. "Please, help us!"

Will bit her lip in hope. She opened her hand to release the orb. And then she peered desperately into the blackness.

It was eerily silent. As dark as a starless night.

Will blinked. Had she seen something?

The darkness was retreating. Will saw a pin-prick of light floating somewhere in the darkness.

The light began growing. Before long, the hole in the blackness was fist-sized. Shafts of brilliant light spilled through it. It pushed back the darkness like a willful bird, struggling to break from its shell.

All four girls seemed to be gravitating closer and closer to her. Finally, Will felt them touching her. They all sank to the floor and huddled together. Will was surrounded by a wall of friends, and, in their center, the Heart of Candracar glowed and pulsed and finally exploded.

The blackness blew into a thousand pieces that flew toward every corner of the room. Then, just as quickly as it had arrived, the darkness evaporated.

Will heaved a sigh of relief. But the feeling didn't last. When she glanced up at Cornelia's ceiling, she realised that, while the blackness might have disappeared, its source remained.

The Seal of Phobos continued to float above them, nestled in a small cloud of blackness.

The Heart of Candracar wasn't going to let it just stay there. It rose from Will's palm up toward the ceiling. The Heart and the Seal hovered next to each other, poised for battle. It was a standoff between light and dark, Candracar and Metamoor, good . . . and evil.

Evil had nothing with which to fight its battle but the Seal.

But good had the Heart of Candracar *and* the five Guardians.

Will rose to her feet. She stood directly beneath the glowing Heart.

Wordlessly, her friends formed a circle around her. It was as if they, too, knew instinctively what to do.

Slowly Will felt something warm well up in her chest. It felt like joy or hope. It was the feeling she had whenever she made a new friend, or won a swim meet; when her mother arrived home from a long business trip; whenever life was at its best and sweetest.

And now, it filled Will with peace. She closed her eyes and relaxed into the joy. She felt it grow and grow within her until the feeling burst from her chest. It emerged as a shaft of light.

When Will opened her eyes, she saw that shafts of golden energy were also emanating from the hearts of her friends. The beams rose upward and joined together in a blinding halo around the Heart of Candracar.

They were feeding the heart – filling it with their magic.

And together, they were conquering the Seal of Phobos. With an angry *fzzzzz-ZAAPPP!* the Seal rushed straight toward the Heart. Instead of shattering the delicate glass sphere, the Seal plunged into it. The Heart of Candracar had completely consumed the amulet. In the next moment, the blue book that had held the Seal shot into the Heart as well.

Just like that, the magic disappeared. The Heart of Candracar swooped back into Will's body with a little *thwip*. The girls each slumped to the floor and exhaled in exhaustion.

Will watched Hay Lin flick a bead of sweat from her forehead. Irma rubbed her eyes blearily. But Cornelia looked at the door in alarm. Will followed her gaze.

The door was opening!

What now? Will wanted to scream. What horrible thing has Metamoor cooked up for us this time? Enough already!

A blonde head popped into the room, well below the doorknob. Lilian! The little girl's mouth was smeared with chocolate and her blue eyes were scrunched into two mischievous slits.

"I bet you were talking about boys!" Lilian announced. She slammed the door and disappeared. Will could hear her little feet thumping down the hallway.

Will's racing heart began to slow. She looked at her friends wearily.

"Uh," Cornelia groaned. "*That* was definitely worse than maths homework."

"I don't know about you," Irma added. "But after that ordeal, I need a snack!"

"Or at least a change of scenery," Cornelia said, lurching shakily to her feet. "Let's get some air!"

"And sunlight!" Hay Lin piped up. She slung her pink-and-purple backpack onto her shoulder and said, "Let's go."

The girls trooped downstairs, stopping in the kitchen for iced tea and a plate of the cookies Lilian and Mrs. Hale had made. Then Cornelia pointed to the balcony off the kitchen.

"There's plenty of air out there," she said with a smile. "What's more, it's fifteen stories up, and Lilian is afraid of heights!"

"A sister-free zone?" Taranee asked with a smile. "I'm there."

The girls carried their munchies through the sliding glass door, then sank gratefully into the comfy patio chairs on the balcony. Will leaned back into her creaky chair and took a deep, long breath of salty air. The ocean was only a couple of blocks away from Cornelia's building. There were even seagulls flying nearby.

All Will wanted to do was talk about going to the beach. Or boys. Or the horrible Sheffield Institute gym uniforms. Anything but what she was about to talk about.

"Listen," she said wearily. She picked up a cookie and turned it around in her fingers without taking a bite. "I can't explain what just happened. But it does tell us one thing. We found that book in Elyon's basement. There's definitely a link between Metamoor and Elyon's house. What we don't know is if Metamoor and Elyon's family are linked, too."

Cornelia stared at Will with a clenched jaw. Will knew Cornelia still didn't want to believe that her best friend, Elyon, could have had anything to do with Metamoor or, worse, come from there.

"That book doesn't prove anything," Cornelia said. "It could have been in that basement for ages."

"Right," Hay Lin said, jumping in. "Maybe Elyon and her parents were just unlucky and . . . they moved into a haunted house! Like the ones you see in the movies."

Taranee walked to the edge of the balcony and leaned on the railing. She gazed wistfully out at the squawking seagulls.

"I think this whole town is haunted," she announced. "A portal inside the gym. Another in Elyon's house. And a third in Mrs. Rudolph's attic . . ."

"And there are nine other portals," Hay Lin pointed out. She reached into her backpack and pulled out a yellowed, dusty scroll of paper. She unfurled it on the wicker coffee table.

"Oh, right," Cornelia said, rolling her eyes. "We were forgetting your wonderful map."

Will eyed the map. It had been Yan Lin's last gift to her granddaughter before she had died. But it was more than an heirloom. It was a detailed, overhead view of Heatherfield, complete with all the portals to Metamoor – well, the three portals that they'd already found, that is. Each time the girls happened upon a portal, its location on the map took on a pulsing red glow.

"It's the most useless thing in the world," Irma cracked. "The only map that shows you something *after* you've found it."

Will sighed in agreement. But Hay Lin was optimistic as always.

"There must be a good reason, if Grandma gave us this map," she said.

Hay Lin turned to Irma, with expectation and just a little challenge in her playful almond-shaped eyes.

"Or maybe, Irma," she said, "you know the answer."

Irma said nothing. She looked as though she had no clue.

Will felt that since she was the leader, she

should know what to do. She was about to shrug off the whole "leader" thing, but before she had the chance, the Heart of Candracar spoke for her. She felt its power throbbing in her palm and, without thinking twice, she held her hand out toward her friends.

There – once again – was the pulsating glass orb. It floated easily out of Will's palm.

Practise makes perfect, Will thought, as she watched the medallion levitate toward the coffee table. I wonder if the Heart of Candracar is feeling as weary as I am.

She steeled herself for another mysterious message from the glowing object. When it halted over the map and spat a pink flash down onto it, Will gasped.

For the first time ever, the Heart didn't present the girls with a mystery, but with a destination.

A house on the elaborate map began to glow a brilliant red.

"That's Elyon's house!" Will cried. Then she looked around at her friends. And this time, she didn't see indecision or fear. They were each nodding with resignation.

"The message," Will said, nodding in agreement with their silent decision, "is clear."

TEN

It was time for the Oracle's meditation. He floated through the corridors of his home, the Temple of Candracar. The temple floated, too. It was nestled in silvery, ethereal clouds, in a place where night never fell.

That didn't mean the Oracle never saw evil. On the contrary, he saw all the evil in the world. He also saw all the good. *And* he saw the fragile Veil that separated the two.

In those moments of contemplation, he also saw the Veil's Guardians – the five young girls he had chosen to close the perforations in that gossamer Veil.

Those were the humans whose final destiny was to save the world.

As he came to a halt in his favourite chamber

of the temple – a room containing a perfect, turquoise lily pool – the Oracle closed his eyes. He folded his legs gracefully beneath him. His white, silken robes fell in smooth folds around his knees.

He saw the Guardians gathering in a room. It belonged to Cornelia, the angry one with the yellow hair. She was still fighting her magic. But the Oracle knew that, in her heart, she was beginning to embrace it.

She will have to, he thought with a small smile.

He watched the girls open the book of Phobos. The Seal emerged from the book. As the Oracle witnessed the ensuing battle, his own muscles contracted. He felt the magic that surged through the keeper of the Heart of Candracar. He felt the leader finding her power, her confidence. He felt every emotion and every bit of energy that she felt as she fought off the blackness of Phobos.

The battle ended as quickly as it had begun. The Heart usurped the place of the Seal of Phobos.

The Oracle opened his eyes and smiled.

He had not been wrong about those little

ones, with their rubber-soled shoes and pink-and-purple clothes. He knew that some members of his congregation had feared the girls' youth, their weaknesses, their affection for boys, their attachments to their families.

Up here in Candracar, we have forgotten, the Oracle thought, *that in the messiness of humanity, there is a source of strength. Humans call it love.*

That's something Luba, for instance, would never understand, the Oracle thought with a chuckle. *I can feel her storming her way through the temple hallways right now.*

When the Oracle cocked his head, he could hear her too.

"Get out of the way," she snarled. "Let me through!"

The Oracle closed his eyes and envisioned Luba's long, silvery pelt, the pointy ears that jutted from her head like the fronds of some exotic plant, and her feline face, which wore a permanent expression of indignation.

Luba was the protector of the Guardians' magic. Today, she had been quite busy. The girls had faced many foes. But none like the challenges that awaited them.

The Oracle had known that that would trouble Luba. She was a loyal congregation member, but an anxious one – always quick to see dangers and mishaps. She didn't have the Oracle's vision.

She was determined, however, to have the Oracle's ear.

"I must talk to the Oracle!" she demanded.

She was blocked by Tibor, the Oracle's adviser.

"This is not the right moment," he barked at Luba. An ancient man, with a four-foot-long beard and white mane, Tibor was nevertheless as strong as a bear. His sole purpose was to stand sentinel behind the Oracle, protecting the Oracle's peace.

It's as if he and I were one person, the Oracle mused. Tibor is the body, a brawny, stalwart presence. And I am the mind – mysterious and weightless.

The Oracle's small body was so light, in fact, that he had levitated right off the ground as he meditated. With his legs still tucked beneath him, he was now floating over the lily pool, enjoying the fragrant breezes wafting off the water.

Thus he was untroubled by Luba's impudence. But Tibor didn't know that.

"The Oracle can't see you right now," the adviser insisted.

But Luba tossed a jolt of magic energy at Tibor. The gesture's impertinence startled Tibor so that Luba was able to push past him, muttering, "That remains to be seen."

"Stop!" Tibor called after her.

But the Oracle held up his hand.

"Let her in, Tibor," he said.

Then, without turning around to face Luba's angry, yellow eyes, the Oracle continued to speak to his adviser.

"I already know Luba's thoughts," he said quietly. "And Luba already knows my answer."

The Oracle felt Luba crouch to the floor, placing her claws beseechingly on the edge of the lily pool.

"This must not be, Oracle!" she cried. "The Guardians are not ready yet! They are still too inexperienced!"

"What you are saying is true," the Oracle allowed with a serene nod of his head. "But it must be. I cannot do anything about it."

"That is not true!" Luba insisted. "You can stop them if you want. You must!"

"What impudence," Tibor gasped as he stole up behind Luba. He glared down at her disapprovingly.

Luba shot Tibor a defiant glare and said, "Should they fail, the Veil will remain without *any* protection against Phobos."

The Oracle closed his eyes. Ah, Phobos. The Guardians had now gotten their first glimpse of the dark Metamoorian prince. His Seal and its darkness had almost conquered them. But the Heart of Candracar had prevailed. Even the Oracle had uttered a sigh of relief when the quiet, red-haired girl had willed the Heart into the darkness, when the Power of Five had shattered the Seal's tremendous strength.

"Those girls are brave, Luba," the Oracle said to his distraught servant. "Try to understand them. Ten thousand years ago, you, too, were as young as they are now."

And as vulnerable, the Oracle added inwardly. Luba wasn't wrong to worry about the Guardians. That was her duty. Everyone had a duty to perform in the face of the certain peril that lay in front of him or her.

ELEVEN

I can't believe we're going back to Elyon's house, Cornelia thought, with a small groan. She and the other girls had left her apartment building immediately after the Heart of Candracar had illuminated Hay Lin's map. Now they were trudging across town toward Elyon's eerie, abandoned house.

Let's see, Cornelia mused, looking up at the increasingly grey, dusky sky as she walked. The last time we paid a social call to Elyon, she turned into some kind of strange, empty-eyed ghost. She melted through a wall in her basement and enticed us down a dank, brick-lined tunnel. Then the bricks came to life and tried to bury us alive. And to top it all off, Elyon introduced Hay Lin to her new best friend, a huge, blue meanie who tried to drag Hay Lin through a portal to Metamoor.

It's getting harder and harder to remember a time when *I* was Elyon's best friend, Cornelia thought wistfully.

The mystery surrounding Elyon's disappearance was still gnawing at her, like a cut that refused to heal. She still wouldn't allow herself to believe that Elyon had knowingly gone to Metamoor, that she was really the one who was luring Cornelia and her friends into danger.

Maybe we'll finally find some answers here, Cornelia thought as the girls arrived at Elyon's house. They paused for a moment inside the front gate. Unraked leaves skittered around the unkempt and neglected yard. The windows in the house were dark. The newspapers piled high on the front porch were damp and yellowed with age.

Everything about the abandoned building seemed to broadcast a warning: stay away.

I'd love to stay away, Cornelia thought, looking up at the forbidding house. This is about the last place I want to be. But when Hay Lin's map says jump, we jump. Just as when some anonymous elders in some imaginary place called Candracar tell us to save the world, we just agree. We change into magical form, no questions asked.

And my friends just *accept* it all, Cornelia thought indignantly. She shot a sullen glance at Hay Lin, Irma, Will, and Taranee. Maybe *they* don't mind taking orders. But *I'm* used to being the one who makes decisions about my life – what to do after school, whom to hang out with, what cool new clothes to buy.

Now, she thought bitterly, those days are over. I have to follow the herd, or at least, Will. I just hope she's up to leading us.

Actually, that's exactly what Will was doing just then. She was the first one to tromp across Elyon's overgrown lawn and climb the stairs to the front porch. As she placed a firm hand on the front doorknob, Taranee whispered, "This place gives me the shivers."

Will nodded in agreement.

"I don't like it either," she admitted. "But it's the only clue we have to find out what happened to Elyon."

Solemnly, Cornelia and the others followed Will into the stale-smelling, echoey house. They tiptoed across the living room to the unassuming door under the stairs. Then they descended the curving staircase into the creepy, circular basement. Just as it had the last time she had been there, the room reminded Cornelia of a giant tin can. Its walls were made of curved, metal slabs. The floor was stubbly, gray cement. The boxes and bicycle propped up beneath the stairs looked even more lonely and dusty than they had the first time.

The one thing that was different was the huge gash in the wall opposite the stairs. Cornelia stared at the jagged hole. It was hard to believe that she was responsible for it; but she was. She'd flung her arms out and assaulted the wall with waves of green magic. She'd literally moved the earth to help her friends discover the tunnel deep beneath Elyon's house.

Cornelia couldn't help but smile proudly as the girls once again stepped through the doorway she'd created.

Slowly they began walking through the tomb-like tunnel. It was damp and chilly. The yellow lights on the wall cast a dingy glow over everything. Even Cornelia's pretty, pink shawl and long, purple skirt looked worn and droopy there.

"Here we are again," Irma sighed. Nodding, Cornelia looked up at the arches that divided the tunnel into sections.

"Now what?" Irma asked.

"There must be a reason the Heart of Candracar led us here," Will declared. So the girls walked on in silence.

I'm glad *she* has so much faith in that little piece of glass, Cornelia thought sourly. Me, I'm not so sure.

And clearly, she wasn't the only one. Suddenly, Taranee's frightened voice broke through the gloomy, silent air.

"Listen!" she shrieked to her friends. "Listen!"

Cornelia cocked her head and looked warily at Will, Hay Lin, and Irma. They all looked totally perplexed.

"Um, Taranee," Cornelia said gently. "We can't hear anything."

But Taranee ignored her. Her eyes were bulging with fear and her hands were clenched and trembling.

"It's the same voice!" she insisted. "It's whispering a name: Phobos! Over and over."

That's when the Heart of Candracar made

another surprise appearance. It popped out of Will's palm, glowing insistently. The girls peered at it. Inside its pulsating glass orb was the distinct shape of the Seal of Phobos. Its circular emblem and pointy ends were distorted by the sphere, but it was definitely still there.

"What can we do?" Irma wondered. "The Seal's inside the Heart."

"And it oughtta stay there," Hay Lin said determinedly.

Cornelia shivered. Hay Lin was right. It would be a long time before she could forget what that Seal had done to her bedroom.

But Will was gazing trustingly at the Seal locked inside the medallion.

"The Heart of Candracar always knows what's right," she said.

"Oh, please!" Cornelia blurted out suddenly. She had *so* had it with following a silly necklace all over Heatherfield. "I don't like this at all. I don't want that thing to tell me what to do."

The other girls – even more freaked-out than Taranee – stared at Cornelia in surprise. It was as if she'd committed some terrible blasphemy or something. Why couldn't they see how ridiculous this situation was?

"True," Cornelia continued. "The Heart got us out of trouble. But one day, it could fail to do that. It could . . . I don't know . . . its energy could run down."

As Cornelia folded her arms stubbornly across her chest, she heard Hay Lin say something to Irma. Cornelia spun around just in time to catch the last snatch of her whisper.

"Can I turn her into a crow now?" Hay Lin was asking her friend.

"Nobody would notice the difference anyway," Irma replied with a giggle.

"I heard that!" Cornelia said, bearing down on Irma. "Why don't you tell me what you think to my face?"

Cornelia clenched her fists and braced herself for a retort. Irma always had a wisecrack in her pocket. Especially for Cornelia.

Well, maybe not *always*. In fact, right now, Irma was speechless. Her lips quivered and the only quip she could manage was *"Eeep!"*

Cornelia laughed.

"Oh, what's wrong, Irma? Are you *afraid* of me?" she asked snidely. "Well, at least you're not making fun of me anymore."

"I– I'm not afraid of you," Irma said. "I'm afraid of what's behind you!"

Cornelia gaped at Irma. *What–*

Then she spun around.

"Aaaahhh!" Cornelia screamed.

"The portal," Taranee cried from somewhere behind Cornelia. "It's open again!"

Tell me something that's *not* painfully obvious, Cornelia thought, desperately. She fell to her knees and clutched at the cold, stone floor. The portal had erupted from the wall, spewing stone and bricks all around Cornelia's head. The mouth of the tunnel was ringed with silvery, swirling vapour. And inside, Cornelia could see the same throatlike ridges she'd spotted in the corridor that had led them here. The ridges were contracting and rolling, like an animal trying to swallow its prey.

And the prey? She was it! Cornelia was closest to the portal. She could feel it trying to pull her in, with powerful, greedy gulps. She clawed at the floor, trying to resist the pressure.

"Hang on!" Hay Lin cried to Cornelia. Irma and Taranee stared at her in horror.

It seemed that Will had eyes only for the Heart of Candracar, which was still floating above her palm. The Heart was shooting spears of silvery magic toward the portal. Cornelia cringed as the magic whizzed by her head. She was surprised it wasn't setting her hair on fire.

But the Heart wasn't targeting Cornelia. It was focused on the portal. Shafts of magic extended between the orb and the tunnel, linking the two with a sort of magical net.

"I think I've got it!" Will cried, over the roar of the swirling portal. "The Seal of Phobos is the key to entering Metamoor!"

Will gulped and looked at Cornelia. Will's brown eyes flashed at her. In them, Cornelia saw a spark of adventure, a flicker of fear, and a whole lot of determination.

"Are you thinking what I'm thinking?" Will asked.

Cornelia glanced over her shoulder at the predatory portal. It seemed to be sucking at her harder, now. She longed to have enough power to fight it off.

And that power could only come from one thing.

Narrowing her eyes, Cornelia turned back to Will and nodded.

Immediately, Will threw back her head and

thrust her palm out toward her friends. Cornelia gasped as she watched the Heart of Candracar explode in a rainbow of lights. A watery, blue teardrop shot toward Irma and whirled around her, replacing her jeans and pale blue jacket with a tiny purple skirt, springy, striped leggings, and a pair of iridescent wings.

A silvery *whoosh* enveloped Hay Lin, transforming her into an elfin, airborne blur.

The Heart's pink magic infused Will, rounding out her skinny torso and lengthening her arms and legs.

Taranee's bright-orange teardrop changed her fearful expression into one of sheer, fiery ambition.

Finally, Cornelia felt her own shimmery, green teardrop swirl around her like a mossy cloak. It whisked around her and bathed her in the scents of damp earth and freshly cut grass.

Cornelia threw her arms above her head as her W.i.t.c.h. clothes appeared on her body. She loved the long, swirly, purple skirt, the midriff-skimming top and the supple boots that hugged her calves as if they had been custommade just for her.

Most of all, she loved the wings that had sprouted painlessly from her back. She could feel them fluttering in her hair, which was longer and silkier than it had been before. The ticklish feeling would have made her laugh out loud if this had been a happy transformation.

But it wasn't.

The girls had turned into their magical forms, so that they could plunge into the portal. And on the other side of that pathway was Metamoor – a place filled with unknowns.

"Okay," Will said, glancing at her witchy crew. "We're ready!"

Whoooooooshhh!

As Will spoke, the mouth of the portal erupted into hot, angry flames.

"Maybe not," Will said.

"Oh, brother," Cornelia complained. She'd been just about to hop into the tunnel. She would have been smoked in a second!

"Are we supposed to jump through that ring of fire?" Irma demanded, backing away from the crackling tunnel. "Forget it! I'm not working in a circus."

Will looked at Taranee.

"Well," Will said with a shrug, "these aren't

your usual sort of flames. But your powers might work anyway. It's worth another trip."

Cornelia saw Taranee bite her lip for just an instant. Will and Taranee exchanged an empowering glance. It reminded Cornelia of Elyon. They'd had a bond like that between Will and Taranee – a sort of silent, best-friend language.

The thought made Cornelia want to see her friend more than ever.

But, she wondered as she stared at the ring of flames, is the risk too great?

She didn't have much time to ponder the question. Taranee was gearing up for action.

"Well," she said to Will, "I guess we're about to find out what my powers can do."

She braced her purple boots on the stone floor and held her hands out in front of her. As orange bursts of magic flowed from her palms, Taranee scowled at the fiery tunnel.

"Do you hear me?" she shouted at the fire. "Get out of the way!"

SSSsssssssszzzzttt.

"Wow!" Taranee gasped. "It did what I told it to!"

Cornelia gasped. The fire had indeed disappeared the instant Taranee had issued her order. After the flames fizzled out, the portal seemed to cough a little, expelling a wan puff of smoke. And then it was still. No fire. No steamy swirls of air. No pulsating walls.

It was just an ordinary, brick-lined tube leading to . . . who knew where.

"Come on!" Will said, running towards the opening in the wall. "Let's go!"

"Wait a minute!" Cornelia cried suddenly. "What happens if we get stuck on the other side?"

Will shrugged and tapped her palm.

"We have the Seal of Phobos," she said. "If it worked to get us in, it'll also work to get us out."

Cornelia gaped at Will.

"You make it seem as if you'd known these things all your life," Cornelia spat. "Little Miss I-Know-Best!"

Cornelia saw Hay Lin and Irma exchange irritated glances. Will merely smiled at Cornelia.

"You're right," she said quietly. "But something tells me it will work."

"And maybe Elyon is on the other side," Irma piped up. "That's enough of a reason to go. Don't you think?"

"Right," Will declared. "Now who's coming with me?"

Cornelia scanned her friends' faces. They were all looking at their leader. Will's usual sheepish smile was gone. Instead, her forehead was furrowed with determination and her mouth was twisted into a rakish smile. She was ready for this mission, no matter what it held.

Well, Cornelia thought defiantly, if she's ready, *I'm* ready.

With that, she followed Will into the portal.

The girls crept along the brick pathway. Cornelia felt off balance on the curved floor. She supported herself against the walls as she moved through the tunnel.

Soon a left turn popped up. Cornelia couldn't help but feel glad that Will had been the first one to peek around the corner.

But there was nothing there. The tunnel just continued on.

After a little while, the girls came to another corner. And this time, when they veered around it, they saw something. It was a light at the end of the tunnel – literally. In fact, it looked like sunlight!

The tunnel began to slope upwards. The girls were climbing up – and out – of the portal. Cornelia began breathing harder. What on earth would they find at the end of the portal?

What am I thinking, Cornelia asked herself, shaking her head lightly. The question is, what on this *non*-earth will we find? We're not in Heatherfield anymore.

Suddenly, Will stumbled. She slapped one hand onto the wall and used the other to support her head, which suddenly seemed too heavy to hold upright.

"Huh," she muttered woozily. "It's that sensation again. It's really strong this time."

"Of course," Hay Lin said, running up to throw a sympathetic arm around Will's shoulders. "We're in Metamoor now."

Will nodded weakly. Then, as it had before, the dizziness seemed to leave her quickly. She straightened up and squared her shoulders. The girls were only a few yards away from the end of the tunnel. Light was streaming in now, bathing them in a golden glow.

Will rushed towards the exit and hopped out into . . . Metamoor? As Cornelia poked her head out of the portal, she gasped.

This wasn't some strange land at all! It was a place with grass and trees, half-covered in autumn leaves. It was a place in which there were both sunlight and Elyon's purple house – with a gaping hole in the wall.

"O-*kaaaay*," Hay Lin said, looking around in bewilderment. "Maybe we're not in Metamoor after all."

TWELVE

Will felt her wings fluttering behind her. She glanced over her newly broadened shoulder. The shimmery feathers were trembling and quaking.

It's almost like having a dog's tail! she marveled. My wings are totally broadcasting my mood. And at the moment, they're colouring me confused.

Because Hay Lin was right. This place the portal had brought them to didn't seem Metamoorish at all. Not that Will had had any idea what Metamoor would be like. But she'd pictured a gloomy place, filled with shadows and sinister figures. She'd pictured anything but this. She noted the same overgrown grass they'd left in Elyon's yard an hour before. They'd finished their crazy journey right back where they'd started.

"Gee," Cornelia said dryly. "Guess we took a wrong turn."

"That's so strange," Will blurted out. She took a few halting steps forward. The grass was flattened silently beneath her knee-high purple boots. Will looked up at some leaves dangling from a branch above her head. They were shimmering in a breeze, just getting ready to break free and fall to the ground.

Will squinted at the leaves. Something was strange about them. But what was it?

Suddenly, Will realised what it was.

"Listen," she said to her friends. "No noises!"

She pointed to the leaves. While the other girls looked quizzically at the branch, Will craned her ear for a faint whistle of wind. For the rustling of the dried-out leaves. A bird. A car whooshing through the street. Anything.

But all she heard was silence.

"There's nobody around," she exclaimed, spinning around in a circle. The sidewalks were empty. There wasn't a bus or bicycle or skateboard in sight. The city seemed to be completely and utterly abandoned.

"Look!" Irma said, interrupting Will's survey of this new, strange Heatherfield. "There's someone over there!"

Irma pointed across the street and began to run towards a tall, stucco house. A man was hurrying up its steps to the front door. He was wearing an ordinary, tan trench coat and carrying a leather briefcase. He glanced over his shoulder as Irma called out, "Sir! Please, sir!"

The man jumped and began fumbling in his coat pocket for his house keys. He moved closer to the door and unlocked it quickly.

"Don't run away!" Irma cried. "Wait!"

By now, all five girls were running towards the man. But before they could reach him, the pale-faced grown-up slipped inside the house and slammed the door shut.

"Sir!" Irma cried desperately.

Will sighed. She couldn't *totally* blame the guy for being weirded-out. How often do you see five teenage girls in matching, slinky outfits parading along the streets of Heatherfield? Will glanced over her shoulder at her twittering feathers.

And I almost forgot the weirdest part of all,

she thought, clapping a hand to her forehead. Our wings! We must make for quite a bizarre picture.

But, Irma didn't seem to understand why anyone would be afraid of them, much less refuse to help them. She thumped up the front steps of the house and began pounding on the door.

"Please open up," she called. "I just want to talk to you– "

Irma's words were suddenly swallowed in a gasp.

She stepped backwards.

"N– now that I'm a magical being," she stammered, "I guess I don't know my own strength!"

Will peered past Irma.

A crack had formed in the middle of the door – right where Irma had been banging on it. Like a spiderweb, the fissure began extending out to the corners of the door. Pretty soon, the wood was divided into several pieces.

"What have you done?" Taranee demanded from the bottom of the steps.

"Don't look at me like that!" Irma squealed, turning around to look at the accusing faces of her friends. "It's not my fault!"

Krrrr-POOOOWWWWW!

"Eeeeeeek!" the girls screamed in unison.

The cracked door had just exploded. Shards of it flew in every direction.

When Will looked up, she realised the devastation wasn't limited to the door! The entire *house* was cracking into jagged pieces. And those pieces were beginning to tumble down upon the girls.

"Aaaaaigh!" Will cried. She watched her friends cringe and collapse to the porch floor, covering their heads in terror. They didn't have time to run.

Will threw her own hands over her head and hoped that somehow her magic would protect her from the shower of bricks, roof tiles, glass, and gutters.

CRA-A-ASH!

Something had landed a few inches from Will's right ear. She jumped and peeked through her folded arms. She expected to see a chunk of splintered stone or maybe a shattered windowpane lying next to her.

Instead, she saw a flat and mysterious object. It was a triangle of something that looked like very thick cardboard. When Will grabbed it, it felt heavy and gluey in her hands. It was of a putty-grey colour.

"Huh," Will said, sitting up slowly. She turned the triangle over in her hands and gasped. The cardboard was painted with incredibly real-looking bricks.

With wide eyes, Will looked up at the still-careening bits of house.

All the pieces were flat and thin! It was *fake*, like a theater set!

The strangeness wasn't limited to that particular house. Gazing down the street, Will saw the entire block collapsing. First, the buildings broke into bits of cardboard litter. Then, after hitting the ground, the buildings evaporated into quickly dissipating clouds of dust.

The entire street – the entire city – was nothing but a facade.

The thing about a facade, Will thought fearfully, is that there's always something behind it.

When the dust from all the falling debris had cleared, Will got shakily to her feet to see just what that something was. Her first glimpse of her surroundings filled her with confusion.

A second glimpse filled her with fear.

It wasn't until the other girls had stood up and clustered around Will in a protective huddle of limbs and wings that Will truly began to comprehend everything she was seeing.

"Gee," Irma whispered. "I think it's pretty clear now. . . . This is *definitely* not our Heatherfield."

Will nodded. She couldn't speak. She was too busy gazing around her.

They were most definitely not in Heatherfield anymore, but they *were* in a city – a city that looked positively medieval. The buildings were tall and narrow, with stone foundations, and were topped with round, wooden battlements. They were supported by creaky ramparts, and their windows were small and dusty.

The girls stood on a muddy, narrow street. Behind them was an austere, stone staircase. It curved around another imposing building – built into a rocky hill – then ducked under a curved aqueduct before snaking up the side of a hill.

Will had seen a movie once that had been set in Shakespeare's time, hundreds of years earlier. It had looked something like this. Except –

"Guys?" Taranee said in a trembling voice. She pointed up at something clinging to one of the stone walls.

Will sucked in her breath quickly.

Okay, she thought in panic, that's *definitely* not Romeo *or* Juliet.

No, it was a creepy creature that resembled an iguana – a bright, blue iguana, splashed with spattery-looking, green markings. Its powder-blue tongue flickered tauntingly. It gazed at the girls quizzically . . . and almost intelligently.

Then Will noticed something else that was odd about the curly-tailed beast. It was wearing clothes! A frayed, brown tunic with a leather belt, to be exact.

Skitter-skitter-skitter.

Will jumped and grabbed Taranee's arm.

"What was that?" she whispered. Out of the corner of her eye, Will saw Hay Lin gaping at a ten-foot-long, orange-and-green tail slithering lazily through the street. It was undulating around a corner. The tail's enormous owner was clearly halfway down the block already.

Will had only to glance up to get an eyeful of more grotesque creatures: a crouching, dragonlike critter wearing a green vest, and figures that walked upright on two legs but definitely did *not* resemble people (it was the pointy ears and ice-blue skin that clued Will in). There were squat creatures and scaly creatures and–

"Hello, Guardians!"

A welcoming committee! Will thought with a shudder.

Together, the five girls spun around. They found themselves gazing down a wide street. It was a dark, dreary stretch of mud made claustrophobic by the half-crumbling buildings looming over it.

"Uh-oh," Will whispered.

She heard the mysterious, threatening voice again.

"We've been waiting for you for a long time," it said. The voice was gravelly and smooth, all at the same time. The voice was also . . . familiar.

Finally, the owner of the voice showed his face – complete with slithering tail, scaly, green skin, razorlike jaw, and jaggedy teeth. His malevolent eyes were cloaked behind a pulsing red mask.

With this scaly beast appeared the giant

blue thug who'd tried to harm the Guardians several times already. Together, the two stepped through the throng of soldiers to confront the girls head on. The beast was dressed in some sort of robe – a dramatic swath of blue fabric, emblazoned with the Seal of Phobos.

Will's limbs started to tremble. But then she clenched her fists and ordered herself not to lose it. She had to be strong! She had to concentrate on whatever the snaky creature had to say.

"As you see," he announced. "I didn't come alone."

Will thought he was referring to his army of thugs. But then, a figure stepped out from behind the villain. That figure was also draped in blue robes with the Seal of Phobos on them. But the blue-draped presence wasn't some grotesque, otherworldly creature. It was Elyon!

"Say hello to your friends, Elyon," the beast said, looming over the small girl with a creepy smile.

Will – with her friends at her heels – ran up to Elyon and grabbed her hands. Will's magical self was several inches taller than Elyon. She leaned down and looked into Elyon's pale eyes. They were vibrant, even laughing. The somber ghost the girls had encountered in the basement was nowhere to be seen.

"Elyon!" Will gasped. "What have they done to you?"

"Nothing! I'm fine!" Elyon said with a grin. "I'm happy to see you!"

Will shook her head in confusion and grasped Elyon's hands more tightly.

"We're going home, and you're coming with us!" she blurted out. "You can't stay here in this horrible place."

Elyon laughed.

"Ah," she said, pulling her hands from Will's and waving her friend away jovially. "You don't understand. This horrible place has a name, you know. Welcome, my friends, to Meridian, the city at the heart of Metamoor. Welcome to my home!"

Elyon looked each one of them in the eye with a warm smile.

"Stay," she said, enticingly. "You'll like it!"

Irma crossed her arms and looked askance at the dank-looking buildings that surrounded them.

"Sure," she said, with sarcasm. "I may ask my parents to rent a house here for the summer."

Seemingly stung by Irma's rejection, Elyon took a step backward, to stand in the shelter of the scaly beast's vast cloak. He loomed above her, framing her in evil.

Elyon's face had darkened as well. Her eyes grew heavy-lidded and her mouth twisted into an ugly sneer.

"You don't want to stay?" she asked softly. "I'm so sorry."

"You leave us with no choice," the snakeman added. Then he glanced over his shoulder at the horde of armed creatures.

"Guards!" he barked. "Take them!"

Hay Lin grabbed Will by the arm.

"I knew he was going to say that!" she wailed. "I knew it!"

Will reached out and pushed her four friends from behind her. Then she raised her own arms in front of her face. Her hands were already shooting forth pink sparks.

"Don't let them get any closer!" Will ordered her fellow Guardians.

And from that moment on, the five girls

began to work as one. It didn't matter that their first practise session had ended in a mud bath. Or that Taranee feared her magic. Or that Cornelia resented hers.

Because, now, the Heart of Candracar – and their friendship – was pulling them all together. And together, they would fight off this army of thugs.

A blast of pink magic shot from Will's palms. It hit a cluster of soldiers right at their feet, unbalancing them and sending them flying onto their backs.

Meanwhile, Hay Lin hurled a blast of air at another charging soldier. It caught him in the gut. He went soaring! The soldier screamed and flailed until he hit a stone building with a sickening thud. He fell to the muddy street and lay still.

Behind Will, a soldier was bearing down on Taranee. Will was sure her friend must be quaking. She started to run to her aid.

But then she skidded to a halt.

"Taranee?" she murmured.

There was nothing fearful about Taranee now. In fact, she was downright bold! She thrust one hand toward the soldier as he rushed toward her. Her palm glowed orange as she began to rev up for magic.

"Hey," Taranee admonished the thug. "Never hit a woman, especially with a red-hot sword!"

With that, she threw a fiery stream of magic. It hit the soldier's sword with a shower of sparks. Immediately, the weapon took on a neon-orange glow. It turned sizzling and molten. The soldier dropped his sword.

Will grinned. Then she spun around to face more soldiers.

We're doing it, she thought incredulously. We're really doing it. We're fighting them off with our magic!

We are powerful.

We are magical.

We are a united force.

We are Guardians of the Veil!

Will hurled another blast at an attacking soldier and watched with grim satisfaction as her power sent him flying.

Her exultation didn't last long, though. The Guardians were winning – she could see that. But that didn't mean this battle was going to be easy. Or quick.

This is just the beginning, Will thought as she gave her friends a grateful glance. We've got a long, hard fight ahead of us. But together, I think we're gonna make it!